# DREAMWALKER

## Natli VanDerWerken

Zenith Star Publishing
Aurora, Colorado

Zenith Star Publishing, LLC
1505 S Norfolk St.
Aurora, CO 80017
www.natlivanderwerken.com

Cover Design © 2024 Natli VanDerWerken.com
Book Layout © 2024 Natli VanDerWerken via BookDesignTemplates.com
Books may be purchased for sales promotion by contacting the publisher.

DreamWalker / Natli VanDerWerken -- 1st ed.
ISBN  978-0-9991750-6-4       (paperback)
ISBN  978-0-9991750-7-1       (ePub)
ISBN  978-0-9991750-8-8       (audiobook)

# Dedication

To Jeremy, Scott. and Tom.
My daughters' husbands.
Inspiration comes in many forms. All of you have
inspired me.

And Forever
To my husband Dan,
who always, always, had my back.

# Contents

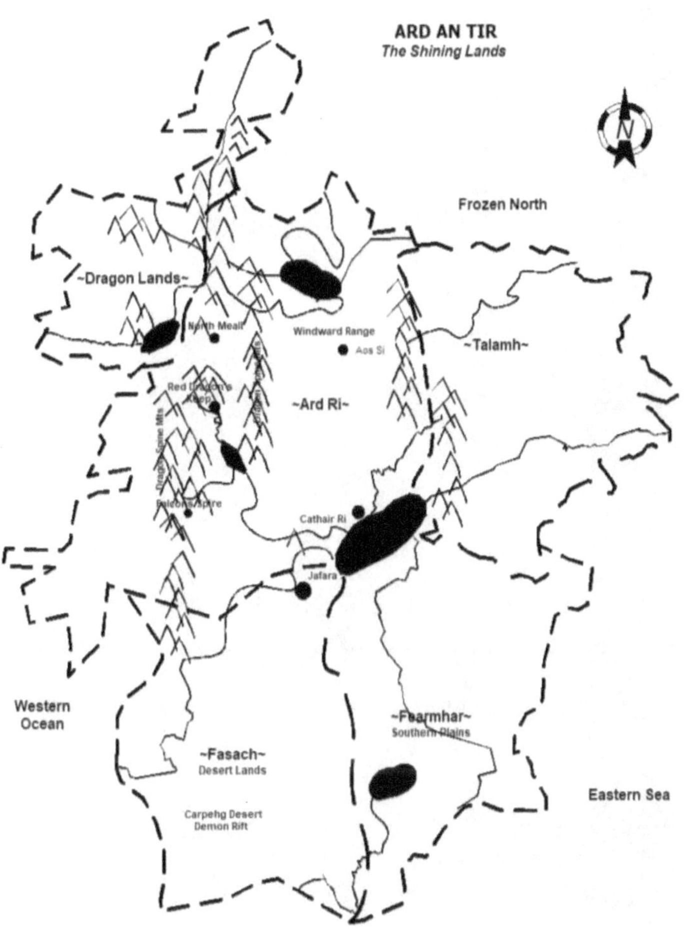

ARD AN TIR
The Shining Lands
Frozen North
~Dragon Lands~
North Meall
Windward Range
Aos Si
~Talamh~
Red Dragon's Keep
Dragon Spine Mtls
~Ard Ri~
Falcon's Spire
Cathair Ri
Jafara
Western Ocean
~Fearmhar~
Southern Plains
Eastern Sea
~Fasach~
Desert Lands
Carpehg Desert
Demon Rift

# ~Fasach~
### Desert Lands

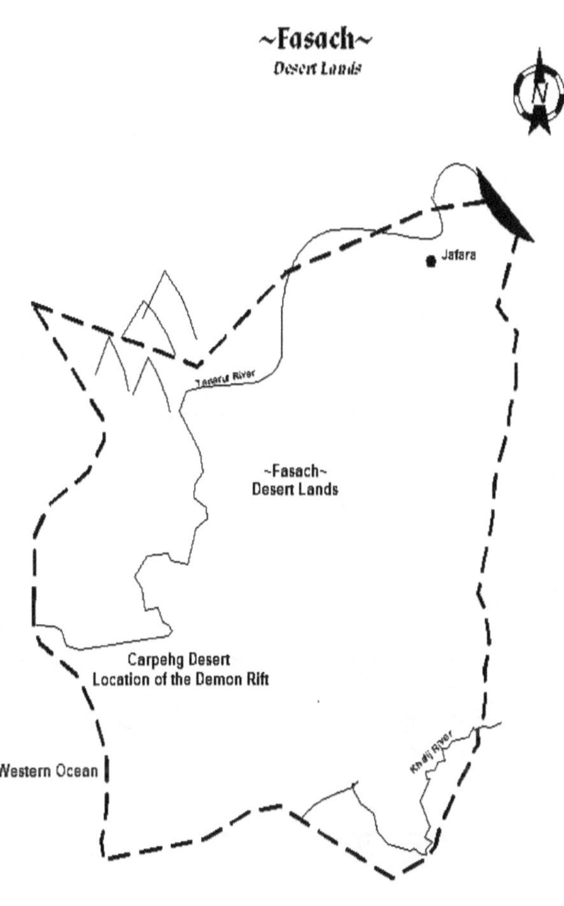

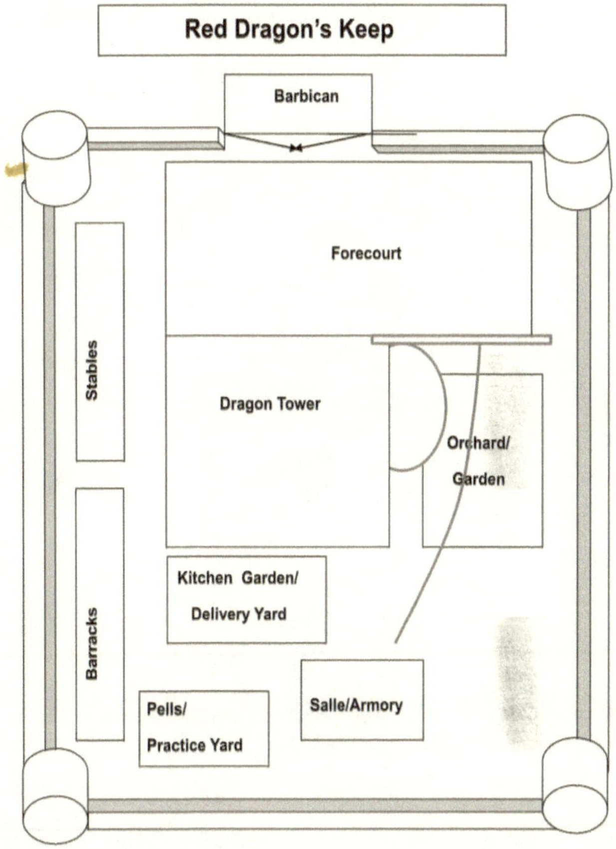

Red Dragon's Keep
Barbican
Forecourt
Stables
Dragon Tower
Orchard/
Garden
Barracks
Kitchen  Garden/
Delivery Yard
Pells/
Practice Yard
Salle/Armory

# AOS SI

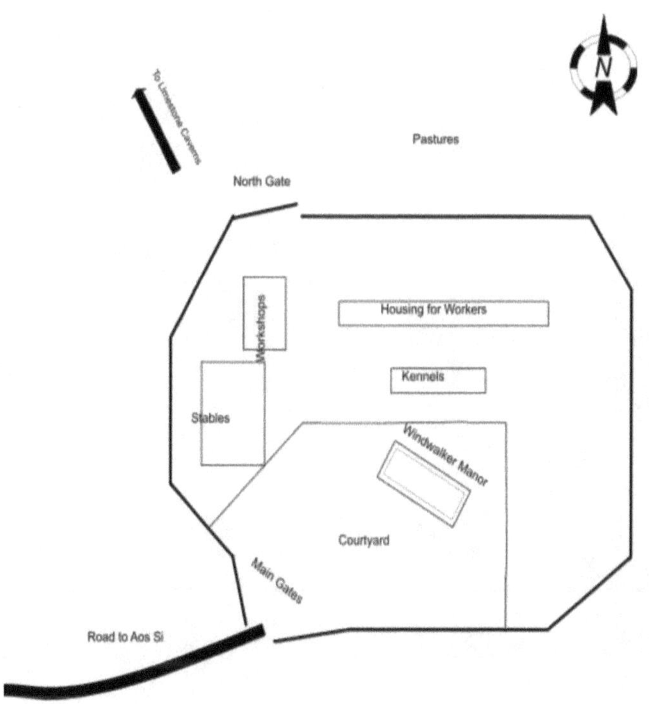

N
To Limestone Caverns
Pastures
North Gate
Workshops
Housing for Workers
Kennels
Stables
Windwalker Manor
Courtyard
Main Gates
Road to Aos Si

# Prologue

Dragons and Demons turned to myths used to frighten children in Ard Ri into obedience. Dragons once flew the skies, helping man battle Demons from another world, but had not been seen in living memory.

The first Demon War was close-fought and almost lost by men. Mages forged Swords of Light by magic and tempered them with Dragon fire. Dragons joined the battle and Claiomh Solas–the Swords of Light–turned the war.

The first mage council fashioned the Cumhacht ar Draigoini—the Power of Dragons—a talisman to control the magical creatures, binding them to obedience or death. Fearing the Talisman's power would corrupt any wielder, the council broke it into five amulets, to be assembled at need, hiding them within the kingdom of Ard Ri. As time passed, caretakers moved the amulets to protect them. The amulets were lost as guardians died or neglected to pass on their locations and the lore surrounding them.

At the end of the last Demon War, the King gave every Dragon to retire to Dragon lands or stay with humans and lose all knowledge of their heritage. Aeden, the Red Dragon, daughter of the King of the Dragons, chose to stay with her humans, the Arachs of Red Dragon's Keep. Her memories faded from her conscious mind as the King bound her from taking Dragon form until her only chance of survival forced her magic to explode through those bindings.

Time passed. Kingdoms rose and fell. Humans fought humans for power or resources. Children were born and elders passed.

Then the Demons returned. Traitors kidnapped the Duke and Duchess of Red Dragon's Keep while they traveled to the capital to attend the King's council. Demons began to prey on the outlying steadings and holdings.

Weapons training ordered by the duke before he left saw Thomas Arach, firstborn and heir, learning the arts of war, governing, and control of the magic he had no idea he possessed. Searching ancient Keep records, Thomas and his two siblings and two cousins found a reference to the Cumhacht ar Draigoini. He searched the hidden tunnels of the Keep and found the first amulet, hidden in plain sight in the greatroom mural.

Then Demons attacked the Keep. When the first Dragon in more than half a millennium transformed, myths shattered, and spells binding magic in Red Dragon's Keep broke.

Thomas sent his brother, Owen, on a mission to bring back needed war horses and war dog replacements from Aos Si, the seat of the Windward Range. As he was about to leave, Navar, a magical WindRunner, arrived at the Keep, choosing Owen as his rider. The two battled Demons and Dark Fey while searching for Owen's parents and the Aos Si amulet.

Demons attacked Aos Si. Owen and Navar, the Forest Lord army, a herd of WindRunners, and his kidnapped family who'd escaped from prison and torture with their Swords of Light, arrived as the Demons were overrunning Aos Si.

The Red Dragon and Thomas reached Aos Si and battled beside them. The gathered heroes destroyed the Demon host.

What looked like the Fasach amulet found its way to Red Dragon's Keep.

The race to find the remaining amulets before the Demons, their controllers, and those in league with them, intensified.

# Chapter 1
# Treachery

*Something is wrong.*

Breanna Arach struggled to wake up.

A dirt path bordered by looming trees stretched before her. Darkness pressed in from either side of the narrow pathway. She could hear the skittering of creatures in the underbrush. An awful smell choked her, triggering her gag reflex.

She heard and felt the pounding of approaching hoofbeats. Dread squeezed her, shortened her breath, her heartbeat frantic. Shadows stretched ahead of whatever was coming down the path. She saw...

Breanna tore herself free of the dream, jerking upright with a shriek of fear.

Her heart hammered. She was panting. Sweat covered her face and body. She trembled with terror in the middle of her bed.

She stared into nothing. The guttering glow of the embers in the fireplace at the end of her bed softened the room's darkness. Her heart slowed its frantic pounding.

A dream. Just a dream.

Breanna swung her legs from under the quilt covering the bed to sit on its side, her feet dangling above the floor. She put her elbows on her knees and rested her forehead on her hands. The untidy braid of deep russet hair swung over her shoulder. She struggled to breathe slowly and deeply.

What am I going to do? This is the third dream this week! I must find a way to stop them.

She pushed herself off the mattress to the floor with a sigh and a hiss. The cold curled her toes. She slipped her feet into soft leather slippers and pulled the robe at the end of the bed over her night shift. Tossing another log on the fire and leaving her Sword of Light in its scabbard on the stand beside her bed, she made her way down the stairs to the small hearth in the kitchen. A cauldron of water sat on the coals, keeping warm through the night. The Dragon Tower was quiet; the only sound was the cadence of patrolling guards.

Pulling a mug from the shelf next to the fireplace, the youngest child of the Duke of Red Dragon's Keep spooned chamomile leaves into its bottom from one of five containers holding tea leaves. She ladled water from the cauldron into the mug, gave it a quick swirl with the spoon, and shuffled to the table in front of the window looking out over the kitchen garden.

Breanna remembered helping Moirra, the Keep's wisewoman, harvest the plants at the end of summer. She leaned over the cup and drew the scent of the tea deep into her lungs. The braid of her hair dangled down her chest, coming close to the tea. Impatience tightened her lips as she flipped it back over her shoulder. Stirring the leaves again to hasten their steeping, she yawned wide, her jaw cracking as she pulled in another deep breath.

"That's attractive," a voice commented from the arch into the kitchen.

Breanna jerked in surprise and swung to face the doorway.

"What are you doing up?" she demanded of Marta, her weapons teacher and, more importantly, her friend.

"I heard your shriek," the young woman told her. Long black hair lying loose down to her waist framed a pale face. Tired, half-open blue eyes blinked slowly.

"Sorry I woke you," Breanna muttered. She pulled the spoon from the tea to let the leaves settle to the bottom.

"That's all right. I wasn't sleeping well myself." Marta said. She walked to the hearth and took down a cup. She scooped in black tea leaves from the canister on the shelf and poured hot water into the cup.

"Really? Why not? What were you dreaming about?"

Marta joined her at the table in front of the window facing the kitchen garden. This deep into the night, it only reflected the dim light from the fire in the hearth.

"Just normal stuff. You know, Demons coming out of portals. Claws reaching out of rifts to grab me. Dragon fire burning me to a crisp. Stuff like that," Marta told her, a crooked smile crossing her face, highlighting the dark circles under her eyes.

Breanna frowned. "You look awful. Have you talked to your mother? Maybe she can help."

Marta brushed the suggestion aside with a flick of her fingers. "I'm fine. It's just a dream about everything that's happened." She looked into her cup, avoiding Breanna's gaze.

"Uh-huh," Breanna said. She took a sip from her cup. "I still think you need to tell your mother about them."

"Why did you shriek?" Marta asked. Breanna recognized the change of subject.

"Something was coming down the path I was on. I knew it was horrible. Just before it turned the corner so I could see it, I woke up." Breanna swirled the liquid in her mug, brooding over her fear. "Well, I don't care if you're not going to talk to your mother. I'm going to find her in the morning and ask her if she can help me control my dreams. I wish my mother was here, or even Aeden. Something is going on. I just know it!"

Marta looked at her for moments, a frown lowering her brows, lips thin. "Fine," she grunted. "I'll go with you. Maybe she can help me, too."

Breanna drank the last of her tea and stood up from the table. "I'm going back to bed and see if I can sleep. See you in the morning."

A miasma of fear and rage reached out for her as she opened the door to her room.

Breanna took an involuntary step back into the hall. Sending a mental shout to SunWalker, Breanna rushed to the sword stand. Nothing answered her.

Shaken by that lack of contact, she hesitated for a heartbeat, then grabbed the Sword, stripping the scabbard from its blade.

Light flared as SunWalker awoke.

The pall of rage and fear vanished as if it had never been.

*Someone bound me!* SunWalker's voice hissed in Breanna's mind. *Someone powerful.*

Breanna plopped onto the bed with a gasp of dismay. If she wasn't safe in her room with a Sword of Light, nowhere was safe.

*How? How were you bound? Can you feel anything? Anything that will tell us who did this?*

Her courage stumbled as the Sword was silent. *Finally - No. I feel the remnants of a spell. It is not from someone in the*

*Keep. That much I am certain of. It triggered when you began to dream.*

She slid the scabbard over SunWalker's blade with slow precision and replaced the Sword on the stand. Breanna flinched as a log burning in the fireplace across the room popped, sending sparks up the chimney.

*What can we do to keep this from happening again? Is there a counter-spell that we can use?* Breanna was shaken to her core. She had thought the Sword was invincible.

*Thomas, HellReaver, and the Dragon return today from the battle for Aos Si. We must ask them when they arrive,* Sun-Walker responded.

Breanna's mood brightened.

*Oh good! I'm glad he's coming back,* she told SunWalker with a smile. *I can't wait to hear what happened at Aos Si. That dream was scary enough, thank you very much. If I never walk through a Dark Fey's dreams again, it will be too soon. I knew Thomas needed to be there for us to win.*

She lay back on the bed and pulled the quilts over her body. The room was still cold despite the fire.

*I shall remain on guard until they are here,* SunWalker told her.

Breanna closed her eyes. She remembered the dream of a horde of Demons attacking the home of her aunt and uncle. She'd seen an army of Forest Lords marching toward the walls of Aos Si as she walked through the dreams of a deadly Dark Fey, a being from another world trapped in hers, bent on killing every human it could find. She'd seen her brother Owen leading a sweeping herd of WindRunners, as black as ink spilled across a new page, coming to the aid of all. She drifted into a dreamless sleep.

§ § §

The light of the dawn sun made its way through the shutters covering Breanna's windows and laid itself across her cheek. She stretched and yawned, pulling air deep into her lungs.

She sat up and swung herself out of bed, yawning again. The clothes she'd worn yesterday were good enough.

Breanna pulled the much-patched tunic over her head and slid her legs into the trousers. She unbraided her hair and swept it into a tail at the back of her head, tying it with a strip of leather. Excitement spiked with the knowledge that Thomas and Aeden were coming home. She shoved her feet into her boots, grabbed SunWalker, and charged out of her room, slamming the door behind her.

She hurried through breakfast of oatmeal and a mug of cider. A cry from the watchtower was taken up by the guards on the wall. "Dragon!"

Breanna jogged through the great hall and out the entry's double doors. She raised her hand to shield her eyes from the blinding light of the rising sun, now shining over the ramparts of Red Dragon's Keep. She stood on the apron of the stairs that descended to the forecourt, bouncing on her toes with impatience.

She pumped a fist over her head in happy celebration as the Red Dragon spiraled into the space between the wall and the Dragon Tower. Villagers and visitors coming through the gates scurried to the walls as wind from the Dragon's wings pushed dust and pebbles across the ground.

Thomas, oldest son, and heir to the Keep, sat between two of the spines that rose from the Dragon's back close to her neck. Her hind feet touched down first, then front feet settled gently to the earth, wings flipping closed to shroud her sides. Thomas unclipped the straps around his waist that attached him to a leather collar circling the massive creature's neck.

He swung his right leg over the Dragon's neck and slid down her left side along her leg to the ground. He pushed himself away, glancing up the side of the tower. Breanna followed his look, drinking in the sight of the Tower and the stone Red Dragon rising up its east side that gave Red Dragon's Keep its name and sigil. Thomas turned and jogged toward his sister when he spotted Breanna at the top of the stairs.

The Dragon stretched out her long neck and roared. The air above her head began to rotate, becoming a whirling column as red as blood, dropping lower and lower until it shrouded her entire body. The whirlwind slowed and dissipated. Aeden walked toward them from the heart of the tornado.

Breanna launched herself toward Thomas from the second stair. He caught her and swung her around. A broad grin stretched his mouth as he set her back on her feet.

"I'm so glad you're home. I want to hear all about the battle. Are Owen and Navar all right? What about Aunt Debra and Uncle Scott? Did the Forest Lords help? When will everyone arrive?" she demanded in one breath.

"Whoa," exclaimed Thomas. "Slow down. First, Mother, Father, and the Gobhlans are alive."

"By the Three Gods!" Breanna shrieked, jumping up and down, a huge grin splitting her face.

Thomas laughed out loud. "They escaped from North Meall and found us with the Forest Lord Army. All of them have Swords of Light! Let's go inside, and I'll tell you all about it." He turned to Aeden. "Lady, would you join us?"

"Yes, I will," she told him, giving each of them a grave nod. Then she grinned. "There is much to tell." The three walked up the stairs and into the great hall.

Thomas tapped the shoulder of a skully wiping down one of the tables. "Please find Gregory and Evan Gobhlan and have them meet us in the Library." The man dropped his rag on the table and scuttled from the hall. Thomas turned to Breanna. "Has Cameron come back to the Keep?"

"No," she told him. "We haven't heard a thing. I'm going to find Marta. She should hear this too."

"Tell her that her father made it and is on his way back," Thomas shouted at her retreating shape.

Breanna hurried out of the tower through the kitchen and toward the fields. She knew Marta was already out in the training pen with the yearlings.

She waved her arm over her head and saw Marta catch sight of her. Marta turned to the bay filly she was training to walk on a lead with a saddle. She started unbuckling the cinch. Breanna slipped through the fence rails, scooped up the saddle, swung around, and set it on the top rail of the round pen. Marta took the halter from the young horse's head and set her free. The little filly jumped away, kicking her heels up in delight.

"Thomas and Aeden are back. Your father is alive and on his way home," Breanna told her. "Thomas wants us to meet in the Library. I'm going to make sure Evan is awake."

"I'll put the gear away and meet you there," Marta said.

Breanna knocked on Evan's door and pushed it open. Evan sat on the side of his bed, pulling on his boots. His blond hair stood up in spikes, and his face still bore the creases of his bedcoverings. He stood up and stomped his feet into the boots.

"Is Cameron back?" he asked his cousin.

"No," she told him with brusque regret. His face lost expression. "Your mother and father and mine are alive!" Evan's eyes went huge, his mouth fell open. "Thomas is going to tell us about the battle for Aos Si."

"What?" Evan shook his head. "What?"

"Thomas said they escaped from North Meall and found him and Aeden right before the battle. Hurry up. I want to hear the story."

"I've got to get something to eat first. I'll be right up." Evan scooted past her body blocking the door.

"Ask one of the skullies to bring up a pitcher of cider and some mugs," she ordered as he jogged to the stairs. He waved his left arm without looking back.

Everyone gathered in the Library on the third floor of the Dragon Tower within half a candlemark. A pitcher of cider with six mugs sat on a tray on the side table against the wall. Breanna and Marta came in together.

The Library occupied the entire third floor of the five-story tower. A massive table with legs carved in the shape of Dragons sat in the center of the room, books piled haphazardly in its center. Large windows on all sides of the room gave a view to the east of the road winding up the mountainside to the Keep. To the south and west, cattle, sheep, and goats grazed on the stubble fields. The north windows looked out on the forecourt and the main gates where traders, farmers, and every kind of goods entered the Keep and the village beyond.

Thomas was speaking as the girls entered.

"...and then Aeden landed next to him, and he about jumped out of his skin when he saw me sitting on her neck. Navar's ears were rigid, and his eyes so wide, I thought they might fall out." A chuckle rippled around the room.

Breanna and Marta sat down at the table. Evan clumped into the room, a bowl of porridge clutched in his hand. Thomas reached out and put his hand on his cousin's shoulder.

"Evan, your parents are alive."

"I know. Breanna told me," he said, a beatific smile lighting up his whole face.

Thomas frowned, glanced at Breanna, and patted Evan's shoulder. "I was hoping Cameron would be here so I could tell him, too."

His gaze swept over everyone in the room.

"Owen found the Aos Si amulet. He also found Mother's belt knife in the circle of standing stones where he and Navar spent the night. We caught up with the Forest King's elven troops. They were on the way to help Owen battle the Demons at Aos Si. When Owen closed the Rift in the Darkened Forest, he broke the spell that imprisoned the Unseleigh Sidhe, the Dark Fey, within the Forest."

"A horde of them headed toward Aos Si to join the Demons gathering there. The Forest King, Owen, and I decided it was best not to leave an enemy at our back. Sergeant Haloran," he nodded at Marta, "and the men he brought with him joined the elven army, and we attacked the horde. Not one survived."

"Aeden burned our dead with all honor. We rode on toward Aos Si. The Demons attacked the walls and broke through at least three places. I led half of our men in an attack on the right flank, and Owen and Navar attacked from the left. A herd of more than fifty WindRunners swept in and joined the battle. The Red Dragon," he gestured toward Aeden, "flew overhead and sent fire over the Demons. The Forest Lords attacked from the west along with our parents. Not one Demon escaped," he finished with satisfaction.

Thomas stood at the head of the table, looking out the east window, his mind far away.

"You should have seen Aeden," he whispered. "She came swooping in, laying down rows of fire along the Demon lines." Heads swiveled to look at Aeden leaning against the wall between the windows at the end of the table, her arms crossed over her chest.

"It was astounding." He paused. "Terrible glory." He shook himself back into the present and looked at Aeden. She gazed back with no expression.

"We almost lost. The Demons breached the walls and attacked anything that moved inside. Warhorses and war dogs were fighting alongside Uncle Scott, Aunt Debra, and the people of Aos Si. When the Demons outside the walls realized we were attacking, they broke and tried to run. The defenders were able to kill those left inside." Thomas lifted his mug of cider and drank half of it.

"Marta, your father is on his way back here with any warhorses and war dogs that Aos Si can spare. I'm hoping he'll be here in a fortnight."

"Evan, your parents and mine escaped from North Meall and caught up with us and the elven army." Thomas reached out and grasped Evan's shoulder in support as Evan began to shake. "It's all right. They've decided to continue to Cathair Ri and find out what's happening with the King. Oh, and a WindRunner chose each one of them."

Thomas stopped talking. The room went even more still.

"And the Swords of Light that each of them carried woke up when Demons attacked them on the way to the Forest Lord army."

"What?" Everyone in the room started talking at once. "That can't be right. How did they know to choose those swords?"

"What about Owen and Navar?" Breanna whispered.

Thomas heard her, even over the babbling of the others. He turned his head to look at her.

"A fairyfly in the Darkened Forest captured and killed Sir Mathin and all but two of his men." The others in the room fell silent again. "Owen and Navar rode into the Forest with twenty soldiers, recruited help from the elves and Agni, the creatures that the elves use like horses. The Agni think Owen is something special. Owen and his allies killed the fairyfly, then closed the Rift that allowed the Dark Fey into the Darkened Forest. Aeden and I found him at the standing stones on the Windward Range. He'd already recovered," he paused dramatically, his hand on his heart, "the Aos Si amulet from the caverns north of the manor."

Everyone sat stunned by the tale.

"Navar and Owen are going south to Fearmhar to find the amulet Navar insists is hidden there. Alberick, the Forest Lord king, sent a scout, Saleth, and his dire wolf with Owen. A Forest Lord prophecy about a hero's journey includes an elf and a dire wolf."

"Is Owen still as nasty as he was before he left," Breanna asked.

Thomas shook his head. "No," he said. "He's changed. He grew up." A half-grin lifted one side of his mouth.

"It's about time," Breanna declared.

After a moment, she continued. "You need to know that something bound SunWalker last night when I started to dream. It only broke when I pulled the Sword out of the scabbard."

Thomas shook his head. "It never ends."

Breanna's lips tightened as a scowl crossed her face. "So, what are we going to do? Just wait until the next attack? Something bad is happening and it's right here," she exclaimed. "We need information. We need to find out who is behind all of this. We need to figure out how to stop them." She pounded the table with her fist at each suggestion.

Everyone looked at her with resignation. As usual, Breanna had cut to the heart of the situation. Her bluntness was irritating at best.

Thomas looked around the table. "Here's another question. Why did the Dark Fey head toward Aos Si? How did they know to go there?"

# Chapter 2
# Trader

High Mage Mannan gasped and doubled over. He crouched in the middle of the empty corridor outside his rooms in the Mages Enclave of Ard Ri. "No," he moaned, clutching his head.

The Rift in the Darkened Forest was gone. He'd invested his magic for a very long time to widen and strengthen it and make it impervious to elven magic. Nothing could have closed it except...Dragon magic.

He stumbled to the wall for support. With the suddenness of a clap of thunder, he was sure it was the Dragon of Red Dragon's Keep, the Black King's daughter, who had lent her magic to destroy his work.

He pushed himself slowly upright with grim determination and moved into his tower quarters. It would take time and many deaths to rebuild his magic. He had to do something to remove the Red Dragon and the Arachs from the board of his great plan.

He made his way with careful steps to his desk and sat.
He pulled a sheet of parchment from the pile on his left
and began to write.

*To the King's Mage*
*Your presence is required at the Mages Enclave.*

$ $ $

Breanna flipped the lid closed on the small bottle of
ink sitting on the right side of her place at the Library table. She rolled the ink from the nib of her feather pen
onto a cloth with careful precision and straightened the
stack of papers she had finished. She'd taken over the
duty of maintaining the Keep records when her mother
left for the capital. She continued the task even after
Thomas returned from the Battle for Aos Si a fortnight
ago and reported their parents alive and on their way
again to Cathair Ri to find out if the King was a traitor.

"Deadly boring," she muttered to herself. "How did
Mother stand this?"

She pushed herself out of the chair she was using. The
chair's feet screeched unpleasantly against the slate floor.
Picking up her stack of papers, she glanced out the window that faced the training yard to the southwest. A
smile flirted at the corners of her mouth as she saw Marta
and Thomas trading blows with practice swords.

Breanna walked to the window and put her records
down on the wide windowsill. She leaned close to the

glass and watched the pair practice the dance of death. *I need to train*, she thought.

She turned away from the window and picked up her work, cradling the stack of papers in her right arm. She grabbed her Sword leaning against the table as she passed it and clipped its scabbard to the left side of her sword belt. She left the Library on her way to the Seneschal's office.

§ § §

Marta Haloran swung her sword back across her body to block her opponent's slash. She caught the tip of his sword with the flat of her blade just as it reached her chest and pushed it up and away. She brought the wooden practice blade back down as she disengaged and whacked her opponent's shoulder on the padding protecting his neck. Had it been a steel sword, she would have cut him to the bone, possibly taking his arm. As it was, he dropped his weapon with a shout and grabbed his shoulder.

Fuming with frustration, Thomas shook his arm and rubbed his neck. "That's the third time you've done that. Is HellScream helping you?" he demanded.

"No. It's all me," she smirked.

The sound of clapping began from the seats bordering the practice yard. Thomas and Marta turned to see who had been watching them. Master Sergeant Faolan Haloran, Marta's father, sat on the second row of benches arranged on the north side of the yard. He had arrived the night before with the men who had followed him from Aos Si and the warhorses and war dogs that the WindWalkers had sent.

Thomas reached down and picked up the wooden sword he had been using. Marta could tell he was embarrassed. His cheeks were red, his eyebrows drawn down in an angry frown.

He looked up and caught her watching him. She grinned at him. His frown began to smooth out and he gave a small grin, gradually widening, until he burst out laughing.

"Good job, Marta. I just can't get through your guard," Thomas told her.

Faolan joined them as they walked to the horse trough placed next to the benches. "Not bad, Marta," her father congratulated her with a laugh in his voice. "Not many can disarm the lord of Red Dragon's Keep."

"Three times in a row, sir. I'm going to make her teach me what she's doing so I can protect myself," Thomas told him. He smiled at Marta.

*Perhaps I* should *help you, Thomas.* HellReaver's voice echoed in all their minds.

"No thank you, HellReaver. I need to learn this so I can train my muscle-memory just in case you're not around." Thomas politely declined the offer from his Sword of Light.

*As you wish.* The sword sounded disgruntled.

Thomas and Marta shared a look.

Reaching the trough, they both splashed water on their faces, washing the sweat and dust away. Thomas wiped his face off with his hands and dried them on his trousers. Marta used the tail of her shirt to scrub her face dry.

Breanna came running out of the Dragon Tower and sped toward the practice yard, the long red-gold braid of her hair thumping against her back.

Thomas turned to her, alarm written across his face. "What is it, Breanna?"

She stopped at the fence between the yard and the Tower grounds, leaning against it, out of breath. "Gregory says he needs to talk to you right away. Something to do with the Traders," she gasped out. "When you're done, I need to talk to you and Lady Aeden."

Thomas began stripping off his protective clothing. "Faolan, will you come with me?"

"Aye, Lord Thomas." He unfastened the buckles on the back of the gambeson padding, lifting it up and over Thomas's shoulders.

Marta placed a hand on Breanna's arm. "Are you all right?" she asked, concern deepening her voice.

Thomas unlaced his leather leg guards with quick fingers and handed them to Haloran.

Breanna reached up and gripped Marta's wrist, looking at her with wide, intense green eyes. "Don't leave," she mouthed.

Thomas turned to the two girls. "Marta, would you take the gear to the armory? This sounds urgent."

Haloran handed the equipment he held to Marta. Breanna ducked through the fence and grabbed the helmets and practice swords lying on the ground. The girls watched as Thomas and Marta's father swung over the fence and jogged toward the Tower.

"What's going on?" Marta asked.

"That Trader, Maaike Soth Lahri from Fasach, was caught in the Tower, trying to snoop in the family quarters. One of the guards found her outside Thomas's room. She's been asking all kinds of questions about defenses and supplies, weapons, and Dragons." The information seemed to spill out of Breanna in a flood. They started walking toward the salle and the armory. "Gregory wants Thomas to use HellReaver to find out what she's doing. It's a mess!" she declared. "I had another dream last night."

Marta stopped abruptly and grabbed her companion's arm. "What? Why didn't you tell me this morning? I dreamed, too," she exclaimed to Thomas's sister.

Breanna pulled her arm from Marta's grip and continued walking. Marta hurried to catch up.

"I didn't remember until Gregory asked me to get Thomas. The dream was about that Maaike. I don't like her. She's up to something, something bad. What did you dream?"

Marta slowed her steps, forcing Breanna to slow as well. "I saw her wrapping Thomas in rope and trying to hang him from the front wall of the Tower. You were there and helped me cut the ropes away from him and get him down. I haven't got a clue what it means."

Breanna looked at her, mouth open in astonishment. She snapped her mouth shut. "Let's get this stuff put away. We need to talk to your mother right now. We should have done it before, but I keep forgetting." She stopped dead in her tracks. "Why did I keep forgetting?"

Marta stopped beside her. A frown crossed her face. "Why did I?"

$$$

Raina sat on a bench pulled into the window alcove across from the main door of the Haloran suite of rooms. She was eternally grateful to Lord Thomas for giving her family the suite when they had arrived at Red Dragon's Keep as refugees.

She finished stitching the rip in Faolan's tunic and set it aside. Reaching into the basket sitting on the floor next to her, she pulled out a brown shirt. She rested her hands on her lap and watched as her daughter and Breanna pushed through the door and hurried across the room.

"How are you, Mother? We looked for you in the still-room, but the cook told us you were up here. Breanna and I need your advice," Marta said.

"Then I'm glad you found me," Raina answered.

"Tell me what you need."

"Both of us have had dreams about Trader Maaike. They're not good dreams," Breanna declared. "She's trying to find out why the Dragon came to the Keep and helped Thomas defeat the Demons."

Marta listened with a deepening frown growing between her eyes.

"I think she's looking for a way to bind or kill the Dragon and Thomas," Breanna added.

"Have you had this dream before?" Raina asked.

"I've had this one for the past week," Breanna whispered, dropping her gaze to the floor. "I was going to come and talk to you, but I kept forgetting."

"DreamWalking is a gift," Raina told the girls. Breanna snorted. You know this," Raina continued. "Some people can walk through other's dreams and know what they are going to do. It's like precognition and it's a very rare talent. Marta dreams of people whom she will meet in the future, as did my mother," Raina told her.

Breanna hesitated then admitted in a rush, "I dreamed about Thomas and Aeden at Aos Si, and I told him. That's how he knew to go. I'm also having dreams about a great danger that keeps coming closer." She shook her head in frustration. "I don't know what it is. I always wake up right before I can see it."

"Not seeing the danger means you're not ready for it. Give it time." Raina pulled Breanna into a hug and kissed the top of her head. "Marta, what have you dreamed?"

Marta told her about Thomas bound in rope and hanging from the castle wall. Raina inhaled sharply when she heard the tale. "How often have you had this dream?" she asked urgently.

Marta stared at her mother's tone. "Since Thomas and Aeden came back," she told her in a small voice.

"This is important," Raina said as she looked at them with a frown. "We need to let Gregory know as soon as possible.

"Gregory sent for Thomas a half candlemark ago, something about a guard catching Maaike snooping in the family quarters," Breanna told her.

Raina surged to her feet, the shirt she was holding falling unheeded to the floor. "We need to see him right now. Quickly," she demanded.

She put a hand on each of the girls, urging them across the room and into the corridor, pulling the door closed behind her.

Raina and the girls hurried through the corridor and down the stairs to the great hall. They went through the arches and turned to the left, the girls almost running to keep up. The closed door to Gregory's office greeted them. Raina knocked hard enough for the sound to echo in the hallway.

A guard pulled the door open. Within the room, Thomas, the men, and a woman whom Raina knew as Maaike turned to look at them. The woman's dusky skin gleamed with nervous sweat that beaded on her temples, her brown eyes glistening with anxiety. A loose caftan of deepest turquoise covered a long dress the color of cinnamon. She wore sandals on her feet.

"My Lord, the girls and I have information that you need to hear. In private, please."

The others shared a look. "Please escort Trader Soth Lahri to the great hall and ask for some refreshments," Thomas ordered the guard. Maaike tried to hide her fright but failed as the guard took her by the arm and walked with her from the room.

Raina closed the door gently behind Marta and Breanna as they entered the room. She walked to Haloran's side and placed her hand on his arm. "Girls, tell them what you told me."

Thomas, Gregory, and Faolan listened as first Breanna, then Marta, told them what they had dreamed.

"How dependable are your dreams? I know you dreamed about the portals and the battle for Aos Si, but..." Thomas asked.

"I can tell when I'm in someone else's dream," Breanna told him. "It's like I see things through their eyes. Most of what they are dreaming about is what they are going to do. Sometimes it's really scary. This one just made me mad." She punched her fist into her left palm in agitation.

Thomas looked at Marta.

"I've had dreams that came true many times. Just like the one about the portal locations. Mother knows about most of them," she conceded.

Raina nodded her head and added, "My mother often dreamed of what was to come. The gift can skip a generation, as I don't have it."

Thomas crossed his arms, the conflict of his thoughts pulling his eyebrows into a deep frown. His face relaxed as he made a decision.

"Maaike is a spy from Fasach." He shot a look at Aeden and Gregory. "We questioned her right after she gave me the Fasach Amulet. She doesn't know that we did, and she doesn't know it's the Amulet, or what we think is the Amulet."

He looked out the window, his eyes fixed, staring into the distance. Breanna thought he might be shuffling scenarios through his mind.

Abruptly he looked back at all of them. "Does anyone know where Neulach might be? Has he come back with Cameron?"

A chorus of "no's" responded to his question. He shook his head in disappointment. Neulach, the King of the Dragons and Aeden's father, disappeared with the

Arach's Gobhlan cousin Cameron while they were investigating an unknown tunnel under the Keep.

"Could you find him, wherever he is?" Thomas asked Aeden.

"No. He has hidden himself from me. I can feel other Dragons far away, but nothing from him," Aeden responded.

Thomas frowned. "We've been following the trader ever since the questioning. Sometimes we lose her, but we know most of the people she talks with. Neulach and I spoke about what to do in just this event. He seems to think that getting rid of the problem immediately is the answer. I think we should continue following her and see what she does."

Silence greeted his statement.

"How would you follow her more closely?" Haloran asked after some thought.

"I've been practicing a spell that Aeden taught me. It's based on the disks that were sent into the Dragon Tower before the first battle. The wording of the spell is important. I'll need all of you to help me. Maybe we can place it on the pin that she uses for her cloak."

"What about on the coins in her pouch," Breanna suggested.

"Good idea, Breanna. She might spend them, though, and then the spell will go with someone else." Breanna nodded in understanding.

"I can set the spell to let a team of scouts follow her without being seen. She can't lose them, even if she tries."

"What do you hope to learn?" Raina inquired.

"Any others she meets with, where she goes, does she pass anything to anyone, things like that. Each scout will follow her for a short time and then another will pick her up. HellReaver, would you please follow the tracker and listen in?"

*Yes, I will. Much will be gained from more closely observing her actions. HellScream, SunWalker, would you shadow the scouts?*

Gregory and Raina jerked in reaction to the voice of the Sword of Light in their minds.

"I should be used to that by now," muttered Gregory. Raina gave him a sympathetic look.

"Haloran, could you get, what - five?" Thomas gave a sharp nod of his head. "Yes, five scouts and bring them back here? Aeden, the Swords, and I will create a spell to transfer to her brooch. Marta, when that's done, will you find a way to attach it to Maaike's cloak?

"Of course," Marta said. "Breanna, can you distract her while I do it?"

Breanna nodded and grimaced with distaste. "I really don't like her."

$$$

"I think these are new contacts," Marta said into the quietness of the others in the Library. The group met following last meal a week after the meeting in Gregory's office.

*That's eight people she has contacted,* HellScream reported. *Every one of them holds secrets that we must uncover.*

"I think she's recruiting spies," Marta continued.

Thomas frowned. "Why?"

"I asked around after she contacted them. They've all arrived at Red Dragon's Keep within the last three years. None of them are from Ard Ri. There are three from Fasach, which makes sense, probably sent by their master of spies. Two are from Talamh and the rest are from Fearmhar."

Thomas's frowned as she gave her report. His lips compressed and his head started to nod in agreement. "I think you're right. She's setting up a network of her own to let her follow what's going on here. Then she becomes the spymaster and will look competent to her superiors."

His eyes narrowed as the muscles of his cheeks flexed. "Breanna, have you dreamed anything about this? Marta?"

"No," Breanna shrugged and shook her head. She looked at the top of the table and traced the grain of the wood with the fingers of her right hand, running them back and forth with absent precision, refusing to look up.

Marta echoed her negative.

Thomas sat silent, his gaze far away.

With a suddenness that startled Breanna, he was back.

"Aeden, do you know anything about dream work, or dream training? Can you help them learn how to control it? HellReaver, no, all you Swords of Light, do any of you know how to control dreams?"

No one answered.

Aeden cleared her throat. "DreamWalking is a Dragon talent. I have not used it myself, but I remember other Dragons who did. We three should meet and explore this."

OathKeeper, Aeden's Sword, who very rarely participated in conversations, spoke.

*DreamWalking is exceedingly rare. In all my time, I have only known five who could do this, and then only after much training. They seem to appear when the need is very great. I remember some of the training they endured. It is urgent that this training happens quickly. I can feel the threads of time shifting.*

Indrawn breath greeted his pronouncement.

Thomas looked at the three.

"Start today, please."

# Chapter 3
# The King's Mage

The short voluptuous woman spun slowly in a circle, causing the heavy black skirt of her long-sleeved dress to flare out and flash as candlelight caught the runes etched in gold and blood-red sigils worked into the fabric. She let her head fall back and threw her arms wide. Her ruby earrings flashed. As she slowed, the flash and gleam of the runes faded from sight. Her white-blond hair settled into an artful cascade down her back.

Her brilliant blue eyes caught her image in the new mirror that graced the wall above her dressing table. Pots of creams, lotions, and crystal bottles of perfume cluttered the table's top.

She scooped a generous amount of cream from one of the jars with the tip of her finger. She rubbed it over her hands and arms, leaving them soft and smooth. Picking up a small brush, she dipped it into a tiny container of kohl. She leaned in toward the mirror and outlined her eyes with the black substance.

Drawing back, she looked at her face and nodded with satisfaction. An illusion of mystery and power enhanced her features.

A loud knock at her chamber door boomed through the suite of rooms.

"Enter," Siubhan murmured. The door swung silently open, revealing a tall, liveried servant, his hand raised to knock again.

He took a hasty step back from the doorway. "The King demands your presence," he said.

"Does he?" she responded. "Are you sure he didn't request it?" she asked with a mocking lilt in her voice. Returning the brush to its tray, she looked one last time in the mirror, turned away and swayed toward the door.

The servant took another step back, his face twisting in disgust, as if smelling death and decay. A wave of the woman's hand filled the chamber with the scent of roses. The servant's eyes narrowed at the blatant display of power.

He bowed deeply. "My lady, the King requests your presence."

"I'm aware of his request. How lovely that he sent an escort."

Siubhan swept into the hallway and made her way along the corridor and down the stairs descending to the second floor, the King's wing of the palace. The servant trailed behind her.

Rich red carpet bordered with gold thread deadened her footfalls as she walked toward the guards standing in front of the doors to the King's chambers. They stepped aside as she approached. The doors swung slowly open without human assistance.

Rudraige Mór looked up from the manuscript he was reading. His blue brocade tunic, heavily woven with gold thread, covered a fine linen shirt over deep brown trousers. Sparse brown hair was combed over the top of his shiny scalp. Amber eyes rose to hers.

"Welcome, Siubhan," he greeted her and pushed his large, powerful body out of his chair as she walked to the table. His chamberlain hurried over, set a dainty cup and saucer at her place, and poured it full of fragrant tea.

"This is an unexpected summons, my king. Isn't there a council meeting scheduled?" she responded as she languidly took her place at the table.

"There is, my lady." He gestured at the table covered with scrolls and books. "I've been reading the contents of the councilors' deliberations and their advice about the Demons."

"Worthwhile, is it? I'm sure they've made particularly good suggestions," she replied with a sly smile. *The idiots couldn't think themselves out of an unlocked room,* she thought.

"Nothing that hasn't been proposed before," he sighed, tossing the manuscript to the table. "Enough of this. I've received a request from High Mage Mannan. He asks for your immediate presence."

Had the King not known her so well, he would have missed the moment of utter stillness that enveloped his mage. He slanted his head in question. "Is this a problem?" he asked.

"No, Sire. I'm surprised that he would ask me to travel now, at the end of winter and with the rising of the Demons."

"Perhaps I should request his presence here," Rudraige mused aloud.

"No, that's all right, Sire," she responded, not wanting to arouse his curiosity. "I will go to him at the Mages Enclave. Did he give a reason for his request?"

"The missive only held his invitation. It *is* rather odd at this time of year. I would ask that you send a message bird to me with a report," the King told her. He walked around the table and laid his heavy hand on her shoulder. "I need you by my side to weather the coming storm. Return as soon as you can. Take whom and what you need."

"Yes, Sire. I'll leave tomorrow." Siubhan sipped the cooling tea and grimaced. It was much too bitter.

Rudraige sighed again and picked up a scroll that sat next to her cup. "Some of these ideas are just stupid," he remarked, wandering closer to the fireplace as he read.

"I'll leave you now, Sire. I have much to prepare."

He gave a nod of his head in dismissal, already absorbed in his reading.

Siubhan's lips thinned in dislike. She rose gracefully from the table. "Thank you for the tea. It was lovely," she told the chamberlain.

"You're welcome, Lady," he answered with a smirk.

No hand touched the doors slowly opening as she approached them. As she walked away, they closed.

$$$

Siubhan watched as her maid folded clothing and packed it into the trunk for her trip to the Enclave, a day's travel south of Cathair Ri. Undergarments followed dresses and shoes into its depths. Cloaks, shawls, and hair coverings were nestled on top. She languidly set her pots of creams and lotions into a small case set on the table below the mirror. Her mind was working furiously.

*What does he want? The King is suborned. Ard Ri will fall. I can do no more. What must have changed to necessitate this summons?* She gave a small shake of head in frustration, her lips compressed. A frown marred her unlined forehead. She noticed and relaxed her muscles. It wouldn't do for lines to mar what she had spent ages preserving.

"My lady, will you ride or stay in the carriage?" the maid asked.

"I'll stay in the carriage. It's much too cold to ride a horse."

"The green wool travel dress and cape, my lady?"

"Yes, that would be fine," she snapped, thoroughly irritated at her the girl. *Really. She knows what I need to wear on this odious trip.*

Siubhan stood still as the maid loosened all the fastenings on the back of her dress. She stepped out of her clothing as it fell to the floor. "Make sure you pack that and my box," she ordered.

She stepped into the skirt that the girl held for her and raised her arms for the blouse and tunic. She shrugged to settle the garments in place. She sat on the bench at the end of her bed and pulled on the short boots that stood on the floor by her feet as the maid picked up her dress, folded it carefully and placed it in the trunk, fetched the box on the mirror table and tucked it down the side next to the clothing. The girl lowered the lid and buckled the travel straps closed.

Siubhan rose and walked to the trunk. She placed her hand flat on its top and sent a surge of power through the wood. Red light glowed around the trunk and slowly faded.

"Send for Sharlay," she snapped with a sly glance at the girl's wide eyes and pale face.

"Yes, my lady." She bobbed a small curtsy and scurried from the room.

Siubhan threw her head back and laughed in delight. *Mouse,* she thought with contempt.

§ § §

The carriage jolted from side to side as the road to the Mages Enclave deteriorated to a rut-filled track. A heavy, wet, early spring snow had fallen overnight and covered the budding trees and bushes with a coat of white ice. Siubhan cursed as her shoulder jarred against the hard wooden side. Sharlay sat across from her on the thinly padded seat, staring stonily out of the window, swaying with the movement of the vehicle.

Siubhan could feel the simmering resentment that radiated from her apprentice.

"So, you don't want to come with me to meet our esteemed High Mage?" she asked.

Sharlay whipped her head toward Siubhan. Her tight lips and narrowed pale blue eyes, as well as her flared nostrils gave the lie to her words. "Of course I do, my lady. He is, after all, the most powerful mage in Ard Ri," Sharlay mocked. Tendrils of white-blond hair, enhanced by magic, curled at the sides of her face. Her short, pleasingly plump figure was fetchingly clad in a mahogany brown travelling jacket and skirt. The hood of the heavy brown wool cloak protected her head. An ermine muff covered her hands to keep them warm.

Siubhan's left eyebrow rose as she contemplated the ignorance of her apprentice. "Keep a civil tongue in your head or you will pay the price," she advised with a light laugh. "You have no idea what's coming."

"Have you practiced the spell and shield exercises I set for you?" she continued with a small smile and a coquettish turn of her head, watching the woman from the corner of her eye.

Sharlay glared at her. "Of course I have."

Without hesitation or warning, Siubhan cast her spell, pushed Sharlay's head back against the wood of the carriage and locked her body in a coil of magic. Sharlay grunted as her head hit the wood and the air left from her lungs.

"Why don't you have your shield up?" Siubhan asked sweetly.

She held the other woman in her magic until Sharlay began to struggle frantically, trying to draw a breath.

With a nod of her head, she released the woman. "Don't ever challenge me again. You will regret it."

Hate narrowed Sharlay's eyes and tightened her jaw. She dropped her eyes to her hands, clenching them together. She sat rigidly on the seat, as if frozen in place. Siubhan felt magic surround Sharlay as the woman raised her shields. They really were quite strong.

Siubhan reached out and patted Sharlay's clenched hands. "Come, come, my dear. We'll be at the enclave soon and really should present a united front." She sat back and turned to watch the empty snow-covered fields pass by.

$ $ $

The sun had almost touched the edge of the world when Siubhan's carriage pulled to a stop in front of the gates to the Mages Enclave. Stone walls, rising taller than the top of the carriage, extended to the right and left of the road. The setting sun turned them a deep blood red. A pair of closed wooden gates blocked entry. Siubhan stuck her head out of the window of the carriage and eyed the gates. She frowned. They should have stood open.

She unlatched the carriage door and pushed it open. The footman jumped from his place at the back of the carriage and hurried to her, extending his arm to give her support as she descended the small stairs beneath the door.

Once standing on the ground, she turned to the gates and frowned again. She reached out and let her magic touch the wood. A mental shove coaxed the gates to start moving. She watched impassively as they swung open.

A man stood in the middle of the road on the other side of the gates. A coldly handsome face neither welcomed nor repelled. His black hair swept across his forehead and fell to his shoulders. He wore a white robe trimmed at the bottom with gold runes. It flowed unbelted from his shoulders to his feet. Long sleeves fell to his fingertips. He gripped a golden staff in his right hand, the end of it grounded next to the black boots she glimpsed on his feet. A white cloak covered the robe, its hood pushed back, hanging down his back.

Siubhan sank into a deep curtsey. "My Lord Mage, the King sends his greetings. I am here as you requested."

Without a word, the High Mage of the Ard Ri Mages Enclave turned and walked away toward the main tower of the grounds.

Siubhan turned back to the carriage, accepted the hand that the footman held out to her and stepped in. "Drive on" she ordered the driver.

# Chapter 4
# Dream Training

The sky was the faded blue of early spring, small puffy clouds dotting the expanse as the girls made their way from the Tower to the armory following the meeting in the Library.

"I wonder what Aeden thinks about all this," Breanna mused.

"We'll find out," Marta said, pulling the right-hand door open and holding it for her young companion.

"I've seen you and Thomas talking after last-meal. Do you like him?" Breanna asked with a wicked gleam in her eyes.

Marta's eyebrows rose. "What's not to like? He's smart and considerate. He worries about everyone else and takes his duties seriously."

"He's pretty good looking, too," Breanna laughed as she ducked away from the shove she knew was coming. They crossed the practice floor and walked toward the south door.

"Stop it," Marta threatened. "He and I are friends. Leave it at that."

Breanna lost her laughter as she turned to her friend. "I'm sorry. I won't say anything again."

Marta gave her a small smile. "It's fine."

They reached the back door of the armory and pushed through it. Beyond was the cottage that Aeden used as her home. She sat on a low stool to the left of the blue front door set in the middle of the whitewashed wall. The rasp of her whetstone filled the air as she ran it along the length of OathKeeper's blade. She glanced up as the girls approached. The windows on either side of the door stood open.

Aeden picked up the oiled rag lying across her leg and slid it down the Sword.

"Glad you could make it," she said, her voice as dry as high summer in the desert.

"Thomas told us to hurry, but I needed to get the training gear put away properly," Marta told her, shamefaced.

"Pull up a seat," Aeden gestured with the rag at the logs cut to sitting height standing by the front door.

The girls obliged, Breanna struggling to roll the heavy wood. She unclipped SunWalker from her belt as she lowered herself onto the log, pulled her own whetstone from the small pouch hanging at her side and began to sharpen her Sword.

"Might as well do something useful while we talk," she said, irritation lacing her voice as she noticed the raised eyebrows on both of her companions.

Giving a sharp nod, Aeden slid OathKeeper into his scabbard and leaned it against the wall behind her.

"Tell me about your dreams," she said to Marta as she rested her hands on her knees, back ramrod straight.

Marta stiffened with apprehension, a frown flashing across her face. "I'm...I don't know what to tell you," she responded.

"When was your last dream?" Aeden asked.

"Two nights ago," Marta mumbled.

Aeden cocked her head to the right. "What was it about?"

"I saw," she hesitated for a moment, then finished with a rush, "the trader on the Traders Road back to Fasach. Breanna and I were with her. We were riding camels, although I knew that our horses were with the others that the trader has. Four guards were with us, except they weren't dressed like guards. They were dressed like traders! There was a man riding with us wearing a purple cloak."

The rasp of Breanna's whetstone against SunWalker's length slowed and stopped as she listened. As Marta spoke of her dream, she couldn't help the gasp that escaped her.

"I had the same dream," she exclaimed, "except Maaike was thinking about what she was going to tell her master when we got to Fasach."

Aeden sat in stillness as the girls looked at each other in astonishment.

"There is no doubt that both of you dream true," she said at last. "The question is how can you control who you observe and the timing of your dreams."

Breanna slumped on her seat. "I've been having nightmares every single night for weeks," she told Aeden. "I'll wake up, then go back to sleep and have another dream, like this last one about the trader."

Aeden reached out and put her hands on the girl's shoulders. "What you are going to learn is called lucid dreaming. You will be asleep and will recognize that you are asleep, but you will wake within the dream.

There is a path that you must follow to enter and return from the dream world. It begins with quieting your mind and setting your thoughts on that path." A picture of a path through a quiet forest bloomed in the girls' minds. *It is a path walked by many as they enter the dreamtime*, the Red Dragon said. *Most do not go past the gate to wake in the astral realms of dreams.*

*Come inside and let us practice*, OathKeeper said to them.

"Remember when I taught you about how to shield your minds when you first learned of your magic?" Aeden asked.

The girls nodded in unison as they stood and followed Aeden into her home. Aeden pointed to the chairs set in front of the fireplace that dominated the room. A fire gently popped and crackled at the back of the hearth. The warmth it radiated was comforting.

"That is the essence of controlling the dreams. Shielding your sleeping mind from attachment to others is just another step for you to learn. Before you sleep, create a mirror shield that will bend the thoughts of others away from you. The spell I will teach you creates the shield."

Breanna's eyes brightened. "I can do that. Maybe I'll finally be able to sleep through the night."

Aeden interrupted. "You must repeat this spell before every journey into dreams. Hold your hands out, palms away from you, and repeat these words three times."

> Capture eyes and make them see
> The things that hide behind me
> Show the air and show the land
> Reflect the image that I planned.
> Keep me safe, three by three,
> With harm to none, so mote it be.

Aeden snapped her hands up into the air, as if throwing something into the sky. "When you awaken, use this gesture, and release the spell with:

> Thanks to those who gave me peace
> To follow that which drew my dream
> Free you are to seek your rest

Until I have another request

"You must both repeat this until I am satisfied with your control."

$ $ $

Marta sighed. "How can we be sure we're not sharing our dream between us?" Both she and Breanna drooped with exhaustion.

A smile tugging at the corners of Aeden's mouth. "You can practice walking in each other's dreams. Set the thought of the one you wish to observe firmly in your mind as you go to sleep.

The only thing you must remember once you learn this is to leave your shields down at least once every three or four days. If you leave them up for much longer than that, you risk losing your ability to disguise yourself from the dreamers you are following.

Learning to sift through past dream memories and fragments that your target still remembers will keep you from missing anything important. It may also help to keep notes about your dreams."

Breanna wrinkled her nose and pursed her lips. "Like I'm doing for the Keep records."

Aeden nodded in agreement. "Sometimes our minds won't let go of something until it is brought back into the world," their teacher told them. "There is also this. You will learn to recognize the person in whose dreams you walk. Keeping them from seeing *you* is more difficult. We call it astral remote viewing, watching from above and behind. Practicing on those you know will give you control. There may come a time when you can do both mirroring and viewing while you are awake."

Breanna and Marta sat spellbound by the warrior woman's words.

"Can we practice now, just like we did with the mindshield?" Breanna leaned forward.

"Of course you can," Aeden said. "Relax, quiet your mind, and let's begin. OathKeeper, if you would join us?"

# Chapter 5
# Mannan's Quandary

Siubhan swept into the room assigned for her use at the Mages Enclave. Sharlay followed closely, carrying Siubhan's heavy chest of magical implements, powders, and herbs. Siubhan gracefully waved her hand toward a bench at the foot of her bed.

"Put the chest there," she ordered. Sharlay marched to the bench and let the chest thud to its surface. "Careful," Siubhan barked at her apprentice. The box, made of exotic dark wood and intricately carved with protective runes and sigils, seemed to squat on the bench, much like a toad.

Skullies carried a trunk and boxes into the room, depositing them in front of the wardrobe that stood on the wall opposite the door. They began to shake out the clothing from the trunk and hang it up. Siubhan's box of powders and brushes found a home on the vanity across the room. Sharlay stood by the door, waiting impatiently to be dismissed.

"Oh, go on," Siubhan snapped at her. "See that savories are sent up from the kitchen within the half-candlemark."

Sharlay scowled and left the room as quickly as she could without running, shutting the door behind her. Siubhan chuckled.

The skullies finished unpacking her trunks and boxes and curtsied as they left the room. Savories were delivered along with a pitcher of watered mead and a silver goblet. She reveled in the luxury of being served.

*I shall have a bath and meet with the High Mage in the morning,* she thought as she sampled the delicacies on the tray by her bed.

$ $ $

A scarlet robed second year apprentice arrived at her door. "Cailleach, the High Mage requests your presence in his chambers."

"Tell him I'll be right along," she said with a casual wave of her hand. The apprentice bowed and left her.

*Mustn't appear as if I'm...afraid,* her thoughts flitted. *Perhaps the blue gown. Yes. It sets just the right tone.*

$ $ $

The High Mage looked up from the scroll that he was reading. Siubhan stood framed in the doorway, demurely waiting for him to notice her.

"Come in," he invited as he rose from his chair behind the heavy ornate table that served as his desk. He was taller than she remembered. His white robes seemed to shine with an inner light.

His chambers were on the highest floor of the Mages Tower. A small fire burned in the white brick fireplace behind him. A picture frame draped with white fabric hung above the mantle over the fireplace. A cushion-less straight-backed chair sat to the right side of the table. Books on white shelves lined the walls. A door to the left of the fireplace stood partially open. Leaded windows on the walls to the left and right of his desk gave a glimpse of blue sky and the roofs of the Mages Enclave.

"It is good of you to grace the Enclave," he murmured.

"I'm concerned at the timing of your summons," she responded.

"As well you should be. A certain missive that you sent to Red Dragon's Keep and the young whelp that holds it has provoked a response that I neither expecting nor wanted. The Black Dragon 'removed the messenger. Were you aware that he had returned?"

Siubhan leaned away from the mage in dismay and then quickly narrowed her eyes in suspicion. "How do you know of this, my lord?"

"It is not for you to question," the High Mage rumbled, his face a study in menace, eyes narrowed and glittering, lips bared across clenched teeth, hands fisting on the table. Magic pulsed in the air. Siubhan shivered. His anger darkened the room.

"I merely sent a message requesting his presence at Cathair Ri, to help the king." Siubhan quavered, her voice trembling in sudden fear. She did not reveal that she had bespelled the wax seal on the scroll to poison Thomas Arach as soon as he touched it. "The spell on the words would have made the brat sick every time he looked at or smelled food. It would have rid us of his presence. Isn't that what you wished?" she whined.

A spark of fire flashed deep in the High Mage's dark eyes. His nostrils flared. Faster than Siubhan could blink, he was in front of her, lifting her by the neck without effort. She gagged and began to struggle, hands grasping his wrists, feet flailing. His fingers tightened.

"One shake is all it takes to break your neck, you foolish woman," he roared in her face. His fingers loosened slightly, allowing her to breath. "Your arrogance has cost me the element of surprise. That Keep is the key to the rest of the kingdom. It must be broken. Every center of magic must be obliterated. You shall pay the first price for your stupidity."

"I'm sorry, High Mage. You didn't make yourself clear about your plans. Had you shared, I wouldn't have sent the messenger," she whined again.

"You are useless," he spoke through gritted teeth. He thrust his magic into her heart and began to strip her of her power. She shrieked in pain and fear. He stopped her screams with a twist of magic down her throat. He laughed in glee as her magic filled him. When she was completely drained, he broke her neck with a snap of his hands and threw her body against the wall next to the door. Her head hit with the thud and crack of a breaking melon. Her body fell to the floor and did not move, blood seeping from ears, nose, mouth, and the back of her head.

He pulled the door open and ordered his secretary into the room. "Have that removed and call her apprentice," he told the man as he waved his hand at the body and blood, the chill of ice in his voice.

§ § §

Sharlay stood transfixed at the door of the High Mage's chamber. There was blood on the floor. A third-year apprentice in dark blue robes knelt by the pool, wiping it up with an old rag, wringing it out into a half-filled bucket of water. She raised her eyes to find the High Mage staring at her. She felt the blood drain from her face. Her breathing quickened.

"Your name," he snapped at her.

Sharlay swallowed against a dry throat, almost choking.

"Sh...Sh...Sharlay," she stammered. She heard him audibly grind his teeth. "High Mage," she added hastily.

"Your mentor is dead." He waved his hand at the blood on the floor. The apprentice rose from his knees, picked up the bucket of red-tinged water and carried it out of the room. "She overstepped her authority and has paid the price. You will take her place."

He flicked the fingers of his left hand, and she felt a massive jolt of energy slam against her shields. The energy pushed her back two steps, but her shield held.

Mannan threw magic attack after attack at her. Energy flashed across the space between them. Sharlay retreated one step at a time, back into the hallway outside of Mannan's chamber. She countered everything that he sent. Spectacular fountains of dissipating energy filled the room and reached beyond into the corridor as his magic rebounded from her shield.

Gathering her nerve, she dropped her protection and shot a bolt of energy at the High Mage, quickly snapping her shield back in place. She was tiring rapidly. Her stomach cramped. She was fast losing her ability to maintain her shield at all.

Her attack pushed Mannan back two steps. He looked at her with contempt. "You grow weak," he taunted. He threw back his head and laughed.

Sharlay saw red. Her rage, always kept bound deep inside, instantly rose, and filled her body. She dropped her shield, raised her arms, and flung bolt after bolt of red energy toward his body and head. He staggered back against his desk.

A sneer twisted his lips. He bared his teeth. His eyes glittered with internal fire. He straightened slowly. Raising his arm, he pointed his finger at her. A thread of power reached out and slammed into Sharlay's heart. She gasped in agony and clutched at her chest.

He began to suck the power out of her body. She shrieked in pain and flung a last waning bolt of magic toward her tormentor. She dropped to her knees, straining to breathe. She slumped to her side, unconscious.

Mannan broke his connection to what was left of her power. Her mind was gone as well.

He stood tall in his white robes, exalting in the magic that he had taken from her. *I should do this more often*, he thought.

"Come and set this mewling idiot outside the gates," he shouted to his assistant.

He'd felt a flash of power when the second amulet was found in the far north of Ard Ri. The sorcerer's jaw clenched, hands curling into fists. His heart began to beat a furious tattoo. His fury knew no bounds. He'd made sure that the Aos Si amulet was hidden well and then forgotten. *Who is meddling in my affairs? Whoever it is, they* must *be stopped! I'll wager it's the other Arach whelps.*

Mannan closed his eyes and took several deep breaths, quieting his anger, sending it to the place in his mind that he kept walled away from the present. Slowly, his anger cooled, his heartbeat returned to normal.

He walked to the window that looked out over the roofs of Caithar Ri and braced his arms on the window-sill.

*There is no one to send as the King's Mage.* He straightened and stood in reflection for several moments, chin in hand, as he listened to two apprentices lift the woman he had broken and carry her from the room.

"I suppose I'll have to do it myself," he spoke to the room and gave a dramatic sigh, hand to chest, rolling his eyes to look at the ceiling.

# Chapter 6
# Dragon Dreams

Breanna built her dream shield one layer at a time. It reminded her of watching the bricklayers raise a wall to keep the dirt in the garden, brick by brick and row by row. She repeated the spell that Aeden had taught her. Going to sleep early for ten days was making it easier and easier, both to raise the barrier and fall asleep quickly. Tonight, she planned to practice finding Marta in the dreamscape.

As soon as Breanna raised the shield, she let it thin. Her path stretched before her with the gate at its end. She set eager feet along it and pushed through the gate into the astral plane. What looked like a rolling fog covered the area. Breanna set her mind firmly on Marta's life pulse. She saw a glow through the fog off to her left. She sent her mind across the rolling fog toward the light. The fog thinned and she could see Marta, a thin reflection of her, but Marta, nonetheless.

She damped down her own life pulse until it was but a dim flicker in the fog. Slowly she approached Marta's light until she stood right behind her. She watched as Marta's dream unfolded before her.

Her friend was riding a horse along the banks of a rushing river. The sound of the water drowned out the drumming of hoofbeats. Marta threw herself from the horse as it leapt into the river and swam to the other side. Marta floated above the horse and landed lightly on its back as it emerged on the opposite shore. Breanna followed, finally reaching out and setting her hand on Marta's shoulder.

Marta turned her head and grinned at her friend. "I knew you'd come," she giggled. "Wake now and come to my room. It's time for us to practice together."

$ $ $

Breanna let her dream shield fall and opened her mind to possibility.

She walked on a path made of crushed black rock. A glittering mist billowed about her, as if breathed from mighty lungs in gentle gusts. She stood on the side of a mountain, a mountain she had seen before through Marta's eyes, the Dragon's Mountain.

She armored herself in a cloak of mirroring with quick flicks of thought. Thank goodness she and Marta had been practicing every single night for the past fortnight. The shield formed itself around her, deflecting attention from her essence. Something brushed against the side of her protection. The contact felt like silky fingers trailing along her shield's surface.

*I see you, Arach's daughter. Why have you come here?* The deep cold voice rumbled through her dream, vibrating in her chest.

Breanna looked at the speaker sitting next to her. A Dragon clad in purple scales, from deepest midnight purple on his spines to a beautiful shade of palest lilac on his belly curled his tail around his feet. The edge of every scale sparkled with silver starlight. One slanted eye of clear radiant amber set on the side of an enormous head stretching into a muzzle filled with triangular teeth that showed below the edge of his lips watched her without blinking. She shivered as her shield dropped.

*You know who I am. What may I call you?*

The great head turned to look at her with close attention.

*You may not call me at all,* the creature said.

*Then I shall simply say "Purple" to refer to you. I have come to ask about my cousin Cameron. The Arach Dubh was with him when he went missing from the Dragon Tower.*

*They are not missing,* the Dragon told her, arrogance and disdain clear in his voice. *They are here.*

Breanna paused, choosing her words carefully. *Thank you. I will find them now.*

She felt the Dragon reach with his mind to keep her from leaving his side.

She thought of the Dragon King as she had last seen him, a tall man clothed in supple black leather, black knee-high riding boots, and a midnight cape sprinkled with starlight and trimmed with the white fur of mountain dire cats. His black eyes were set above a large prominent nose on a long saturnine face. She gasped as her thought brought her to him. A shiver of unease raced up her spine.

Neulach stood in the center of a vast great hall, the white walls gleaming in the light of thousands of candles. The polished black floor reflected millions of white stars from the candle flames. Dragons in human form sat in groups on elegant furniture placed around the room or milled about at the edges of the space. Artwork, both Dragon and human, hung on the walls.

Neulach cocked his head and looked at her, left eyebrow raised, amusement glinting in his eyes.

*Breanna. You come to find your cousin. He is well.*

In her dream, Breanna bowed deeply before Neulach. *Yes, my lord, I've come about Cameron. She hesitated, then continued despite her fear, "I've searched for him in dreams. I need to know that he's all right. We all need to know. Why did you take him? What is he doing here? Why haven't you come back?*

The Arach Dubh stiffened. *Your cousin is an extremely powerful mage. He is in training to use his talents in the safest place I know. No one and nothing can find him to corrupt him or his power.*

Breanna stood speechless, shock coursing through her body. Cameron, a mage? A powerful mage? She shook her head from side to side in wonder.

*Please. Tell him that his mother and father live. They are on their way with the Duke and Duchess to find out if the King is a traitor.*

Neulach went still. Though his eyes were locked on her, Breanna knew that his thoughts were far away.

*Perhaps I should visit to calm fears and question my daughter. Others will guard Cameron. I shall send a messenger to you. Ah, I see you have met... "Purple" is it?* Humor at her choice of name and the reason she had chosen it tumbled through Breanna's dream. *He will find you. Return to your dream world, young Arach.*

Breanna woke with a start as her body sat up straight in bed. "By the Three Gods," she breathed. Her stomach clenched as she remembered the purple Dragon she had met. "I need to tell Thomas."

# Chapter 7
# Mannan's Plan

Mannan took another sip of the red wine that he favored. Only bones remained of the excellent meal of pigeon and roasted vegetables the Cathair Ri cooks had produced. The fingers on his other hand beat out a soft pattern on the table as his thoughts moved from strategy to strategy, searching for a way to exploit this turn of events.

The Dragon King and the Arach cousin had disappeared. He'd felt the instant that the Arach Dubh and his young companion vanished. Plan after plan flitted through his mind as he considered and rejected each one.

*I could search for them using magic, but Neulach will recognize it. I can't risk him knowing where I am. I might set a trap for them should they return. Or is there some way to use Neulach's power to call a pack of Demons and perhaps end him?*

He shook his head. *I'll have to promote one of the five on the council to High Mage,* he thought. *Then I will return as the King's Mage to "guide" him in his rule.*

Decision made, he pushed his chair away from the table and stood. "Invite Mage Trison to join me in the oratory," he ordered the acolyte assigned to serve him. The young boy hurried from the room.

§ § §

The High Mage scanned the palace with his mind as the seneschal ushered him into the audience hall. He felt intriguing tendrils of power but could not tell where they came from. He dismissed his guide and, once the man had withdrawn and closed the doors, sealed the chamber with a spell of silence. He approached the throne and bowed with a flourish before the King of Ard Ri. He straightened and looked him in the eye. "Sire, I regret to inform you that your Mage, Siubhan and her apprentice, were slain by unknown forces that I am tracking with my magic. I have returned to you in her stead."

The King paled, then flushed with anger. He regarded Mannan, head cocked to the side, eyes narrowed, lips compressed in a thin line. "You would do well to find the murderer quickly. Suibhan was my strong right hand and someone I wished to keep close," he spoke through gritted teeth. "You are the High Mage. Why do you step down from that position? You have all the power over magic in Ard Ri at the Mages Enclave. Here you are only my advisor. Why?

"Sire, you and I both know that the Demons must prevail in this war. I seek but to help with that task. Mage

Trison has been appointed High Mage. He is easily led and will serve us well, monitoring and reporting on the other mages in the kingdom," Mannan answered the king, his words backed by the subtlest of power.

The king sat silent, pondering the mage's words, running his thumb and forefinger from the corners of his mouth to his chin as he thought, eyes filled with suspicion. Finally, he nodded in agreement. "Very well. You may serve as the King's Mage. Join me for last-meal this evening. We will discuss what must be done to support the Demon Lord in his plans."

Mannan bowed in response. "As you wish, Sire." He turned in a swirl of black cloth trimmed with white ermine and strode from the chamber, dismissing his spell as he left. His first order of business must be to search for the amulet he was convinced lay hidden in Cathair Ri.

# Chapter 8
# Mission to Fasach

Breanna stalked from one side of her room to the other. Her hands were clenched in anger, her face scrunched in a scowl. She stopped and stamped her feet.

"You arrogant lickspittle. I'm going to kill Neulach! This is unbelievable!"

The Dragon shapeshifter she'd met in her dream materialized as a human, making her shout as she jumped away. "Purple" smirked at her and lounged back on the chair next to her fireplace.

His black hair gleamed with purple highlights. Eyes the color of amber glittered at her. When he smiled, the sense of menace increased in the room. He wore a silver tunic and black trousers, with a purple cape draped over his arm. Right leg crossed over left, black riding boots covered his feet and legs to his knees.

"Why are you here?" Breanna demanded. "You shouldn't even be in my room. How did you get in here?"

The shapeshifter laughed.

"The mighty Neulach required that I come to you," he mocked her. "I have come as my king commands."

Breanna felt a trickle of power from her Sword of Light. She stopped her pacing in front of the sword stand.

The Dragon's black vertical pupils dilated a tiny amount as the power bloomed. He frowned.

Breanna's gaze sharpened, aware of his disquiet.

"Have you met a Sword of Light, "Purple"?" she purred.

She leaned back and grabbed SunWalker, stripping the scabbard from the blade in one swift movement as she turned to face him. Light flashed along its length as it burst into flame.

He sprang to his feet and backed away from the duo.

Breanna grinned with glee and advanced on the Dragon in human form. "So, there IS something you fear. Good thing to know," she said.

"I fear nothing," the Dragon shapeshifter responded, his haughtiness evident in every line of his body.

"Really." Breanna's sarcastic tone lashed at the Dragon. "Let's test that."

She lunged forward, SunWalker at full extension. She stopped an inch from the Dragon's chest as he tried to press himself through the stone wall behind him.

"Stop," he exclaimed.

"Why should I?" Breanna taunted back.

"The Arach Dubh sent me to protect you. I regret my...insolence. Let us be at peace."

Breanna slowly withdrew. "Then I suggest you arrive as a Dragon above the Tower and land in the forecourt. It is unseemly to be in my room alone with me. You obviously have never dealt with humans. Do as I say," she told him, ice in her voice. "Now."

The shapeshifter disappeared.

Within a tenth of a candlemark, Breanna heard the pounding of booted feet in the corridor outside her room.

"Dragon," someone shouted. "A purple Dragon above the forecourt."

With a snort, Breanna retrieved the scabbard she had dropped on the floor and slid SunWalker into it.

*Why did you stop? He was clearly threatening you,* the Sword asked her.

*I wasn't sure he was afraid until he apologized, and I didn't really want to hurt him,* Breanna murmured to her companion. *I just wanted to teach him a lesson.*

She hurried from her room, making sure to spell the door locked, clipping her sword to her belt. She shook her right hand as if trying to fling water from it. A grimace tightened her lips as the pain in her hand receded.

"Thomas, wait," she shouted down the hall as she saw her brother exit his room and stride toward the stairwell to the great hall. He stopped and turned as she ran to him. "The purple Dragon was sent by Neulach. He thinks I need protection."

Thomas's eyebrows rose in surprise. "What? How do you know?"

"Because the idiot appeared in my room about a quarter of a candlemark ago. I had to threaten him with SunWalker before he'd leave. I told him to arrive in the forecourt. That's him." She jerked her head toward the great hall.

"Well, let's go meet your 'protector'," her brother ordered, unsuccessfully trying to hide a grin as he gestured for her to precede him.

The two siblings made their way down the stairs and through the great hall where skullies scrubbed down trestle tables and spread fresh rushes on the floor. Thomas pushed the doors open. They were just in time to watch a Dragon the color of the evening sky as it shaded from deepest blue to purple to black land in the space at the foot of the stairs.

The Dragon's wingbeats raised a cloud of dust and blew small rocks and debris across the ground. The silver edging on each of his scales glittered in the rising sun. Nostrils flared as wings folded neatly along the black spines that lined its back.

Lady Aeden strode out of the opening to the Lady's Tower on the east side of the forecourt as the Dragon landed. She trotted up the entry stairs to stand behind Thomas and Breanna.

The Dragon was abruptly hidden by a whirlwind that looked like purple smoke. As it dissipated, a young man walked out of it, anger evident in every line of his body. He was dressed in black trousers tucked into knee-high black boots, a silver tunic, and a voluminous purple cape that billowed out as he stormed toward the trio. The heels of his boots beat out a thudding pattern of ire.

Breanna skipped down the stairs and gave an elaborate bow to the approaching man. He came to an abrupt halt, rocking back on his heels, trying to avoid running her down as she straightened. She raised taunting eyes to his face, eyebrows arched, eyelashes fluttering.

"Welcome, Lord Dragon, to Red Dragon's Keep. I am Breanna Arach, daughter of Duke Arach." She gestured to the top of the stairs. "This is my brother, Thomas, heir to the Keep, and this is Lady Aeden, the Red Dragon." Her words mocked him.

A growl of frustration escaped him. "I know who you are, smart mouthed girl." He bowed to those still standing at the top of the stairs.

Lady Aeden arched a brow at him. His cheeks colored in embarrassment. He bowed with a flourish to the daughter of the King of the Dragons. "My Lady, how fare thee?"

"I am well, Corcra. What brings the King's Voice to this Keep?" A warning was given in her tone.

Corcra straightened slowly and took a step back. "The Black Dragon has commanded me to visit and assure those here that the human named Cameron is well and learning magecraft at his side. No human has ever had such a teacher."

Breanna squealed and whirled toward him, punched him in the arm. "Why didn't you tell me, you oaf? We've been worried sick about him. I wasn't sure if that part of the dream was real."

Corcra recoiled from her blow. He turned his head to glare at her.

"Be careful whom you touch and how, human," he growled through clenched teeth.

Aeden took the ten steps down to the forecourt in a rush. She ranged herself next to Breanna. "Be careful whom you threaten, Corcra." Her words were threaded with threat and power.

"Forgive me, Lord Corcra. I meant no disrespect." Breanna spoke slowly and distinctly, trying desperately to diffuse the situation she had created with her actions. "We've been very concerned about his wellbeing."

The tension radiating from both Aeden and Corcra eased. Hands curled ready to strike relaxed. Tightened muscles in arms, legs, and backs lengthened. Heartbeats slowed.

"Neulach also commanded that I accompany this one," he jerked his chin toward Breanna, "on her journey."

Thomas frowned as he joined the group at the bottom of the stairs. "What journey?"

Corcra glanced at Aeden. "Time is mutable," he murmured.

"Learn to live in the moment," Aeden advised.

"What journey?" Thomas raised his voice.

Corcra stepped away from the group and bowed to Thomas. "I cannot say, Lord Thomas. This must be of you and your sister's choosing."

A frown lowered Thomas's brows as his lips narrowed with irritation. He turned and started up the stairs. "Dragons," he muttered, sarcasm dripping from the word.

The others followed him into the Dragon Tower.

§ § §

Thomas led them through the great hall and down the corridor to his father's office. He pushed the door open. A beast, black as night, huge claws extended from massive paws, mouth gaping wide revealing teeth as sharp as daggers, launched itself at him from the middle of the room. Thomas stumbled back with a shout of fear, pushing the others aside as he fell. A claw grazed his shoulder, cutting it to the bone. Blood gushed.

Swords hissed from scabbards as the two Dragons and the young girl drew them. SunWalker burst into flame as Breanna swept the blade up into the neck of the leaping creature. The head flew from the demon and bounced across the corridor. Its body landed next to Thomas. He rolled away and surged back to his feet.

"AHHH!" he shouted. Adrenaline surged as he ripped HellReaver from its sheath and plunged it into the body lying next to him. Blue heatless flame flickered and spread over the body, consuming it.

The two humans stepped back and leaned against the wall, both panting. "What was that?" Breanna gasped. The flaming swords extinguished their fire.

"It's not like any Demon I've seen before," Thomas gasped out. "Not even close to those that attacked the Keep before Aeden transformed into a Dragon.

Aeden and Corcra slid their Swords into their scabbards. Aeden knelt next to Thomas.

"Better question is how did it get in here?" Aeden hissed.

Blood still trickled down Thomas's arm. Aeden reached out and laid her fingertips on his shoulder. She gasped. With quick hands she ripped the tunic from his body. Black lines radiated from the wound on his shoulder down his chest toward his heart. Thomas lost what little color was on his face as he slid down the wall to the floor.

"Why are you not healing? Corcra, he usually heals within minutes."

"What?" Breanna gaped at her brother.

Corcra reached out and laid his own fingers on Thomas. "Poison."

"Thomas, you must center and ground yourself," Aeden commanded, pulling him forward to lean against her shoulder. "Breanna, lend your strength to his."

Thomas quieted his mind and found his center with difficulty. He sent tendrils deep into the earth beneath the Dragon Tower. His body quieted. His mind calmed. Breanna knelt and put her hand on his arm sending him a trickle of power, boosting his own. HellReaver and Sun-Walker joined in the effort. As they all watched, the black lines began to recede, magic burning out the poison coursing through Thomas's body. He grunted with pain.

Black turned to grey and disappeared. The wound on his shoulder began to close as his own magic surged. The wound sealed shut, leaving a long pink scar in its place. Thomas sighed as Aeden leaned him back against wall.

"We will sweep the room to find how that abomination gained access," Aeden told them, her voice as chill as ice. She gestured at Corcra to follow her into the office.

Breanna put her hand on her thigh with slow deliberation. "How long have you been able to do that?" she murmured to her brother. "Do Mother and Father know?"

Thomas didn't answer. He leaned his head back against the wall and closed his eyes. "Can you let it go for right now? I'm very tired."

"Do they know?" Breanna asked with quiet persistence.

"I don't know. I wasn't hurt during the battles, so there was nothing to heal. I didn't even think about it to tell them," he grumbled. "And don't you tell them either."

"Why not," she demanded. "They should know. Can you heal other things, or just yourself? When did you find out you could do it? Is there..."

"Just stop. This isn't yours to tell. Go in and help Aeden and Corcra find out where that beast came from," Thomas ordered.

"Well," Breanna harrumphed and surged to her feet. She stomped down the hall and into the office.

§ § §

Breanna helped herself to the boiled beef and vegetables from the large tray that Aeden ordered from the kitchen. She took her heaping plate behind her father's desk and sat in his chair to eat.

Thomas sat in one of the wing-backed chairs in front of the fireplace on the left side of the room, his face gaining color as he ate. He'd paid the price for using his healing magic and was exhausted and famished. He forked food into his mouth without pausing. When he'd cleared his plate twice, he set it on the floor next to his chair.

Breanna looked up at the thump of the plate on the rug. Her eyes narrowed as she watched Thomas lean his head back against the chair. He still looked drained and spent. She inhaled to ask a question, releasing it at an index finger raised by Aeden. She frowned, her mouth scrunched in mulish stubbornness.

Corcra lounged in the chair next to Thomas. His eyes followed Breanna's every move. At her expression of displeasure, he laughed outright.

"Have patience young Arach. All answers come in time." His regard shifted to Thomas. "Are you well?"

"I'm better, thank you." Thomas looked at Aeden. "What did you find?"

"This was a Demon from no world that I know. It is not from the world of the Demons that we fought before. It is linked to a very powerful Demon; one might almost say a Demon god. The rift opened in this office powered by that Demon. It was sent specifically to kill you."

Thomas turned his head and looked at Corcra. "You mentioned a journey. What journey? Where is she to go?"

"It is your choice, Lord Thomas. Given the questions that must be answered and the things that must be found, where would your sister be of best use? She could stay here and continue her machinations and disruptions, or she could be sent to find those answers."

"Hey," Breanna protested, her voice rising. "I don't 'machinate', whatever that means, and I don't disrupt."

"Do you not? Did you not almost bring Lady Aeden and myself to blows? Did you not chivy your brother to find out about his healing power? Did you not question the wisdom of the Dragon King himself, prompting him to send me to accompany you?"

Breanna's mouth snapped shut. Thomas's and Aeden's eyes got larger and larger as Corcra listed her misdeeds.

Quiet settled on the room. Eventually, Thomas cleared his throat. "I need to stay here and so does Aeden. I think you're right, Corcra. Breanna should travel to Fasach with Maaike. Marta can go with her. That way they can watch each other's backs and gather twice the information."

Aeden snorted and added, "There is also this. Marta dreamed that she and Breanna were riding camels along a trail following Maaike. Breanna dreamed there was a man wearing a purple cloak riding with them. They told me about their dreams when I first started to teach them." She looked at Corcra. "Indeed, time is mutable." She smiled.

Thomas leaned forward in his chair and swung to face Breanna. "Are you willing to go to Fasach as our eyes and ears?"

Breanna looked from Thomas to Aeden and last to Corcra. "I guess I'm going, whether I want to or not. The dreams spoke true."

# Chapter 9
# WindRunners

The sun rode the sky toward sunset, its light dimmed and brightened as clouds moved across from the northwest. Jenni Arach rode beside her husband, the Lord of Red Dragon's Keep. Deep in thought, she absently guided her horse to the right, closer to him. Her leg bumped his. He twitched his head to the left and glanced at her from the corner of his eye.

"What are you thinking?" he asked, knowing that look very well.

"We need to learn how to ride the WindRunners. We couldn't take the time before we left Aos Si. We should be doing that now. What will their magic do to us when we ride them? How will we stay on when they use the wind to run?" The WindRunners had chosen them in the courtyard of Aos Si after the battle against the attacking Demon horde was won with the help of their Swords of Light, the WindRunners, and the Forest Lords.

Both felt the amusement sent to them by BattleSworn and FireGuard.

Tom frowned.

"I know, I know," she continued, her own frown creating deep lines between her brows. "We've been working with our Swords, but we also need to plan what we're going to do when we get to Cathair Ri," she told him. "Do you think the king is really behind all of this?"

Lord Tom looked to his right at the four black WindRunners that paced beside the column trailing behind them. He listened to the hoofbeats of the horses Anne and Jeremy Gobhlan, the Duke and Duchess of Falcon's Spire, rode just behind them. He glanced to the left at his wife and lifted his eyes to scan beyond her to the empty prairie that stretched away into the distance. Nothing had changed in the four days they had been on the trail.

"Yes, I think he is," he replied with a sigh. "It's the only thing that fits all the things we've been through. Who else could have ordered our kidnapping, or our imprisonment? We were lucky to survive."

"We've not been involved in palace politics," Jenni said. "Why are we important? Why would we need to be removed? It just doesn't make sense," she exclaimed as she fisted her hand and thumped it against her leg.

Tom looked at her, a grin lightening his somber features. "Look to your right."

Jenni turned her head and saw the WindRunner.

"What is your hand resting on?"

Jenni snatched her hand away from the leather-wrapped pommel of her Sword of Light.

"Oh," she muttered as realization bloomed in her mind. She was silent for a time. "But we didn't have the Swords or the WindRunners when we were kidnapped. What else would make us important?"

Tom shook his head. "Who does the king have around him? The King's Mage - I've heard it's a woman -, the Chancellor of the Treasury, the general of the armies, the High Mage of the Mages Enclave, and anyone who wants to curry favor with the king. He's asked me to attend innumerable times and, thank the Three Gods, there's always been something to keep me away. It's a nest of vipers." He grimaced with distaste.

Jenni sat easily in the saddle, moving with the rhythm of her horse. "I wonder if someone knew that Lady Aeden was Neulach's daughter. That would mean that they knew about her before she broke the spell binding her magic and shapeshifting ability. Who could possibly know that?"

Tom's forehead knotted as he frowned in thought. His eyes absently scanned the land around them, regardless of the scouts he'd sent out as sentries.

*BattleSworn, do you have any idea who might have known about Lady Aeden?* He sent the thought tentatively toward his Sword of Light. He was still uncomfortable carrying a weapon that held magic and could talk to him. His discomfort increased as the Sword responded after several seconds.

*There are those Dragons who elected to remain with humans before the Arach Dubh cast his spell of binding and forgetting. The Red Dragon is one of them. They did not remember that they were Dragons and could not shift to their Dragon form.*

*One attempted to shield himself from the Forgetting but did not have the power to stay the Binding. He hid himself among the people, disguising his Dragon essence so that neither the King nor the Swords could sense him. There is suspicion that much of the chaos through the ages has been instigated by him and others who thirst for power over humans.*

"Huh," Tom grunted, his thoughts racing. He relayed what BattleSworn had told him to his wife.

"So, any one of the King's councilors could be a chained Dragon?" Jenni grimaced and shook her head. "Wonderful."

Tom straightened in his saddle as he noticed a large pillar of dust or smoke beginning to rise to the southwest. He raised his right hand in a signal to halt the convoy. Jeremy and Anne rode forward and joined them. Anne raised her hand to her forehead, shielding her eyes from the glare of the sun.

One of the scouts raised his own dust cloud as he galloped toward the column. He pulled his horse to a sliding stop as he reached his lord. "Sir, reavers are attacking a fortified manor." He nodded at the smoke. "I counted twenty of them."

"That's got to be the Roury Manor," Tom told the others. "Malachi Sandston's been a good friend. Sergeant, form the men. We ride to the manor. Have the wagons follow as they can, four men as guards," he ordered.

The column came together with quick efficiency. Tom heeled his horse into a canter as the others followed in quick succession. WindRunners glided beside them. The horses began to run.

Tom pulled his horse to a stop at the top of the last rise before the mile run down the slope to Roury Manor. The stone building rose three stories high, bordered on the west by the Claring River. Barns and outbuildings stood to the south of the manor. No wall marked its boundary.

Half of the reavers shot flaming pitch covered arrows at the unglazed windows, setting the interior alight. Fire and smoke billowed from the roof and windows. The other half chased after crofters trying to flee from the attack, killing them as they rode them down. Flames raced toward the outbuildings in the dried grasses allowed to grow too close to the walls.

*Shing.*

Tom drew BattleSworn and held it aloft. "CHARGE," he bellowed. The horses jumped into a full out run. Brilliant white light engulfed BattleSworn. Jenni pulled

FireGuard from its scabbard and leaned forward over her horse's neck, Sword extended. A rope of blazing light erupted from the tip and took the head of the reaver watching the burning manor instead of the land behind her.

The reavers turned in surprise as the riders thundered down the slope. The hooves of horses and WindRunners shook the ground as they descended toward the brigands.

Slow to react to the threat, the reavers closest to the racing horses tried to scatter. Then the rescuers were among them. Tom used BattleSworn as a lash, lighting the reaver in front of him with a burning flash. The reaver screamed in agony.

Anne and Jeremy swung wide to the right and rode toward the river and the back of the manor, drawing their own Swords, racing to cut off the reavers running pell-mell away from the charge.

A WindRunner reared high over the leader of the bandits as the reaver shouted orders to his men. Black hooves, each at least a foot across, slashed out in a lighting fast strike at the leader's skull, crushing it. His body reeled out of the saddle as his horse bucked the body off and fled in terror.

The remaining reavers were ridden down and executed by WindRunners and the rest of the men-at-arms. As the last one fell, Tom pulled his horse to a stop and dismounted near the door into the manor, now fully engulfed with fire. The bodies of a man and child lay halfway over the threshold.

*BattleSworn, can you stop this?*

BattleSworn unfurled magic toward the burning building. *Lend me your power,* the Sword requested.

Tom closed his eyes as he tried to send what he didn't know he had to the Sword. He felt a drawing deep in his mind and on the *ki* at his center. BattleSworn wove his magic into a cone like a candlesnuffer over the manor. Deprived of oxygen, the fire guttered and died as Tom opened his eyes and watched. The Sword released his magic with an abruptness that made him gasp in shock. Tom reeled with exhaustion and leaned heavily against his horse.

Jenni stopped next to him and twisted to her left to reach into her saddle bag. She pulled journey cake from its bottom and slid from the saddle. She stood next to him, shoving the food into Tom's hands.

"Eat," she ordered as she took a bite herself. "Remember? Thomas told us to eat after we use magic."

Tom bit into the dry salty-sweet bar and began to chew the leather-like strip. Some of the energy he'd expended began to return as he ate. Jenni handed him dried fruit and her waterskin.

"Thanks," he told her. He finished eating as quickly as he could.

He turned toward the bodies in the doorway. Jenni put a restraining hand on his arm.

"Let the men check," she said, compassion alive in her eyes as he glanced at her.

Tom stared at the burned-out interior of the fortified manor, its thick stone walls branded by the smoke of the flames that had consumed it.

"No. I need to see to this," he said, pushing himself away from his horse. He walked toward the body of the man whom he had called friend. Two of his men followed.

"I'll have camp set up for the night as soon as the wagons arrive," Jenni called after him. He raised his hand in response.

$ $ $

Jenni gestured to the top of the small rise above the burned-out manor. The wind from the northwest blew the lingering smoke and smell of death away from them. "Set up camp just on the other side of that rise close to the river," she told the sergeant in charge of the thirty men-at-arms who rode with them. He saluted and hurried away to begin the process. The supply wagons crested the rise and he shouted at the driver, gesturing for him to follow the soldiers.

Jeremy and Anne rounded the corner of the manor from the side closest to the river. Blood covered their clothing and horses. Both rode with a weary slump. They stopped next to Jenni. Anne dismounted, pulling her waterskin from the saddle, taking a long pull from its spout. She handed it up to Jeremy. Blood seeped from an arrow hanging from his shoulder.

"I'll ride to the fire," he told them.

Jenni took one look at his exhausted face, grabbed the reins of his horse, and started leading them toward the picket line the men had already set up near the river. "At least you had the good sense not to pull that arrow out. Let's get to the campsite and see what we can do about it," she told them.

The tall winter-cured clumps of grass caught at their feet as she and Anne walked. "The horses will have plenty of grazing," Jenni said as she stumbled over one of the clumps.

Reaching the fire the men had started, the women helped Jeremy slide from his horse. He grunted with pain as the arrow grated against the bone of his shoulder. He gasped and grabbed his arm to hold it still and fell to his knees. Anne dropped down next to him. Jenni pulled her saddlebags and blanket from behind the saddle and handed the reins of the horses to a soldier who led them away. She dropped the saddlebags next to Jeremy and unrolled the blanket on the ground behind him.

Jenni glanced up the slope of the hill as movement caught her attention. She watched through narrowed eyes as the WindRunners drifted closer.

*Lubach?* Jenni took several steps up the hill, reached out to the WindRunner, not sure how to communicate with the mare.

*Yes?* The instant response startled Jenni. She took a step toward Lubach, her hand half-raised, wanting to touch, not sure if her gesture would be rejected. Lubach rested her nose on the extended palm.

*Do not be concerned, my friend. I am here to help you save our world.*

Jenni's mouth dropped open with astonishment. Her hand fell away from the WindRunner.

*What?* she asked.

*There is grave danger in what we go to do,* Lubach responded. *This man needs our help quickly.* The WindRunner tossed her nose toward Jeremy.

A deeper voice joined the conversation. *Can there be a greater danger than a Dragon and a King bent on betraying a country?* Tom's WindRunner Anial sent from where he grazed on the dried grass.

"Jenni, I need some help here," Anne called to her.

Siomh and Gaoth came to hover behind Jeremy and Anne. Jenny frowned as she turned to look at them. She strode over to the pair by the fire with quick steps. Kneeling, she grounded her *ki* as she had been taught by Aeden and her sons following the battle for Aos Si.

"What's wrong?" she asked her sister.

"I need more hands to get the arrow out of his shoulder," Anne said.

"Jeremy, we're going to help you lay down," Jenni said as she and Anne linked hands behind his back. Once he was lying flat, she pulled her belt-knife out of its sheath and notched the arrow on both sides. She snapped the arrow off at the notch and set it aside. She raised her eyes to Anne.

"We're going to have to cut it out," Jenni said with matter-of-fact bluntness.

Anne held her gaze steady. "I may be able to push it out using the same path it went in."

Jenni stared at her.

"You need to hold him steady and block the pain."

Jenni compressed her lips. "I can do that," she muttered. Placing her hands with care to not jar him, she let her magic trickle into Jeremy's chest. The heat of inflammation and shriek of torn flesh almost swamped her awareness. She sent magic along the lines of pain with grim determination, stopping each surge as it tried to make its way on the nerves. Jeremy sighed and relaxed into the sea of magic that she cradled him in.

Anne held her hands above the hole where the arrow had entered. She extended her awareness along the path that the arrowhead had taken. She formed a covering of magic surrounding the tip of the arrow and the remaining shaft. Careful slow pressure began to move it up the channel created by its entry. She sealed veins and drew flesh together as the arrow withdrew. Her magic began to fade.

Jenni felt Anne's magic stumble and almost fail. She sent a tendril of thought to Swords and WindRunners with frantic haste. *Please. Help us!*

Jeremy groaned.

The sparkle of strange magic rushed along her pathways and into both Jeremy and Anne. Jeremy's awaking retreated.

Anne clamped down on the flood of power to keep the arrow from exploding out of the wound. She resumed the slow work of healing the path as she pushed the arrow out. A soft pop sounded as the tip of the arrow finally exited the wound and rolled down Jeremy's chest.

The hole closed to a red pucker as Jenni watched. The shared power from their companions withdrew. She lifted her hands and released her own magic into the earth. Anne sat back on her heels with a sigh of exhaustion.

Someone handed each of them a journey cake. They ate with ravenous intensity. The pain in Jenni's middle slowly receded. She pushed herself back to sit on the cold ground. She put her elbows on her knees and rested her forehead on her hands, content to simply sit. Tom squatted down next to her.

"That was impressive, both of you," he complimented them.

Anne gave him a tired smile as he handed her another bar. He handed his wife dried fruit wrapped in waxed cloth. She carefully pulled the cloth away from the stickiness and held it to her nose. Just the scent made her feel better. She tore off a piece and popped it into her mouth.

"Thank you," she mumbled around the food. "Jeremy should sleep for at least a couple of candlemarks. He'll be fine."

"I hate to mention it, but there are others who need your tending. Not as serious as Jeremy but needing care just the same. Is there anything I can do?" he asked as he pushed himself to his feet.

"Set up our tent and put the injured there," Anne said. "We'll need time to finish eating. We'll be there as soon as we can."

Jenni looked up at Tom. "Was it...?"

"Yes," he answered, jaw clenching, lips thin, instant fury in his eyes.

She reached out and touched his hand. "I'm so sorry."

"I have the men burying him and his son in their graveyard. The men are seeing to everyone else who were slaughtered. There's no one left," Tom told her. "I think his wife died birthing their son." He shook his head. "What king would allow reavers to run wild in his country? This is happening everywhere."

Jenni's hand dropped away. She frowned. "I didn't know it was that bad. How do you know this?"

"Just because I don't live at the court doesn't mean I don't know what's going on there, and around Ard Ri," he told her. "Aeden and our seneschal are wise councilors." He gave a crooked grin that didn't reach his eyes. He stood up.

"I'll have the tent set up and the wounded brought in. Come as soon as you can."

# Chapter 10
# Purple Dragon

Last meal was long over. Candles in brass holders with glass chimneys flicked in the drafts that moved the air in the Keep's Library.

Thomas, Breanna, and Aeden sat around the table in the center of the room surrounded by shelves holding hundreds of books and scrolls the Arach family had collected over generations. The words of the spell that Thomas had fashioned sprawled across the latest parchment he had used to craft the incantation. It rested on top of the others he'd spent a week creating.

> "Set the time and set the place,
> Mark the route and seek the pace
> Watch the travelers, keep them safe
>
> Take the trail to far off home
> Carry greetings to your country's throne
> Tell the Sayathia we wish to know
> Of stranger things and places that glow"

"Finally," Breanna remarked with a smirk, absently rubbing the fingers and palms of her hands. "I like this one."

Thomas looked at her across the table, a scowl on his face. "You know, Breanna, if you'd help instead of criticize, we might get this done quicker," he barked at her, irritation lacing his voice. "I'm tired of your constant harassment."

Surprise crossed Breanna's face. "I'm sorry," she told him. Thomas was slow to anger, but when he got mad, she knew to keep quiet.

"An apology is only good if you change the behavior," he growled at her. She looked down at the table.

Aeden broke the tension. "This is good, Thomas. I would add a fourth line after 'Watch the travelers, keep them safe' - perhaps 'Against the war for which we brace'." Thomas dipped his quill into the inkwell placed to the right and above the stack of parchment, adding the line to his spell.

"When do you want to cast it?" Aeden turned her head toward the window looking out to the east.

"The new moon is in three days. That will be the best time to start a new journey."

"Do either of you know if Maaike has finished buying merchandise to take back to Fasach?" Thomas asked. "I think it would look suspicious if she went back with only half of her wagons loaded." His glance lingered on Breanna. He turned his head to Aeden.

"If she has, I'd like to send them on their way within the week. If you could find out and let me know, we can set a time to complete this." He pointed at the parchment. "Breanna, you should pack and be ready to leave. Please tell Marta to get ready as well."

Aeden pushed her chair back and nodded. "I'll find out now."

As she left the room, Thomas crossed his arms and leaned them on the table. He focused on the reflection of the room in the east window shrouded with the darkness behind it. "I wonder if Corcra can ride a horse. I wonder if he's ever even been around one. Huh." A fleeting smile crossed his face. "Guess we'll find out."

He looked at Breanna. "Do you think you can ask him about his experience with horses without creating a war or getting killed by a Dragon?"

"Yes," she answered as she pushed her own chair away from the table.

She walked out of the Library, head down, shoulder slumped forward, dejection evident in every step.

§ § §

*I can't do anything right.* Tears threatened as Breanna dragging steps took her down the stairs to the family's corridor. She lingered along the hallway, looking at the old tapestries hanging on the walls to block the chill radiating from the stone. She'd offended just about eve-ryone in the Keep in one way or another as she'd gone from weapons training to horse breaking to herb gather-ing through the day. Maybe her entire life.

She reached her door and slid her hand over the han-dle, removing the spell that locked it. She slid SunWalker into the sword-stand next to her bed as she removed the belt that held it at her waist and hung it on the peg at the end. She fell gracelessly to the mattress and covered her face with her hands. They ached.

*What is wrong with me? Why do I always make comments that no one likes? I'm just telling the truth.*

She rolled onto her side and curled up, dragging a pil-low to her stomach and pulled it in tight. *I'm so stupid. I've even made Thomas hate me. I should just leave and never come back.*

The same thoughts ran through her mind repeatedly until she finally fell asleep. Within moments she found herself walking the path that had become all too familiar. She tried to turn and run back the way she knew she had come, but she had no control.

She listened to the thudding of what she thought were hoofbeats, looking ahead to the curve in the road where golden light glowed as if sunset sent its rays to splash against the trees. The trail she trod was left in deepening gloom.

She felt a presence off to her right. She looked between the trees and saw a young boy running toward her, his gilded hair gleaming with some internal light, dodging around trunks, and jumping shrubs and thickets blocking the way. As he drew closer, she recognized him.

Evan jumped from the small rise that bordered her path and landed next to her. A spectral hand and arm reached out from the forest behind him. He shrieked in terror as it snatched his arm and ripped him away from her.

Breanna reacted without thought. She turned and jumped into the forest, knowing full well that she must not leave the path. She raced after Evan's blond hair and the guttering light that tried to engulf him as they receded away from her. Anger replaced fear.

*How dare they. How dare they try to steal Evan.* She held a flaming Sword in her hand. She noted its presence with distant wonder and focused on catching up. She raced on through the trees.

The figures ahead gradually grew closer.

She felt as if she had been running forever. The body of a purple Dragon appeared in front of the running kidnapper and its prey. The terrible head, teeth gleaming, snaked forward and its open maw engulfed the body of the thief. Massive jaws snapped shut. Evan was thrown to the ground by the suddenness of his release. His momentum pitched him into a roll, bringing him to a jarring stop at the base of a tree. Breanna stumbled to a stop next to him. The flames from her Sword winked out of existence.

Evan pushed himself to his hands and knees, shaking his head. He looked up at Breanna with no recognition in his eyes. Between one breath and the next, a huge wolf crouched where he'd knelt, lips wrinkling up and away from gleaming teeth. It snarled.

The Dragon's head lowered between Breanna and the wolf. When it lifted away, the wolf was gone. Evan was nowhere to be seen.

Breanna stared at the place where her cousin had landed. She started to turn to the Dragon.

She shouted as something shook her shoulder. She sat bolt upright on her bed and let out a shrill yell.

*What is going on?*

§ § §

Marta stood next to Breanna's bed; her face twisted into a scowl. "Are you all right?"

Breanna lifted her hands and scrubbed her face. She shuddered as she recalled the fear that she had felt while running after Evan. "I don't know. Something is wrong."

"Tell me," Marta demanded, sitting down on the chest at the end of the bed.

The tale poured out of Breanna. She couldn't seem to stop until she reached the end.

Something pounded on her door. It flew open and re-bounded from the wall behind it. Corcra and Evan stood in the opening. Marta jumped to her feet.

Evan was shaking uncontrollably. Corcra's eyes narrowed to slits; his jaw clenched so tight the muscles on his neck stood out in ridges. He gripped Evan's arm as if to keep him from running away. He grabbed the edge of door as he pulled Evan into the room and slammed it closed behind them. A wave of his hand locked it with an audible snap.

"What. Are. You. Doing?" he snarled at Breanna.

Breanna raised her hands palms up and shook her head, as she pushed herself as far from him as she could get.

"What? I went to sleep and had a dream. I haven't done anything!" Her astonishment flashed to anger. Violence hovered in the room.

"Get out," she growled, swinging her legs off the bed, and pushing herself to stand. She reached toward her Sword of Light.

"What did you do, Bree?" Evan shrilled. "Something tried to kill me in my dream. I couldn't breathe. How did I get there?"

Her arm fell to her side. She stood unmoving, thoughts tumbling through her mind. She looked at Marta. "We need Aeden and your mother."

"Did you set your dream shields?" Corcra grated out.

Breanna froze. She looked at him then dropped her head with shame. "No. I just went to sleep."

"You pulled even me into your dream!" Corcra's outrage radiated from him like heat from a fire.

A quiet knock at the door startled everyone. Corcra winced as his spell on the door was released without his permission. Aeden stood in the doorway, Raina a step behind her.

Aeden looked at each one of them for several seconds, finally settling on Breanna. "You failed to set your shields," she stated. "I felt the result all the way out to the armory." The two women stepped into the room and Raina shut the door quietly behind them.

"I...I'm sorry. I didn't think to set them. I just...I just wanted to sleep," Breanna wailed. She covered her face with her hands, tears leaking from the corners of her eyes, hiding from all of them. Marta reached out and rested her hand on Breanna's shoulder.

Aeden gestured at each of them. "Sit."

Breanna and Marta sat on the bed. Corcra took the chair in the corner in swift obedience. Evan dropped to the floor, leaning back against the side of the bed, his knees drawn up, his arms clasped around them.

"What did you dream?" Aeden asked.

Breanna wiped the tears from her face with her hands and dried them on her trousers. She sniffed and wiped her nose on her sleeve. She refused to look at anyone. She related the details of the dream, misery evident in every word.

Aeden let her gaze rest on Corcra, cocking her head to the side as she listened. As Breanna came to the part where the purple Dragon ate the kidnapper, her body stiffened.

"Repeat that please," Aeden requested, swinging her head to focus on Breanna. Listening closely to the retelling, her concentration made Breanna falter and slow her story, struggling to retell every tiny detail.

Finished, Breanna hung her head and wrung her hands resting on her lap.

Aeden stood quietly. "Corcra, did you recognize the wraith?" she finally asked.

"I did not, Lady," he answered. "Something felt familiar, but I cannot tell you what it was."

Aeden dropped down on her haunches in front of Evan. His eyes were huge and filled with dread as he tried to make himself as small as possible. She put her hand on his knee.

"It's all right, Evan. It was only a dream, no matter how real it felt. I will teach you to shield your mind, just as I did with Marta and Breanna. We will create a trap for any other wraiths that might try to scare you. Remember, Corcra saved you."

Evan twisted around and turned a bashful look on Corcra. "Thank you," he murmured.

"You are very welcome, young sir." Corcra stood up. "Lady, I will return to my rooms." He gave her a short bow, ignoring the two sitting on the bed and walked out of the room.

Aeden stood up and held a hand down to Evan. He reached up and took it. She pulled him to his feet. They walked to the door. Aeden turned to look at the two young women.

"I will think on this, Breanna. You and Marta should seek your beds. There is much to be done tomorrow to get ready for your journey. This time, remember to set your shields."

"Set your shields as well, Marta," Raina told her daughter. "Something is trying to get to both of you. Come now. Let's get back to bed." Raina pulled the door shut behind her as she left the room.

Breanna looked at Marta. "I'm so sorry. I don't know why I didn't remember to set them." She shook her head. "Nothing is going right." She sighed.

Marta stood and looked at her. "You need to remember. Always. I think it might be for the safety of us all." She left Breanna to her thoughts.

§ § §

"Mute and dumb shall she become
Who dares to speak of hidden things
Bind the mind and bind the tongue
Should words be said to which they cling

Of secrets great and secrets small
Amulet and Talisman shall bind them all."

The spell of silence settled like an invisible shroud over Breanna's and Marta's bodies and minds. For a moment Breanna felt like she couldn't breathe, and ants were crawling over her skin, but that sensation quickly passed. Aeden ended the spell with a snap of her fingers.

"Time to go," Thomas pulled Breanna into a hug. She hugged him tight, then released him and stepped back. Aeden laid a hand on her shoulder.

"Remember. Say nothing of what has happened here or of what you search for. If you do, you will be stopped." Aeden looked at Marta. "Take care of each other. The lands of Fasach are treacherous as are the people. It is well that a Dragon accompanies you."

Thomas pulled Marta into a hug. "Pay attention. Danger is everywhere. I trust you, but everyone else is suspect. Be safe," he murmured and released her.

Corcra strode down the stairs from the tower into the forecourt. Breanna followed his glance at the vardo modeled after those used by travelers who occasionally stopped at the Keep, selling things they had traded for at other villages they had passed through. The wagon's wooden sides, fitted with tongue and groove boards, rose higher than normal, to head height. Curved wooden half-hoops arching over the top from side to side, lifting a heavy canvas roof over the bed of the wagon.

Windows with real glass were set into the right side of the wagon and an elaborately carved door opened into the vardo from the rear, accessible with a folding set of stairs whose bottom step now rested on the ground. Boxes filled with supplies and barrels for water were fastened to the outside of the wagon walls on both sides. The large rear wheels, twice as big as the front wheels, allowed the wagon to travel easily over rough ground.

The Maaike and her caravan master strode along the line of twenty wagons formed up in front of the gates across the road leading to the wider world. She approached the highborn group waiting in the forecourt and bowed deeply. "My lords and ladies, are you ready to depart?"

"We are," Breanna answered, her voice a little breathless as the time of leave-taking arrived.

"I ask that you follow the second wagon." The caravan master spoke for the first time.

"Of course," Breanna replied.

"Mount up then," he ordered, waving his hand at their wagon.

Maaike stepped forward. "Thank you for your hospitality, Lord Thomas. We have been well served by your people. I look forward to returning next year."

"As we do you," Thomas responding in the ancient leave-taking reply. He nodded at the spy from Fasach.

Breanna, Marta, and Corcra climbed the stairs into the vardo. Marta pulled up the steps and anchored them by the hooks on either side to the back of the wagon. She stepped into the space and moved aside for Breanna to step back out on the tiny back porch.

The teamster cracked his whip over the back of the oxen hitched to the wagon. It jerked forward as the animals leaned into their yokes. The vardo began to move. Breanna waved at Thomas and Aeden, a huge smile plastered across her face. They were on their way.

# Chapter 11
# Familiar

The sandcat watched as the caravan made its slow way along the track in the hardpan dirt of her home. Her tail twitched. The sand-colored fur striped with narrow bands of chocolate brown on her flanks shuddered, dislodging several flies. The sagebrush that shielded her from sight scented the air. Something intriguing was in that caravan.

The cat's pale blue gaze lingered on each figure as it passed. The wide ruff of brown-tipped fur encircling her neck channeled the sounds of the desert to her sensitive erect ears.

*There. Those three.* The sandcat raised her head from where it rested on her front paws. The figure riding the four-legged runner after the two leaders caught her attention. She stretched her neck forward, searching for a hint of what drew her. The pupils of her eyes dilated to huge disks as she searched.

$ $ $

Breanna hummed a tune under her breath. Someone had sung it at the campfire last night and it was stuck in her head.

She'd been sore from the unaccustomed time in the saddle at the beginning of the trip. The pain in her legs and back had lessened as she rotated from horseback to riding in the wagon. They'd been on the trail a week and, according to Trader Maaike, were a third of the way to Jafara, the capital of Fasach.

She raised her hand to shield her eyes from the light that became more intense each day. That light washed color from the landscape. Not a cloud floated in the cerulean sky arching over her head. The jagged teeth of the Dragon Spine Mountains rose in the west on her right. Foothills, some very steep, stood as a barrier between the plains and the sharp ridges of the mountains. The river flowing to the south that the Traders Road followed had shrunk to little more than a creek.

The far-off shapes of vultures or eagles drifted in the thermals rising from the land. Widely separated grey-green shrubs as tall as her horse's knees grew haphazardly from the parched landscape on both sides of the trail. The plants spread across the hardpan of the ground up to the sides of the mesas and spires of rock to the east and the foothills to the west. The only true green was carried by the budding willows along the banks of the stream.

Breanna swung around in her saddle to check on Marta and Corcra following at a distance, the caravan stretching out behind them. Marta wore brown leathers like hers, while Corcra made do with black leathers, a white shirt and grey cloak. She'd expected purple. His horse still jigged and crow-hopped occasionally, trying to rid its back of what it considered a deadly enemy. The other horses kept a safe distance from the menace.

She turned back to look ahead at Maaike and the caravan master, Khaled Qadir. They were dressed for the desert: cream colored loose cotton tunics, twill trousers tucked into sturdy leather boots, and a cloak with a loose hood that could be drawn up over the head for protection from the unrelenting sun. Breanna was beginning to envy them the lighter clothing.

Restless from the slow plodding pace, she shifted her weight to find a more comfortable position. The urge to kick her horse into a headlong rush into the foothills was a fever in her blood.

*Perhaps you could suggest scouting ahead to look for any signs of bandits,* SunWalker suggested. *The game trail beyond the next hill to the right looks promising* the Sword advised.

Breanna stopped fidgeting as she turned the suggestion over in her mind. She felt a grin of wild delight cross her face as she heeled her horse into a trot, drawing even with Maaike and Khaled. The Trader looked at her with a frown.

"I'd like to take a turn at scouting, Master Qadir, Trader Soth Lahri, with Marta Haloran and Lord Corcra?" she asked, knowing that the trader and caravan master could hardly refuse. Soth Lahri had been in the courtyard when Corcra had changed from Dragon to man.

The two traded a look. Qadir scanned the land around them. Whipcord thin, the man's skin was a deep bronze from constant exposure to the sun. His startling green-eyed gaze came to rest on her face.

"Of course, my lady," he responded. Maaike's eyes narrowed. Her mouth was a slash of disapproval across her face.

*SunWalker, would you please ask HellScream to tell Marta that we are going scouting? Have her tell Corcra,* Breanna sent to her Sword with prim correctness. She twisted in her saddle to look at Marta and Corcra.

Marta jerked in surprise. She looked wide-eyed at Breanna, then looked over at Corcra and said something to him. He raised his head and looked at Breanna with a slow nod.

The two sent their horses into a fast trot with alacrity, hurrying to catch up with Breanna. She turned her horse toward the game trail that SunWalker had pointed out and waited until the others joined her. They trotted along the trail that curved around the flank of the hill next to them. Breanna urged her horse into a canter. Marta and Corcra followed. They rode for three-quarters of a candlemark, alternating between trot and canter.

The trail widened into a regular path. The caravan was quickly hidden from view as the path opened to a lush green valley dotted with groves of trees growing alongside the many streams cascading down the sides of the foothills. The damp fresh smell of grass and trees was a welcome relief after the dryness of the Traders Road.

Rocks had tumbled down the side of the hill, forming a low wall next to the trail. A rhumba of tiger-stripe rattlesnakes curled on the trail, sunning in the heat reflected by the rocks.

Breanna's horse leaped up and away from the curled bodies with a squeal. Breanna's feet lost the stirrups as she desperately grabbed at the horn of her saddle, trying to remain upright. She slid farther and farther to the right. The horse landed and bucked, all four feet off the ground.

The horses following scrambled to avoid over-running Breanna's horse, hind hooves digging into the dirt, forelegs stiff, heads down, and then both jumped sideways as well. Marta sailed in a wide arc, landing head-first on the sagebrush at the side of the trail. Corcra rolled over the neck and head of his animal and landed on his feet, still clutching the reins. The remainder of the snakes seemed to vanish as they disappeared into the border of rocks.

Breanna landed on her back, the impact driving the breath from her body with an explosive gasp. She struggled to pull air into her lungs as she rolled to her side.

A snake coiled in front of her face, its head upright on a swaying body, the rattle on its tail *shirring* and ticked with threat. Its black eyes caught hers. She wanted to push herself away but knew that it would strike if she tried.

The flicking of the snake's tongue was hypnotic, lulling her into stillness. Its head gradually drew back, preparing to attack.

A large tawny body flashed between Breanna and the snake. The head of the snake with its flicking tongue flew in one direction as the body spasmed in the other. It thrashed across the hardpan, throwing grit and small stones into the air.

Breanna jerked her body sideways, rolling several times, coming to rest on her forearms. She raised her head and looked at the writhing body of the snake. Panting hard, she lowered her head and rested it on her fists. She took a few moments to let her heart slow down. Looking up again, she swung her head to her left, looking for the animal that had saved her life. It had disappeared.

Stillness dominated the area around them. Breanna swiveled her head further to the left, looking over her shoulder, checking on the others. Corcra stood next to his horse, holding the bit in an iron grip. The horse did not move. He'd managed to snag the reins of Breanna's horse as it bolted back toward the caravan.

Marta was still on the ground, unmoving. Her horse was nowhere to be seen.

Breanna pushed herself to her knees with slow deliberation, checking for injuries as she rose. The sweet minty musky scent of crushed sage filled the air. She was bruised and scraped, but nothing was broken.

Breanna scanned the area again, searching for any hint of what had saved her. A glint of blue through the sagebrush perhaps twenty feet away caught her glance.

She let her eyes un-focus, looking at everything and nothing. The outline of a large cat appeared with a suddenness that had her inhaling with a gasp. Once she saw the outline, she could pick out the round head framed with a ruff of fur, the tail tipped with brown that twitched as she watched. The lightly brown striped body was the perfect match with the color of the ground on which it rested.

Pale blue eyes gleamed. The cat stood with sudden intent. SunWalker hummed in the back of her mind. Breanna waited.

The cat ghosted closer making no sound as it seemed to stalk her. One slow paw moved forward at a time. Breanna dropped her hand to the pommel of the Sword, uncertain of the cat's intent.

*There is no danger here,* SunWalker told her.

The cat reached her and sat down just out of touching range in front of her, curling its tail around its enormous paws. Its stare never left hers.

Breanna let her mind-shield fall with slow deliberation. Nothing reached out to her. She looked at the cat, head tilted with curiosity and concern. The cat yawned, revealing needle-sharp teeth and a bright pink tongue curling back as its mouth stretched wide. It closed its mouth and reached its nose toward her. Standing, it walked around her where she still knelt, investigating her clothing, the Sword's scabbard, the knives in her boots and finally came to sit in front of her again. It began to purr.

"Breanna, please come see to Marta," Corcra called to her from where he crouched next to Haloran's daughter.

Breanna slowly stood up and turned to walk toward the pair. The cat rose to its feet and paced next to her, still just out of reach. Its shoulders came just above Breanna's knees, its head to her hips.

Breanna looked at Corcra, eyes wide with fear, rolling them down and to the side to look at the cat, then back at Corcra. She was surprised to see an infrequent smile cross his face. "It is a sandcat. They are exceedingly rare. Some have bonded with humans to their mutual advantage. I believe she has...adopted...you," he told her. Breanna's eyes opened even wider. Her mouth fell open in a soundless "O.

The sandcat slipped past Marta's body and sat down near her head, curling her tail with tidy precision over her feet. She cocked her head with what looked like quizzical interest as she looked at the fallen woman.

Breanna knelt next to Marta's still body. She gently put two fingers on her friend's neck, checking her pulse. It was slow and steady. Breanna frowned.

*SunWalker, do you know what's wrong with her? She's breathing fine and her pulse is steady. Can I roll her on her back?*

*HellScream says that she hit headfirst when she was thrown. Her right arm is fractured, and her ankle was twisted when it caught in, and then came loose from, the stirrup. She is lucky she survived, as are you. You may turn her onto her back, Sun-*Walker's tone scolded her.

"Corcra, will you help me turn her on her back. HellScream says..."

"I heard the Sword. I will help you. Support her head while I roll her," the Dragon told Breanna. He stood up next to Marta where she lay on her right side next to the crushed sagebrush she had landed on.

Breanna slid one hand along Marta's spine near her head, putting the other hand at the back of her skull. Corcra put a foot on either side of Marta's body and bent down, placing a hand on Marta's uninjured shoulder, the other on her hip. He looked at Breanna. She nodded.

Corcra slowly applied pressure to Marta's body, increasing the pressure until she began to roll to her left. Breanna rotated her hands to maintain the support under Marta's head and neck. When Marta was lying flat on the ground, Breanna gently pulled her hands away.

"Can you get one of the waterskins?" she asked Corcra as she carefully lifted Marta's leg where it still lay across the injured one and set it flat on the ground. He moved to the horses and returned with his waterskin, unwound the leather tie that held it closed and handed it to Breanna without a word.

Pulling off the scarf around her neck, Breanna put it over the skin's opening and carefully poured out a small amount to wet it. Marta's forehead and cheeks were soon damp. Breanna dribbled a tiny amount of water onto Marta's chest, hoping that the slight chill would shock her into waking.

Marta's breathing quickened, but her eyes did not open.

"Marta, can you hear me?" Breanna leaned close to Marta's ear. She sat back on her heels, shaking her head with frustration.

*HellScream, can you help her? SunWalker?*

*She has retreated far into her own mind,* HellScream's response sounded reluctant.

*We should heal her ankle and arm before she is drawn back,* SunWalker told her.

"I'm not a healer," she muttered to no one in particular. She didn't know what else to do.

The sandcat stood and reached out to Marta, placing her paw on Marta's forehead.

Her eyes flew open and her back arched as she drew in a huge breath. She let it out with a shriek. She grabbed her arm. Shocked into stillness by the shriek, Breanna shook it off and lunged for Marta's shoulders, holding her down.

"Stop," she shouted. SunWalker added volume to the command.

*HellScream, take the pain away!* She sent a desperate plea to the Sword.

Marta relaxed against the ground with a sigh of relief.

"What happened?" she rasped.

"Snakes," Breanna replied with brisk efficiency, leaning back on her heels. After a small pause for thought: "and a sandcat."

Marta's eyes glittered as she turned her head to the right, looking at the animal that sat next to her. "By the Three," she whispered.

The sandcat began to purr.

"The Swords and I will heal her," Corcra spoke unexpectedly from behind the two. "The sandcat will help."

Breanna whirled on her knees, gaping at him. "You can do this?" she gasped.

The Dragon's left brow rose. "Of course," he responded, the bite of sarcasm in his voice.

$ $ $

Marta rested on the ground, leaning back against Breanna's saddle. Breanna insisted she stay quiet as her body coped with the healing magic that had coursed through bone and muscle. HellScream still controlled the nerves to numb her pain. She lifted the waterskin and sipped.

"Thank you, Corcra, HellScream, and SunWalker," she said. "I'm not sure I could have survived without your healing."

She looked at the sandcat sitting next to Breanna. Its blue eyes looked into hers, seeming to see her soul. "Thank you as well," she said with a grave nod of her head.

*She hears you,* HellScream said, a chuckle in his voice. *She hears all of us.*

Marta's eyes opened wide with surprise. She looked at Breanna who looked back at her with a puzzled frown, not being privy to the conversation. "HellScream says that the cat can hear us," she relayed.

Breanna's frown deepened. "I lowered my shields and got nothing," she told her companion.

"Maybe she doesn't want us to know she can hear us," Marta said.

"Why not?" Breanna asked.

"How should I know?" Marta retorted. "Try again," she ordered.

$$$

Breanna's nostrils flared, her lips thinned as her eyebrows lowered. She sent Marta an evil glare. Turning away, her breathing slowed and deepened as she willed her *ki* deep into the earth, dropping the shield protecting her mind. She felt a cool brush of curiosity across her thoughts.

*Who are you?* she sent.

The sandcat tilted her head. *Selgith*, she responded. *You are Bree.*

Breanna's lips flattened in dismay. *Why didn't you respond?*

*Why should I? You were perhaps a danger*, the sandcat responded with cool logic.

Breanna felt the beating of many pounding hooves through her knees. She looked up with alarm as Marta demanded, "Do you feel that?"

A cloud of dust rose from the trail that they had followed.

"It is the trader come to save you," Corcra told them, sarcasm rich in his voice. "As if a Dragon would let anything kill those under his protection," he said with a dismissive snort.

*I will not be far. I do not wish them to know I am here*, Selgith told Breanna and Marta.

She faded back into the landscape. Corcra stepped onto the path in front of the women and stood there, arms crossed over his chest.

Maaike, Khaled, and three of the wagon drivers galloped along the trail toward the group on the ground. The riders slowed their headlong charge and came to a stop in front of Corcra.

The leaders swung themselves off their horses and threw their reins to their followers. Maaike stomped toward the group, little clouds of dust spurting from under her feet.

"What happened," she demanded.

"Snakes," Breanna answered succinctly.

Maaike pressed her lips together in anger, the muscles along her jaw bulging as she clenched her teeth. Khalid put a calming hand on her shoulder. She shrugged it off.

"You have cost us three hours of travel time. We can't make the next waterhole before dark. Get up and get on your horses," she barked at them.

"No." Corcra's quiet declaration slid out and stood between the angry trader and the group.

Maaike's snarled as her face turned red. "How dare you?"

Corcra shrugged and called his purple whirlwind. The horses of the newcomers went mad, pulling and rearing, trying to flee. Breanna's and Corcra's horses stood quiet, too tired to make a fuss. As the wind slowed, the Purple Dragon confronted Maaike.

*I AM A DRAGON. We will overnight in the valley beyond this hill. Bring your caravan here.* The Dragon's voice thundered in all their minds.

Khalid gave a deep bow to the Dragon. "As you command, Lord Dragon."

Maaike sputtered in fury. The Purple Dragon lowered his head toward the trader, lips wrinkling to just show the tips of his teeth. Khalid took her arm in a firm grip as he turned and walked back to their horses, pulling her along behind him. He muttered something to her, and she stopped struggling and let him guide her to her mount. They swung into their saddles.

Khalid pointed at the valley to the right, not visible from the ground. Maaike followed his gesture. Her eyebrows climbing to her hairline in surprise.

"This is a good place. There is water and excellent grass here. We will spend several days to let the animals graze and refill our water supplies," Khalid told her. "Would you stay or return with me to bring the wagons?"

Maaike shook her head in anger, eyes narrowed to slits, lips tight. She shot a glare at Corcra, then at Breanna and Marta. "I'll go with you." She reined her horse around and kicked it into a gallop. Khalid nodded at those on the ground, saluted the Purple Dragon, and followed her, motioning at his men to come along.

"What is her problem?" Breanna breathed, a frown deepening the line between her eyes. "We are ambassadors and we've paid to be in this caravan," she continued with indignation.

*She thinks she is in charge*, the Dragon answered. Purple smoke began to rotate around his body. He stood as a man when it disappeared. "We should find a place in the valley to rest until they arrive."

"Marta, how strong do you feel? Do you think you can walk yet?" Breanna turned to her friend.

"I can try." Marta held out her hand. "Help me up."

Breanna grabbed her hand and pulled her to her feet. Marta wobbled back and forth, caught her balance. She put her hand on Breanna's arm to steady herself.

"Marta, you will ride my horse. Breanna will ride hers."

Corcra stood behind Marta and lifted her by her waist to sit on his horse. Breanna grabbed the saddle and blanket Marta had used for support and threw it on her horse's back with quick precision. The horse began to move as soon as her legs touched its sides. Corcra led them into the valley.

# Chapter 12
# Mage's Training

Cameron raised his arm and sent a burst of magic from his *ki* along his arm and out of his palm in a brilliant bolt of light. The magic splashed against his target, a metal form in the shape of a human's shield hanging from a stone pillar. A hole appeared in the metal as it turned cherry red. The shield exploded with a report that reverberated across the training ground. Cameron ducked as he snapped a mental deflector into existence around his body. Shrapnel bounced off and slid across the ground.

"Hmmph," he snorted in disgust. "Neulach, how do I keep it from exploding?" he asked. "This is the fifth target I've destroyed. I can't make the magic any smaller."

The King of Dragons rolled over in the sandpit next to the arena where he was dozing and raised his head from the warmth that radiated from the sand. He rotated one glittering black eye toward what was left of the target.

With a sigh he stood, shaking his enormous black body free of the sand he'd been wallowing in.

The air began to swirl around him. It increased in strength until a black whirlwind lowered from the sky above his head. It shrouded his body, hiding it from view. The sand surrounding him lay undisturbed. The whirlwind decreased in intensity as it lifted away and dispersed, leaving no sign it had ever existed. The Arach Dubh, King of the Dragons, stood in the sand in his human form.

"You have practiced this for a week. Remember, narrow the focus of your mind onto the smallest area you can on the shield. You are concentrating on the magic, not the shield. Control of your concentration is critical." He gave a small gesture with his hand and another shield was created where the last had been destroyed. "Again."

Cameron readied his body and prepared to draw on his magic. A loud shriek sounded from the air around him. He jumped sideways with a shout of alarm. Neulach laughed.

"Concentrate," he commanded.

"That's not fair," Cameron growled at his instructor.

"Two things, Cameron. There will be amazing amounts of noise in battle just as there was during the battle for Red Dragon's Keep, and..."

"Life isn't fair," Cameron and Neulach spoke at the same time.

"I know. I know," Cameron responded with a grimace. "It's still not fair. I'm trying as hard as I can." He kicked a toe into the dirt with disconsolate despondency.

"The only way to learn a skill is through repetition and then with proofing. If you cannot use your training with almost no thought, you will die," Neulach told him, his voice low and grave. He laid his hand on Cameron's shoulder. "My daughter would never forgive me." He paused. "I would lose a valuable apprentice and ally."

Cameron grinned.

When Neulach took him from the tunnels under Red Dragon's Keep to Arach Sliabh, the Dragon Mountains, he was shaken to his core. Weeks had gone by before he was comfortable in the company of men and women who were Dragons, especially when everyone deferred to whatever Neulach wanted.

Neulach introduced him to the Dragon shifters and named Cameron as his apprentice, throwing the gathering into chaos. He hadn't even raised his voice when he told them "Stop. Some quiet grumbles followed but soon dwindled.

"Cast your first spell in Dragon Lands," he commanded Cameron as the others looked on. The boy looked at him in confusion.

"Which one," Cameron asked.

"Perhaps the one you cast to burn Demons in the last battle," Neulach suggested.

Cameron complied. He was quaking inside but grounded and pulled fire from his *ki* and the earth, directing it to the fire burning in the center of the hall. Flames roared to the ceiling, not just normal yellow and red, but incandescent blue and white. Cameron shuddered as he began to lose control of the burning. Neulach paced to his side and placed his hand on Cameron's shoulder. No words passed, but the flames winked out. He'd looked at Neulach with new respect, and not a little fear.

The Black Dragon started his training the day after they arrived. Cameron already knew how to center and ground his magic. Lady Aeden, Neulach's daughter, had taught his cousins and his brother how to do these most basic of magical requirements. The Dragon King helped him strengthen his mental and physical shields so that not even he, with all his power, could get through them.

Projecting magic was another thing entirely. Defense was not enough. To become a Mage, Cameron would have to face the magic of his mentor and battle him to at least a draw.

With that thought in mind, he focused on the piece of metal, concentrating on its outline. Nicks and depressions covered the surface. He reached out with his perception and ran his mental fingers across the deepest dent.

He concentrated on the dent. He raised his arm and pulled a surge of energy from his *ki*, channeling the power through his arm and out his palm, pushing it toward the metal.

A brilliant thin burst of light streaked toward the target, burning through with quick efficiency, leaving a perfectly round hole. Cameron cut off the light, releasing his power, and let the magic drain into the earth.

"Yes. That is the concentration you must develop," Neulach congratulated him. "Again."

Cameron grinned. "That was fun!" He gathered his power and grounded his *ki*.

# Chapter 13
# Dream of Danger

There is nothing we can do," Corcra told Breanna and Marta, his deep voice rumbling. "He is in charge of the caravan, much like a ship's captain."

Breanna scrunched her face into a mulish tight-jawed grimace. "I know. I don't like it, but I know. We need to get to Fasach and establish relations with the Sayathia and the other things Thomas told us to do." She rolled her eyes, not wanting to talk about the amulet aloud.

The three from Red Dragon's Keep were relegated to riding in the rearmost position of the caravan after their disastrous scouting foray. One good thing came of it. Two days of rest and grazing in that valley gave the oxen, horses, and people a chance to recover from a month of steady travel.

The dust raised by the hooves and wheels of the lengthy line in front of them hovered in the air, even inside the vardo. The sharp sweet molasses smell of varnish was still evident over the dust. It made Breanna's stomach roll, clogging her nose and throat.

She glanced around the interior at the carved cabinets, beds and chairs that made up its interior. An unlit lantern swayed from the highest arch of the roof.

Breanna pulled the brown and cream scarf tied around her neck up and over her mouth and nose, trying to avoid some of the dust. Marta coughed. Corcra sat in stoic reserve on the side bench mounted on the right wall, swaying with the jostling of the wagon.

The caravan followed an ancient roadway of massive stone blocks laid down in a time long forgotten. Covered and uncovered with sand and dirt by wind and time, the going wasn't much better than the wagon tracks they'd followed across the hardpan ground of southern Ard Ri.

The light filtering through the canvas covered roof of the vardo and through the window on the left set into the wooden wall dimmed. The wind speed increased and pressed the canvas tight against the bows that arched from one side of the walls to the other. Marta frowned as she leaned over and looked out of the window. Breanna watched her eyes go wide.

Breanna scooted to the rear door and eased it open. The wind grabbed the edge and whipped it out of her hand, slamming it open against the back of the wagon. She reeled back with a gasp, pushed herself back to the opening, and tried to pull it shut.

"Something bad is coming. It's as black as night on the horizon," she choked out.

The passengers fell against the side of the wagon as it turned to the left and was brought to a shuddering halt. Shouts high with fear sounded from outside. Breanna moved to the door to see what was happening. She sprang back with an oath. A tawny figure leapt toward the opening, its front legs and neck extended. The sandcat flew through the opening, landing on the woven red rug covering half of the floor, sliding into the cabinets under the beds when she could gain no purchase with her paws and claws.

Corcra looked down his nose at the cat and snorted, dismissing her as beneath notice, and turned to look out the window. Marta gasped and leaned back and away from the sliding body. Breanna reached out of the open door and grabbed the door handle, wrestling with the increasing wind to slam it closed. She leaned back against the frame, panting with her effort. Her eyes fell on the sandcat.

The sandcat stood and shook, sending a cloud of dust into the air that settled on every surface. She then sat down, paws covered by her tail curled with neat precision over her toes. Her slanted blue eyes glanced at each of them, then fastened on Breanna.

*The great wind comes. You must find shelter.*

*What great wind?* Breanna demanded.

"It is a sandstorm," Corcra responded, foregoing speaking in their minds. "It can last for days and kills man and beast. We *are* in danger." He rose with studied calm and bent to the door, grasping the handle and pushed it open against the wind. He poked his head out of the door as Khaled Qadir rounded the corner.

"Quick, help me stake the vardo wheels. We haven't much time and the animals must be sheltered," Qadir ordered, the urgency clear in his voice.

Corcra and the women stepped down from the wagon, hurrying to follow. The cat stayed inside.

The man opened the doors that lined the bottom of the wagon, revealing a storage area under the floor of the vardo. He grabbed eight huge u-shaped metal pins, three feet long on one side, as well as a sledgehammer. He thrust them into Corcra's hands. Corcra snorted and let them slip to the ground with a thud.

Qadir picked up two from the pile and scurried to the rear wheel of the wagon. He set the points of the first pin on either side of the wheel rim next to a spoke. He pounded it into the earth with powerful strokes of the hammer, securing the wheel to the ground. Qadir picked up the pin he'd dropped, placed it over the rim beside the next spoke of the wheel and beat it into the ground.

Corcra stepped away from the vardo and gestured at the pins. Two of them rose into the air and floated to the front wheel, positioning themselves over the wooden rims. Corcra extended his hand horizontally and pushed it toward the ground. The pins slid into the earth, immobilizing the wheel. Qadir's stared in amazement.

Corcra walked around the end of the wagon, the pins floating obediently behind him.

Breanna shook her head. "I can't believe this," she muttered as they followed him. The wind snatched at her hair and clothing, ripping the air from her nose as she rounded the end of the wagon. She gasped and turned her back. Tiny pebbles of sand hammered against her jacket.

Corcra gestured and the pins oriented over the wheels. They slid into the ground again on that side, the sound covered by the rising wail of the gale.

Qadir sprinted back around the wagon. The women followed. He reached into the storage space and grabbed a large roll of canvas folded in half, pulling it out and letting it fall to the ground.

"Haul this end over there," the caravan master shouted, pointing to the back of the wagon. Breanna and Marta grabbed the end of the roll, staggering at its weight. They tugged and lifted, struggling to unfold it toward the rear of the vardo.

"Unroll it," Qadir shouted.

With hands and feet, the women complied, all three struggling to unfurl the canvas and spread it on the ground out from the side of the wagon.

A row of huge grommets lined the canvas every foot along the edge closest to the wagon. Qadir threaded a sturdy rope through them. Climbing the barrels and boxes mounted on the side of the wagon with nimble feet, he hauled the corner of the canvas close to the wagon after him. He slid the grommet at the end of the canvas over a hook positioned on the upper curve of the wagon's wall, leaving a tail of rope dangling. He stepped to the next foothold and lifted the fabric over his head, securing the next grommet, and the next, as he moved to his right.

Breanna and Marta watched with close attention. Grasping the grommet at their end of the canvas, Breanna dragged it to the side of the wagon. Marta scuttled up the side and stood on a box of supplies secured to the wall. She reached down for the grommet Breanna held up to her.

Breanna pushed herself under the canvas, using her body to support the fabric. Marta grabbed the next grommet and struggled to reach the next hook on the wagon. Breanna lifted the canvas and pushed it up, giving Marta more slack to raise it. Marta grunted as she reached up and pushed the grommet over the hook.

Breanna followed on the ground, feeding fabric to her friend. Marta stepped on the tops of barrels, anchoring grommets as they moved toward Qadir. The fabric whipped like a snake, threatening to pull out of Breanna's hands. Qadir and Marta met in the middle of the wagon, securing the last grommet.

They jumped down, Marta staggering and almost falling. Qadir raced to the front of the wagon, she to the rear. Grabbing the dangling rope, he wound it in a figure eight around the cleat mounted low on the side of the wagon, pulling the top of the canvas taut. Marta tied her end off at the back of the wagon.

The vardo drover unhitched the team of oxen from the front of the wagon and waited for the shelter to be completed. The oxen tossed their heads in agitation and circled around their handler. Another drover led their three horses from the remuda to stand beside the oxen.

The canvas flapped as the wind tried to rip it away. Qadir pulled heavy spikes from the under-wagon storage and pointed at the outside edge of the canvas. Marta and Breanna rushed after him, grabbing the fabric and holding it to the ground. Qadir staked the canvas to the ground through the grommets on that edge, creating a triangular shelter anchored by the canvas attached high on the side of the wagon on one side, the ground on the other.

Two flaps of fabric rested on the slope of the canvas. Breanna pulled the flap down to the ground on her side. Using the spike Qadir had tossed to the ground on her side, Breanna drove it deep into the ground. The drovers led the oxen and horses they had collected from the remuda into the shelter the canvas created. The men tethering the animals to the wagon, leaving enough rope for them to lie down. A guard pulled a small wagon filled with hay up to the shelter, tossing a pile in front of each ox and horse, and unloading five bales to be stored under the wagon as a windbreak. Marta staked the front flap to the ground.

Qadir stood at the front of the wagon, looking toward the head of the line of wagons that had become shelters against the coming storm. A quarter of a candlemark had passed. Breanna and Marta joined him. Breanna's breath caught as she raised her head and watched the approaching wall of red-gold billowing sand and dirt growing taller and taller, darker and darker, against the sky. Storm clouds chased the haboob, throwing lances of brilliant lightning into the roiling seething gust front of death.

Breanna shook her head in wonder and no small part fear. "Is there anything else we can do?" she asked Qadir.

Corcra appeared around the back of the wagon and stopped short, cocking his head with curiosity, following their gaze up the line.

"The caravan is safe. Find your wagon." His voice thrummed with power, making their insides quiver. He turned and walked behind the vardo. The rear of the wagon sank as he mounted the stairs. Breanna shot a startled look at Marta and the caravan master. She hurried after him, Marta bolting to follow her.

Breanna lurched into the vardo, throwing herself onto the left side bench, breathing hard. Marta followed, slamming the door shut behind her.

"What do you mean, the caravan is safe? How can it be safe?" Breanna demanded in outrage. "There's a huge dust storm about to slam into us and you say we're safe? Why? How?"

Marta put her hand on Breanna's shoulder, trying to calm her. Breanna brushed it off.

Corcra sat on the opposite bench, hands resting on his thighs, regarding Breanna with glittering amber eyes, jaw clenched, anger furrowing his brow.

Marta grabbed Breanna's shoulder and shook it hard. "Stop it," she shouted. "You are going to get us all killed! Except for him! Stop it!"

SunWalker sent a bolt of energy through Breanna's body. "Ouch," she exclaimed. "What are you doing?"

*You are a fool.*

Breanna's mouth dropped open. The voice that she heard in her mind, and in the others' if their faces were any indication, was Selgith's. Breanna swept her gaze around the interior of the wagon and saw the sandcat curled on the top bunk at its far end.

*What did you say?*

*You are a fool. The most powerful creature in this world sits in this wagon. Close your mouth and learn.*

I...I...I. Breanna snapped her mouth shut. She crossed her arms over her chest with a harrumph. She watched as Corcra's eyes filled with amusement, his left eyebrow rising to his hairline. She glared at him.

*I must ask Neulach how he keeps humans in check. No one talks to him as you have talked to me,* Corcra remarked.

"I have set a warding on every wagon in this caravan," he continued aloud. "The pegs will not pull from the ground. The coverings will not slip loose no matter how violent the wind. We are safe."

A gust of wind shook the vardo, the beating of sand hammered against its side. Breanna and Marta flinched away. The wagon shook harder. Corcra looked out the window and the shaking stopped. Breanna cocked her head to the side, watching him in fascination. She thinned her mental shields, just until she could feel the power radiating from the Dragon. She slammed her shields back in place, grunting in surprise. She'd *seen* the power shimmering all around the wagon.

*What did you expect?* the sandcat queried.

*I am as interested in your answer as she is,* SunWalker chimed in.

Breanna rolled her eyes toward the bed where the cat lounged.

*I don't know. I've fought Demons before and have fought beside Aeden. I never thought about their magic, about what else they can do.*

The sandcat snorted.

Breanna's shoulders slumped as she leaned forward and rested her elbows on her thighs, letting her head fall forward into her hands. *I don't know why I can't stop poking at him. He is so irritating!*

The light in the wagon dimmed further. Exhaustion from the heavy work of getting their wagon ready rolled over her. She pushed up off the bench and moved toward the beds.

"I've got to sleep," she mumbled. She stumbled and caught herself against the side rail of the top bunk and pushed herself upright. She unwound the belt from her waist that held SunWalker's scabbard, created a loop, and hung it on a peg at the head of the bed. She pulled off her boots and let them thud to the floor.

"Marta, do you want top or bottom bunk?" she asked her friend.

"I'll take the bottom one," Marta's quiet voice had just enough volume to reach her ears. "It looks like Selgith has already decided where you will sleep."

Breanna hesitated. She raised her head to look at the cat lying at the foot of the mattress. She wasn't sure if she wanted to sleep up there. *May I share the bed with you?* she asked as politely as she knew how, a tiny quaver of fear making its way into her tone.

*Of course,* the cat responded after moments of quiet.

Breanna stepped onto the side rail of the lower bunk and then onto the wooden tread someone had nailed to the headboard, using it to push her body up. She twisted into the bunk and landed on her back.

A quiet sigh of relief escaped. She felt every muscle in her body relax, one by one. The shields on her dreams came slowly as she remembered to fold them around her mind. Turning on her side to face the wall, she tucked her hands under her cheek, closed her eyes and slept.

$ $ $

Breanna recognized the dream space. She knew it now from the practicing she'd been doing for months and even more intensely after what she'd come to think of as the "Dragon Dream". It most often presented itself as a path in a field that led to a gate into the forest. She could choose to follow the path or not. She'd chosen to take the path and stepped into a nightmare.

Danger was very close. She tried to wake up, but neither pinching nor willing worked. It was dark. No light was visible wherever she tried to look. Her heart started to pound with dread. She heard a snuffling rumble off to her left. She strengthened and tightened her shields.

*I must create some light. Not too much, just a little to see by.*

Breanna reached out with her will. She brought a memory of firelight to mind. Using her magic, she created a tiny globe of light far up above the body she wore in this space. The glow, like sparks that rose from a burning fire, gave just enough light to reflect from the red eyes surrounding her, showing massive black shapes to her disbelieving awareness.

Fear quickened her breathing. Light glanced along canine teeth where iridescent green saliva dripped to the ground as the dim outline of bodies jostled and snapped at each other. The putrid rotting-meat stench of their breath filled the air around her. A distant question flickered in her mind. How could she smell in a dream?

A sense of heaviness pressed against her body, sucking the breath from her lungs, trying to push her to the ground. Something worse than the Demons surrounding her had entered the dreamscape. She struggled to breath, mouth open, short panting inhalations, and exhalations, trying to remain silent.

The ground shuddered from ponderous footfalls. The sound of monstrous breathing thundered in her ears. The Demons turned as one to face the oncoming terror.

Breanna watched with horror as the massive misshapen form of a grey Dragon lowered its head and nosed at the Demons many feet away. Loose scales and skin hung from its body, like the loose skin of old animals or people. Power radiated from it in waves. Its muzzle was twisted awry, decaying teeth protruding from misaligned jaws. It looked like it had been hit in the face by a massive force.

Milky white eyes, with no pupil or iris, searched for her. A quick snap and one of the Demons was killed, half its body hanging from the crooked snag-toothed jaws. The Dragon flipped its head and caught the remainder of the body in its maw. The Demons melted away into the darkness, one slow step back at a time.

*I know you are here, Arach daughter. I see your light.* The Dragon swung its head from side to side, nostrils flared wide. *What happens in this space can change the world. You are mine.* Breanna felt the Dragon's glee ripple through her mind. *Come to me. Rule by my side. There is nothing that we cannot do together.*

Breanna stood as silent as the darkness itself, not daring to move, scarcely daring to breathe. She feared that this monstrosity could hear her heart hammering in her chest.

She loosed the magic of her light. The dreamscape plunged into blackness.

*You will regret your choice, human. So be it.*

She heard a massive in-drawing of breath. The Dragon exhaled a river of incandescent blue and orange and white flames, lighting the space with terror. It swung its head from side to side, seeking to incinerate her.

Breanna dropped to the ground and curled into a ball, knees drawn to her chest, arms crossed over her head. Through the onslaught, she kept her shields intact. They began to fray as her energy waned. A flicker of flame touched her arm. She could feel the fabric of her blouse begin to char. She whimpered with the pain.

The Dragon flamed again. Breanna shrieked as her last layer of shielding failed. Her arms and hair began to burn.

She shrieked in agony until her throat was raw.

# Chapter 14
# Cathair Ri

Anne stepped into the stirrup, grasped the pommel and the cantle of the saddle, and swung her leg over the horse's back. Her WindRunner, Gaoth, watched as she drew the reins through her fingers. The other WindRunners who had chosen the Arachs and Gobhlans had already left the camp.

They had been on the road from Aos Si to Cathair Ri for a month and Anne was sick of riding. *Just one more day on this endless journey.*

*It has not been so bad,* Gaoth told her with wistful insistence. *I would that I could go with you.*

*It hasn't been bad,* Anne admitted. *I'm just tired of being on the move all the time. It will be nice to sleep in a bed and eat at a table from real dishes.* She sent a mental smile to the WindRunner. *You know that you cannot come within a mile of the castle. Any closer and whatever is there will be able to sense you because of your magic.*

*I know.* Black eyes glistened as Gaoth tossed her head. *We will stay by the river among the trees and mask our magic from others.*

*Have you been here before?* Anne cocked her head in question, watching as Gaoth gave a tiny crow hop, then reared and spun in a circle. She dropped her front legs to the ground and raised her head high, arching her neck. Sunlight shimmered along her jet-black coat.

*Once, when I was very young. I can feel the change that has come into this land.*

"Huh," Anne grunted, a frown creasing her forehead and narrowed her eyes. *What has changed?*

Her WindRunner was silent for a time. *There is a taint in the magic here, like the smell of over-ripe apples or something rotting. The magic itself is slow, not sparkling, and lively as it should be.* Gaoth gave another toss of her head. *Come. Run with us.* She took two steps toward the other WindRunners, looking back over her shoulder at Anne.

*No, you go,* she told Gaoth, a smile brightening her face. *Find us when you are done.*

Gaoth summoned the wind. Anne felt the magic wrap the WindRunner in its power. Gaoth started to trot, then to gallop, her legs blurring with speed. Her form receded into the distance, following her companions.

Anne touched her heels to the barrel of her horse, sending it into a walk. Empty fields stretch on either side of the wagon track that the cavalcade followed. She studied the horizon to the east, looking for any sign of watchers or humans. She looked to the west, doing the same in that direction. Shaking her head with frustration, she urged the horse into a trot.

*You have trained hard and well these past weeks, Storm-Bringer,* her Sword of Light murmured in her mind. *Together, we have prepared as well as possible for what we face. Gaoth is correct. The magic is tainted by something I half-remember from very long ago.* She sounded puzzled. *I should remember, but I cannot.*

The horse stopped. Anne sat unseeing, unmoving, caught in the remembering of her Sword from long ago. Memories poured through her mind, of battle and killing, of twisted dark hunger seeking power, of magic clashing repeatedly until there was none left.

*Dragons lay dead on the ground. Thousands of men and horses bled and died on the battlefield. Demon bodies bubbled and smoked, turning into mounds of green slime. The ground beneath the slime turning black. A blue Dragon falling from the sky, crashing to the ground with the thunder of breaking bones and dead meat, a spear projecting from its side.*

Anne gasped and shivered as the hair rose all over her body. She pushed her hands out and away as if shoving the vision from her mind. She closed her eyes and dropped her head into her hands, shuddering in reaction to what she had seen.

*I was there.* StormBringer told her the simple truth.

The escort of fifteen men mounted their horses. Lord Jeremy guided his warhorse to her side, a frown carving a deep line between his brows. "Are you all right?" he asked his wife.

Anne quieted the anguish in her mind. She slowed and deepened her breathing, struggling to let go of the fear and dread the images had created. She raised troubled eyes to her husband's face, looking for his calm and practicality. Jeremy reached out and touched her arm. His horse shifted with unease, reacting to his concern.

"StormBringer told me she's been here before. She showed me a huge battle between Demons, Dragons, and men. There were thousands of dead. Gaoth said that the magic here has been tainted and the Sword agrees. I've been feeling like we're walking into a trap for days now. It's getting worse I think." She shook her head with frustration. "I'm not sure we should have come here."

*I was part of that battle.* Jeremy's BloodForged spoke in everyone's mind. *We are all in danger.* Jeremy dropped his hand to the hilt of his Sword. The other Swords murmured their agreement from their places with Tom and Jennifer. *We must shroud our power as we did in the armory before the Demon awakening.*

The Swords drew a veil between their chosen and themselves. Their magic faded from the wielder's minds. *Do not fear. We are aware and will come at need.*

The companions looked at each other.

"I feel like I've lost a part of myself," Jennifer choked out.

"How do we play this? Dumb and stupid or aloof and knowing?" Jeremy asked.

Tom cocked his head to the side.

"I think naïve and appalled, don't you think?" His eyes narrowed. "We've been kidnapped, beaten, and tortured by a peer of this realm. Something must be done." He gave his hand an exaggerated wave.

Anne nodded in agreement.

"The sooner we get there, the quicker we can end this. Let's get going."

The four urged their horses into a walk and then a trot. Two outriders surged to the front and fanned out from the trail. The column followed the high-born. The driver slapped the reins on the rumps of the horses hitched to the supply wagon. Their sturdy bodies leaned into their harnesses, moving the wagon forward with a jerk. The group set off on the final leg of their journey to the capital of Ard Ri.

$ $ $

"There is this, Sire. Without the money, you cannot buy the men and magic to fight." The Master of the Treasury laid a stack of papers in front of the king. Short and pudgy, her clothing bore food and ink splotches down its front. Ink-stained fingers were quickly withdrawn into the large sleeves of her surcoat. She shook her head in resignation. "There is not enough of either."

The King rested his chin on the palm of his hand supported by his elbow on the arm of his chair. His face bore a frown and his lips were pursed in distaste. He was uncomfortable on the hard seat. He'd made sure that all the other chairs in the room had seats just as hard to encourage short meetings of his privy council.

He was bored. "What do you suggest be done?"

The treasurer pursed her lips. "I've suggested any number of ways to raise more money, Sire. You have rejected all of them." She took a step back from his chair.

"I suggest a levy be placed on all land within Ard Ri and on all subjects down to the smallest babe. The army must be sent to collect this tax and bring those who cannot, or will not pay, to justice here. They will be indentured until their debt is paid. Those who are able must be impressed into the army. Set a few examples and I'm sure the funds will flow." She rubbed her hands together; a pinched smile crossing her face. "Torture. Some scourging. That's just the ticket."

Rudraige examined the idea from all sides as he thought, staring at her. "And who will pay for this increase in troops? Who will feed the many new mouths that will fill the castle?"

"Why, Sire, those self-same mouths will be sent to the fields to bring us more food, and money will flow in from all corners of the kingdom."

"Hmm. Send me my secretary. I'll put this into an order."

The treasurer bowed low. "As you wish, Sire."

# Chapter 15
# Spell of Silence

Breanna's back arched as she screamed in voiceless pain. She rolled to her side, drawing her arms and legs in against her body as tight as she could. The heat and acrid smell of burning cloth sent her heart racing. Her mental shields fluttered in tattered ruins around her mind. The grey decaying Dragon continued to wreath her body in red and orange and blue/white flames.

Rolling away from the inferno, she pushed to her feet and tried to run toward the wall she hoped was behind her.

Heat and flame abruptly cut off. Something pushed her hard. She stumbled and her knees hit the ground. Crumbling forward, the right side of her head hit the ground. A heavy weight pressed down on her back. She grunted as all the air left her lungs. Desperation drove her as she pushed up on her elbows and knees, trying to draw in a breath.

Power wrapped her in its coils. Her eyes flew open as she gasped for air and tore herself from the dream that trapped her. She was floating in the middle of the vardo. A portal into the inferno open at her feet shrank to the size of a fist and winked out of existence. She struggled to breathe. Smoke filled the interior. Marta was sprawled on the floor. Corcra stood with his back to the door, arms raised. Breanna could see the pulses of power extending from his hands to the magic that held her.

Corcra flicked two fingers. The air was clear, the smoke gone as if it had never been. The sandcat leapt from the bunk to the floor, violent sneezes shaking her body. She darted to the end of the vardo, clawing at the cabinet door. A claw caught the catch and pulled it from the wood. The door swung open, and the cat disappeared into the small hiding place.

Corcra lowered Breanna until her feet were firmly on the floor, loosening his magic, allowing it to slowly thin and dissipate.

She abruptly sat down. Her clothing was charred in many places. Black ash circled holes pocking the fabric, revealing reddened skin underneath. The smell of burned cloth and flesh filled her nose. She pulled her legs up, circled them with her arms, and rested her forehead on her knees. "What happened?" she mumbled.

Corcra moved forward and knelt next to Marta, laying two fingers against her throat. "She lives," he announced.

Breanna turned her head, resting her cheek on her knees. She tried to focus on her friend and the shapeshifter. Nausea roiled her stomach. She closed her eyes and turned her head back with a groan.

She worked to bring all her senses awake. The roar of the wind outside the vardo, the occasional susurration of sand against its side, the pain of her burns, the dryness of her mouth. She heard a squeal of hinges as the sandcat pushed out of the cabinet.

Dim light fluctuated as the strength of the sandstorm rose and fell. Sand and dust filtered through the tiny openings throughout the vardo, quickly filling the air. The waves of pain from her battered mind made her whimper. A cold nose pressed against the back of her neck.

Breanna felt as if a cool gauze sheet spread over her body and torn mental shields, stilling the pain that throbbed to the beat of her heart through her body. She took a deep breath. Though again filled with dust, it was the sweetest lungful she'd ever drawn. She exhaled and released as much of the pain as she could as her lungs emptied. A breath in. An exhale out. The knotted muscles in her arms and legs, along her spine and neck, began to relax.

Her body drooped with relief. *Thank you* she sent to the sandcat, reaching out to place her hand on Selgith's back.

Breanna slowly ran her hand from the cat's neck to her tail, taking comfort in the softness of her fur.

Breanna turned her head, rested her cheek on her knees and watched with dull attention as Corcra stood from his place at Marta's side. Breanna noticed the charring of the wood along the wall behind the bunk where she had tried to sleep.

Marta's body began to rise from the floor. Corcra placed his hand on her feet and guided her to the bottom bunk. He lowered her with gentle pressure to its surface. The wagon rocked as a gust of sand-filled wind bellowed outside.

Corcra turned to Breanna. He squatted down at her side, looking into her eyes. "Show me what you dreamed."

Breanna closed her eyes in desperation. She frantically tried to keep her thoughts away from what she had experienced. "I can't," she choked out. "I won't."

"You must," the Dragon shapeshifter responded with gentle insistence.

"Why are you being so nice? This is all my fault. All of it. My shields weren't strong enough. That monster knew all about me, all about us. I don't even know who or what it is," she exclaimed, frantic worry choking her voice. She wanted to hide somewhere, anywhere away from here.

Corcra laid his hand on the side of her head. Her mind tried to curl in on itself, tried to hide. She felt the weight of his perception rifling through her most recent memories. "Ah," he murmured.

The sandcat's nose touched her cheek. Calm settled around her.

*You are safe.* Two voices spoke in her mind: the cat and her Sword.

*Where were you?* she asked SunWalker.

*You blocked our link. Why?* the Sword responded.

*It was not she who blocked the link.* Corcra joined the conversation.

Breanna turned that idea over in her mind. Had that grey abomination compelled her into the dream? Just what was it? Why was it trying to kill her? Why was it trying to kill all of them?

Her eyes opened wide as another thought occurred. "Is this storm natural?"

Corcra cocked his head as he looked at her. A long pause. "I thought it was. Perhaps not." He turned and gazed at the wall as if his mind were far away.

"Brilliant," he said. His gaze returned to hers. "You are correct. It is not natural. The source of its power is to the south and west and is very subtle. It is losing strength." Corcra's eyes narrowed as he frowned. "What is to the southwest?"

"A portal to the Demon world," Breanna answered immediately and without thought. Eyes huge, she clapped her hands over her mouth, dismayed at the information she had just disclosed.

"What?" Corcra demanded.

Breanna dropped her eyes from his. "I'm sorry. Marta and I 'dreamed' together and found a map of all the portals throughout Ard An Tir in the High Mage's Tower. We were searching for Cameron after he disappeared with Neulach. Marta saw him at the bottom of a pitcher of water, swimming with Dragons at Dragon Mountain. Thomas swore both of us to secrecy. I shouldn't have told you."

Corcra put his hand over his mouth and rested his elbow on his knee. Breanna looked up and caught the merriment dancing in his amber eyes. Her jaw tightened.

He lowered his hand and straightened his face into suitable sobriety.

"I am not laughing at you, Breanna. I am laughing at the picture you painted of finding Cameron at the bottom of a pitcher. The portal map is astonishing. Who is the High Mage?"

"His name is Mannan. He's been the High Mage in charge of the Ard Ri Mage's Enclave for as long as anyone can remember," Breanna told him. "Someone set portal spells inside Red Dragon's Keep, letting the Demons in when they first attacked. Before the last portal was destroyed, Aeden used a spell to find the maker. Marta's father recognized him. Mannan is one of the King's Councilors, as the High Mage has always been."

Corcra's face lost all expression. Not a muscle moved in his body. He sat carved in stony muteness.

Breanna slowly sat upright with a groan. She straightened her legs out then crossed them in front of her. She kept her eyes on Corcra, abruptly wary. She thought back on the last few things she had told him. What had set him off?

"There are circles within circles, connections within connections," he murmured. "I must go to Neulach as soon as this storm ends."

$$\text{\$ \$ \$}$$

The gusts of wind and sand against the vardo began to weaken. Breanna lit the timekeeping candle and carefully lowered the hurricane chimney frame along its rails on either side of the wax pillar. The pierced metal top meant to keep gusts from blowing the candle out slid into place. She lifted the lamp and placed the loop at the top of its frame over the hook mounted on the ceiling beam. The candle lit the interior of the vardo with a soft glow.

Breanna stepped back and looked at the flame. It had been two days and a night since the sandstorm roared into her life. She sighed. A muffled thump, then a curse, came from the lower bunk behind her. She spun around to see Marta sitting up in the bed, holding the top of her head.

"What happened," Marta muttered, her eyes still closed. She pressed her hand to her forehead. Breanna stepped over to the bunk and gripped Marta's shoulder.

Corcra swung his feet to the floor, pushing up from the padded bench he'd been using as a bed. "Good. You're awake." He stood up and stretched. "How do you feel?"

"Like I was caught in one of your whirlwinds. Something hit me in the head," Marta grumbled.

"I believe it was Breanna's foot, and the wall she shoved you against." Corcra told her. "When I was finally able to drag her from the dream, she was kicking, flailing, and screaming."

"If you were being burned alive by a decaying Dragon, you would have done the same," Breanna barked at Corcra. "I've got the burns to prove it was real."

"The reality was never in question," he responded. "The vardo almost caught on fire. The first inkling of trouble I had was the charring of the wood at the back of your bed. I reached into your dream, much as I did to save Evan. I thought Aeden trained you to prevent this from happening again."

"She did," Breanna's voice trembled. "I thought my shields were stronger. I thought I could hide myself." Her embarrassment was palpable. "I thought I'd dream a good dream to help me relax.

I was sucked into the dream like I was a branch caught in a roaring river. I could *not* get out of it. I tried every trick Aeden taught me, and nothing worked." The volume of her voice rose in agitation. "I won't be able to sleep." Panic narrowed her eyes and tears started to leak down her cheeks.

Marta coughed. "Is there any water?"

"Hold on. I've got some right here." Breanna wiped the tears from her face, turned to the counter behind her, and scooped up the water jug and a clay cup. She took three steps to Marta's bed, filled the cup, and handed it to her.

Marta gulped down the water and held the cup out. "More, please?"

Breanna filled it. "Go slow," she warned. The vardo rocked in a gust of wind. The water sloshed in the cup, coming close to spilling.

Marta nodded in agreement and winced. "I know," she said and sipped.

Breanna set the jug on the counter behind its rail and thumped down on the tiny chair next to the small table to her right, bracing her elbows on her knees and dropping her forehead into her hands. "What am I going to do?" she choked out, anguish tightening her throat.

"There are spells to give you dreamless sleep," Corcra's deep voice jerked her from the dejection that filled her mind. She raised her head, noting the frown that narrowed his eyes and furrowed his brows. She frowned in response.

"What spells?" she demanded.

His left eyebrow rose. "Spells that Dragons know."

Breanna grimaced, tightening her jaw and pressing her lips together.

*Breanna,* SunWalker barked in her mind. *Accept the help that you are freely offered. Control yourself.*

Breanna dropped her gaze to the floor. She snorted in irritation. "Thank you. Can you teach me one of them?" She raised her head and looked at Corcra.

He tilted his head in thought. "Perhaps," he said. "If you are strong enough."

Breanna sat up straight, her spine stiffening with indignation. Remembering the dream, she sagged again.

"Tell me what Aeden taught you."

"First: recite the spell to create a mirror over my mind that will bend the dreams of others away from me," Breanna recited. "Second: before I sleep, I'm to think of the thing I want to follow: human, spirit, or animal. Third: recite the spell that creates a tight shield around my thoughts and mind within the dream. Fourth: always keep a shield over my mind. Every three or four days, I'm supposed to let the shield down and then put it back up. Otherwise, I might not be able to see who is dreaming of me. Oh."

"What?" Corcra asked.

"I was afraid to lower my shields at all," Breanna confessed. "Then I just forgot to do it," she said, her voice very soft.

Corcra waited.

Breanna pushed herself from the chair and took the four steps to the door. Turning, she paced back to the chair, jaw clenched, arms crossed. She shook her head, frustration clear in every line of her body. "I don't know what you want to hear," she exclaimed.

"What else? What else have you not told me?" he asked.

Breanna looked at the floor. Tension thrummed in the vardo. She raised her head and looked Corcra in the eyes. "There are things I'm not supposed to tell anyone, not even you."

Corcra's eyebrows rose in surprise, then crashed into a scowl. "What do you mean you can't tell me?"

"Thomas and Aeden set a spell of silence on Marta and me. If we tell anyone about the amulet or talisman or anything that is happening at Red Dragon's Keep, we will be stopped."

"What things specifically can you not tell about?" Corcra pressed.

"Things like there are five amulets and we have found two, possibly three. We're looking for the Fasach Amulet on this trip and seeing if the Sheik is a traitor." Breanna felt suddenly dizzy, her stomach turning over.

"When did this happen?" Corcra rubbed the fingers of his right hand together. "Silenced how?"

"The day that we left Red Dragon's Keep," Breanna answered, her voice flat. "Aeden added the silence spell when Thomas was finished."

The sound of the wind and the sand against the sides of the vardo fell away into stillness. A fitful gust rattled one of the windows in its frame.

Breanna looked toward the shutters. The light outside that had been shadowy and dim was beginning to brighten through the gaps between the boards.

"Can you tell me the words of the spell?"

She jerked her attention back to Corcra. "I'm not sure. I've tried to remember a few times, but it's hazy, like I'm supposed to forget."

Marta muttered, "I do."

> "Mute and dumb shall she become
> Who dares to speak of hidden things
> Bind the mind and bind the tongue

As she spoke, Marta's voice deepened and began to reverberate, as if in a large hollow space. Her eyes were fixed, as if staring into a void. Selgith crouched and hissed, lips drawn back from razor-sharp teeth, her tail lashing back and forth.

> Should words be said to which they cling
> Of secrets great and secrets small

Corcra shouted, "STOP!"

Marta fell silent.

Breanna whispered the last line.

Amulet and Talisman shall bind them all."

A mental explosion manifesting into the physical plane detonated in the vardo, expanding outward to destroy the interior of the wagon. Marta crumpled to her side on the bed. Breanna's eyes rolled up as she collapsed to the floor. The sandcat slid along the floor until her head cracked against the door wall. Her body came to a stop, and she lay still. Corcra flew backward, body splayed against the wall, head slamming against the solid wood. He fell forward to land face down on the floor next to Breanna.

# Chapter 16
# Fearmhar

The second son of the Duke of Red Dragon's Keep, Owen Arach, slapped at his arm, killing the horsefly that had been bothering him for miles. The eyes of the grey dire wolf, Samanach, glinted as he looked up, padding through the grass bordering the trail with no sound at all. His mouth seemed to grin as he panted, his tongue lolling out of the side of his mouth.

Navar, the black WindRunner that Owen rode, tossed his head and snorted. *A shield to bounce the annoyances away would keep us from their vicious maws,* he sent to them all.

"Finally," Saleth laughed. Elf of the Darkened Forest and one of the heroes of the Battle for Aos Si, he agreed with his King's command to accompany Owen on his ongoing quest to find the pieces of the Cumhacht Ar Dragoini–the Dragon Talisman. Why didn't you use your magic to kill it an hour ago?" His glittering Agni elfmount that he walked beside snorted.

"Huh. I didn't think to do that." Owen's annoyance mirrored the flip of his hand as he flicked the carcass away. He drew in a deep breath of air scented with the fresh smell of new growth.

"I'm glad my father and your king sent us here. I know Navar and I insisted on searching Fearmhar for the amulet, but getting away from the main track was genius. No one knows where we are."

Saleth grinned. "I've been this way in the past. It has not changed."

Owen scanned the land around them. The tall, bright green growth of late spring moving in the gentle breeze swayed and dipped like the waves on the lake near his faraway home. A dark line of trees in the distance told him that a creek flowed at the base of the rise to the west. These weren't hills, but the land wasn't flat. Owen had never seen the sea, but he'd heard enough stories to think that this looked very much like those troughs and peaks.

The far-off trees looked strange. They were not green with new growth. Instead, they stood like a blackened skeletal barrier to what lay on the other side. Navar snorted and halted his steps, swinging his head and pricking his black ears toward the line.

Saleth checked his stride and swung to the right in front of Navar to inspect what the others had noted. He frowned. His eyes squinted in the bright sunlight.

He leaned on the staff of Rowan wood that he carried as a walking stick and a weapon. His elven heritage showed in his pointed ears, fine bones, and the long hair that fell in a thick braid down his back. His latent magic camouflaged his brown tunic and trousers to blend with the grasses they were traversing.

*I can feel the trees' deaths within the magic that flows through Fearmhar,* Navar told them. *There is a taint in the energy akin to that of the Darkened Forest.* Astonishment colored his sending.

Saleth cocked his head and went still, as if he were listening or sensing something that the others could not perceive. He slowly straightened, glancing around them. Raising his arm, he pointed to the south. Owen followed the line of his arm and saw a faint cloud of dust gradually growing larger. Something or someone was coming.

Saleth slid the bow he had stowed from its diagonal sleeve on his back, replacing it with the walking stick. Stringing the bow with quick hands, he checked the arrows in the quiver hanging over his right shoulder. Owen dropped his hand to HeartStriker's hilt. Navar tossed his head in agitation and jigged to the right. Samanach faded into the vegetation. There was no place to hide for the WindRunner, Agni, elf, or human.

The cloud of dust grew as whatever was creating it drew closer. Owen could see figures racing toward him, feel the vibration of pounding hooves through the ground. Within a tenth of a candlemark, he could see a line of at least fifteen riders stretching across their path to the south. He drew HeartStriker.

*I will wait until needed to flame;* the Sword told him.

*Good idea*, Owen sent the wry thought. He rested his fist holding the deerhide-wrapped grip of the Sword on his thigh, the flat of its blade leaning against his shoulder.

The figures grew larger. Long, narrow, with incredible endurance, the fleet horses of the plains, named coursers by the tribes, carried their riders in a wide sweep around the six until they were surrounded. Loosely knocked arrows pointed at the ground from strung bows were held in ready hands as the coursers came to a halt.

Only the sigh of the wind and the rustle of grass stems against each other broke the quiet. Unfriendly stares watched the group. The coursers' ears flicked back and forth, especially those on the right side of the circle. A half-smile lifted the corner of Saleth's mouth. Dire wolves hid very well.

Shirts and trousers the color of ripened wheat served as a kind of uniform for all the riders. Dark tooled-leather armguards rode each archer's bow arm. Calf-high deep brown riding boots protected their legs. A wide, stiff-brimmed leather hat, flat on top, sat on each head or dangled down backs on thin chin cords. Clubbed hair tied with beaded thongs rested at the back of each rider's neck. Several wore beaded bone breastplates.

A palomino courser, coat shimmering with gold highlights, took one step into the circle. The rider's upper arm bore a silver cuff over his shirtsleeve. Bronze skin gleamed with sweat. "Who are you?" his deep husky voice abruptly demanded.

Owen tilted his head to the right. "I am Owen Arach, son of Duke Tom Arach, Lord of Red Dragon's Keep in Ard Ri." He nodded toward his elf companion to his left. "This is Saleth, Forest Lord Scout. And this is Navar, WindRunner from the Windward Range."

Navar struck out at the ground with his left plate-sized hoof, chin tucked almost to his chest.

""This is an Agni, elven mount from the Forest Lords. We're on our way to the court of Fearmhar to talk with the Commanders of the Nations."

Murmurs of astonishment swept the circle. No expression crossed the leader's face. A courser stamped a hoof and blew. The warrior kneed his animal forward, sending it walking toward Owen and Navar.

As he reached the WindRunner, his courser laid its ears flat and snaked its head toward Navar's neck. Navar squealed and struck back, grabbing the courser by the crest of its neck, and snapping his head to the side. The courser staggered and almost went down, spinning away on trembling legs, almost throwing its rider. Owen balanced atop the WindRunner as if there was no movement at all.

Owen locked eyes with the eyes of the courser's rider. He raised one eyebrow. The rider pulled his mount in a circle, keeping a tight hold on the courser's reins, ready to react to a repeat attack.

"Fearmhar is closed to outsiders," he grunted.

"I understand," Owen responded. "However, my message is of such import that I insist we go to the Meeting Stone to tell them what is happening in other lands."

"No," responded the Fearmharan border guard.

Owen lifted HeartStriker from his shoulder and raised it, point up, into the air. *Now*, he told the Sword. A spear of flame burst from the Sword into the sky.

Behind the circle of coursers, Samanach rose from his concealment in the grass. Half of the coursers shied away and bucked in fear. They bolted, racing flat out toward the horizon, their riders trying fruitlessly to stop them.

The leader pulled his courser's nose to his knee, keeping the animal from bolting, spinning it in a circle. Lather coated its neck and flanks. He finally brought it under control, nose still snubbed to his knee. The dire wolf walked into what had been a circle and took up his place at Saleth's shoulder.

"I am Yansa, of the Kheron clan," the rider said through gritted teeth as his mount fought him, struggling to spin and shed the rider on its back. He finally brought it under control, shivering and sweating.

HeartStriker's fire flared once and disappeared. Samanach sat and cocked his head. Saleth stood ready. Navar flared his nostrils. The Agni watched the clansman, muscles bunched, ready to attack. "It is truly urgent that we speak to your council of elders. Why has Fearmhar closed her borders?" Owen asked.

"Something stirs in Fasach and Ard Ri. We don't know what it is, but tales brought by traders tell of Demons on the move," Yansa replied. "We want none of it."

Owen shook his head. "They will come here regardless of what any of us hope for."

Yansa stilled, staring at Owen. After what felt like an eternity, he slumped in the saddle and shook his head in resignation. He pulled his horse around and pointed it toward the line of dead trees. "Follow me."

The bringers of unwelcome news strode forward, following the scout.

§ § §

Samanach swung wide of the riders to the left, gliding through the grass. Owen watched him out of the corner of his eye. The scouts kept their discomfort hidden, but the coursers certainly didn't. The half that had bolted returned, their horses lathered and stumbling with exhaustion. Snorts and nervous sidling marked their passage as the animals tried to keep the dire wolf in their sight.

The sun slid closer to the horizon by a candlemark as the cavalcade rode through the line of dead trees.

Owen shivered.

# Chapter 17
# Aftermath

Marta pushed up from the bedding where she had been thrown, shaking her head in dazed bewilderment, trying to make out her surroundings. Her eyes refused to focus. Rolling up to sit on the side of the bed she groaned, hands grasping the sides of her head.

Peering through narrowed eyes, the interior of the vardo finally resolved. Much of the furnishings were on the floor. Pitchers, plates, and mugs were shattered and jumbled in heaps. Cabinet wood was splintered. The window glass had disintegrated into shards and powder. Two bodies lay on the floor amid the ruin.

Marta's legs refused to hold her as she tried to stand. She thumped back to the bed. She wiped her hands over her face. They came away bloody. Cuts and nicks covered her face and arms.

Pieces of pottery, splinters of wood and dust coated everything. She slid to the floor and crawled with slow careful movements over the debris to the body closest to her. Grasping the shoulder farthest away from her, Marta pulled the body over. Breanna's body rolled to her back. She was breathing.

Marta released the breath she'd been holding. Exhausted, her head fell forward to rest on her forearms. She pushed herself to her knees after a few minutes of rest and edged past Breanna, pushing debris out of her way, crawling to Corcra. He shuddered as she approached, dislodging the wreckage that covered him. Propping himself up on his forearms, head shaking from side to side, he looked at her with dull eyes.

"Are you all right?" she croaked, reaching out to touch him on the shoulder.

"No."

His eyes lost their dullness as he frowned and swept a searching look over the devastation. He sat up with an abruptness that startled Marta. She jerked away from him and pushed herself up to lean against the cabinet frame across from him.

Dismay twisted Corcra's face as he reached toward Breanna.

"She's alive," Marta said.

Corcra drew back. He rested his hands on his knees as Breanna groaned. She turned her head toward them, her eyes squinting open. She tried to bring her knees to her chest and grunted in pain.

"Breanna," Corcra breathed, a question in his tone.

§ § §

Breanna shuddered. Every muscle in her body ached. She brought her hand to her head and felt wetness. She pulled it away and looked at the blood covering her fingers.

She tried to ask, "What happened?" Her lips moved but nothing came out of her mouth. She frowned, tried again. Again, nothing. Fear tightened her face. Realization shortened her breath as she remembered the spell. She remembered what she had told Corcra. Marta put a hand on her shoulder.

Breanna pushed herself up and rotated to sit, swinging her legs around, crossing them. She put her bloody hand on her throat. "I can't speak," she mouthed.

"The spell of silence worked. I'm not sure it was supposed to be that spectacular or destructive." Corcra's grave words filled the ruined wagon. He cocked his head. "There is something else that altered the spell. It might have attached itself while you were in your dream, perhaps from the grey Dragon. I think that speaking of anything about Red Dragon's Keep to anyone triggered it."

Breanna swung her head toward him. Dread tightened her chest as she turned his words over in her mind. She tried to mentally reach out for SunWalker. Her thought met nothing.

A look of horror rounded her eyes as her mouth fell open. She pushed to her feet in frantic haste, stumbling toward the sleeping alcove where the Sword of Light hung on its hook by her mattress. She fell against the support and slammed her hand onto its scabbard. No reassurance reached out to her.

Breanna whirled and stared at Corcra.

The door to the last cabinet at the end of the vardo swung open. The sandcat pushed into the aisle from where she had sheltered after waking from her encounter with the wall. She gave a mighty sneeze, sat, and started to clean her fur. All three of the humans stared at her.

Breanna crumpled to the floor. *What am I going to do? I can't talk or reach SunWalker or Selgith. What am I going to do?* She put her face in her hands, wanting to hide from the world. Tears leaked past her fingers. Arms gathered her close and patted her on the back.

"It's all right. Everything will be all right," Marta murmured into her hair.

*How can she still speak? Why didn't the spell work on her?*

Breanna wanted to shrink and disappear into nothingness.

"Let's get our wounds cleaned up before anything else," Marta said with practical assurance. She reached into the shelving behind her, searching for an unbroken jug of water and a bowl. She found a jug wrapped in toweling, protecting it from damage. Rummaging deeper in the cabinet, she found napkins normally used for the table. She dampened the fabric and started to clean the cut on Breanna's head.

Someone pounded on the door of the vardo and shouted a muffled command.

Corcra rose to his feet and crunched over the broken glass, pottery, and splinters. He pulled the door open just as caravan master Khalid Qadir raised his hand to pound on the door again. The sandcat ran out the door between the two and darted into the shifting drifts.

"What," barked Corcra.

"Lord Dragon, could you help dig out the caravan?" Khaled craned his neck to see past Corcra's body blocking the door. "What happened in here?" He raised his eyes to stare at the shapeshifter's face.

Breanna shifted to peer around Corcra at the caravan master. Her soft groan of pain was muffled by Corcra's snarl. The caravan master took several quick steps backward, down, and away from the stairs. Corcra followed him, stepping down the three steps from the vardo to the ground. Breanna pushed up from the floor, clutching Marta's shoulder for balance. Marta stood and pulled Breanna's arm over her shoulder. They staggered to the door. Marta balanced the pair as they hobbled down the stairs.

Sand drifted high up the side of the wagon, heaped above the tops of the windows. The wind had swept a broad swath of clear ground at the end of the wagon, piling sand in a hill to the right of the vardo, just beyond the canvas animal shelter.

The two stood at the bottom of the stairs and stared out at the rearranged landscape. The sand glittered as bright sunlight struck the dunes left by the storm. The top twigs of the shrubs that lined the trail were the only vegetation visible above the drifts.

"Can you unbury the wagons?" Khaled asked, hesitant hope in his voice.

Corcra crossed his arms and glanced down the line of wagons. "Perhaps."

Corcra looked out across the plains toward the mountains far in the distance. He strode to the other side of the wagon. He shook his head. "I will try to unearth our wagon."

*Corcra, maybe you can create a whirlwind to lift the sand and send it to the North.* Breanna tried to send the shapeshifter her thought. He didn't react. She pushed away from Marta and turned to look at her. Marta cocked her head in question. Breanna twirled her hand in a rotating motion and then pointed to the right side of the wagon.

"You want him to lift the sand in a tornado and move it over there?" she asked. Breanna nodded in quick agreement.

"Corcra, Breanna suggests that you move it over there," she said, pointing to the other side of the vardo. "Maybe use a whirlwind?"

Corcra looked at them. Breanna stared at the ground, away from his obvious scrutiny, embarrassed by her inability to speak. "Perhaps you should go inside and see what can be done to clean up the wreckage," he offered. Marta nodded.

Breanna turned to the stairs and moved into the vardo, one slow step at a time. Marta followed, pulling the door shut behind them. Breanna's legs quivered as she stood by the splintered cabinets, leaning on the counter with one hand. Two tracks of tears carved paths through the dust that covered her face. All she wanted to do was crawl into her bed and hide.

Marta pulled a twig broom off the hook on the door. She passed it to Breanna and grabbed a handful of napkins and a larger piece of fabric. "I think we can use this to hold all of the broken stuff," she said, shaking it out.

Breanna nodded. She began to sweep the litter to the center of the aisle with slow hesitant movements. Marta used one of the napkins to push the debris on the counters onto the floor then pushed it into the pile Breanna was creating.

Breanna stared at the broom and the debris. She coughed as dust rose in the air. She leaned the broom against the wall and went to her gear, rummaging through the bag at the foot of the bed for her riding gloves and scarf. She knotted the scarf at the back of her neck and lifted the front swag over her mouth and nose. Pulling the gloves on, she turned and squatted at the edge of the fabric that Marta had spread on the floor, lifting pottery, glass, food, and splintered wood onto the sheet.

"It's full enough," Marta told her. They gathered up the four corners, two to each, and walked the bundle to the door. Marta went down the stairs backwards, lifting the tarp as high as she could. Breanna strained to lift her end over the threshold and then followed the thumping fabric bundle down to the ground.

At the bottom of the stairs she released the corners and looked at Marta. Marta was shaking her head at the pile. Breanna caught her eye and raised her hands palm up. *What now* she thought, knowing her friend could not hear her.

Marta shook her head again and strode around the corner of the vardo. Breanna followed.

Corcra was two wagon-lengths away, guiding a spinning sand-filled column of air into the desert to the south. Khaled stood slightly behind him, arms crossed over his chest as he watched. Growing drifts of sand and earth defined Corcra's work. A steady wind from the northeast lifted the cloud of dust he raised away from the caravan.

Breanna leaned against the side of the wagon as Marta strode toward the two men. Khaled moved up to stand next to Corcra, looking to the southwest. Khaled pointed to the horizon where a dark grey cloud boiled into the sky. It wasn't sand.

She couldn't hear what was said and shook her head in frustration. Her heart started to pound, and her body shook as thoughts of her life going forward shortened her breathing. *I won't ever be able to talk to anyone again. I've failed everyone. I can't do what I need to do to find the amulet. What will happen to Selgith and SunWalker? I can't even talk to the ruler of Fasach. How can I possibly be an ambassador?* Breanna covered her face with her hands.

Every thought increased her panic. Dizzy, she sat down hard on the ground next to the rear corner of the vardo. Her thoughts slowed as a low-pitched humming filled the air. She stared at the ground and listened.

The sound rose and fell over and over. It shook her bones. Bellows of pain from the oxen boomed across the desert, rising in volume.

Breanna's heart slowed to match the rhythm of the sound. She could barely draw a breath. Looking up, she watched Corcra and Marta turning toward the southwest as if moving through some kind of thick honey instead of air.

She followed their gaze with her own. A dark hole in the sky was rotating in the distance. The outer edge of the darkness separated into a spiral around the hole that grew larger and larger until it stood at least a man and a half tall. The pounding of the sound increased as the spiral drew closer. She opened her mouth to scream, but nothing came out. She watched as people digging out their wagons all along the caravan took one look and moved to take shelter under, in, or on the other side of the flimsy protection. Some grabbed weapons and stood ready.

A blur of brown and tan raced past her, knocking her out of the rhythm, sending her sprawling on the ground. The sandcat bounded up the stairs and into the vardo. Breanna lay on the ground, trying to steady her breathing. Selgith flowed down the stairs, SunWalker's scabbard gripped in her mouth. She dropped the Sword on Breanna's legs and bolted back into the desert.

Breanna's awareness snapped into focus. *I can still fight. Whatever is coming, I can still fight.* Fierce joy filled her. She reached down and grabbed the Sword by its grip, rolled to her stomach and brought her knees to her chest, using them to push her body upright. Breanna staggered to her feet.

She ripped the Sword from its sheath.

A hoard of black Demons flooded from the rotating hole in the sky, red eyes gleaming, teeth bared, long grey claws on thick paws and thicker legs churning up sand. A portal from the Demon world lay open.

SunWalker burst into flame. Breanna ran toward the line of charging monstrosities, swinging the Sword back over her shoulder. She whipped it forward as the beasts from nightmare drew close. A long lash of flame reached out and impaled the three that were running toward her.

She bared her teeth in fury. She lifted SunWalker and its rope of fire up through the Demon bodies, gutting them. They dropped to the ground and stopped moving. Blood fountained and smoked. She drew the Sword back and flung the fire vertically, beheading the Demons following their leaders.

A lash of fire from her left startled Breanna. She whirled to face the threat. Marta had joined the fight, using her Sword of Light as a whip. Demons exploded as the fire touched each one.

The bellow of a Dragon's roar echoed across the sands. A whirlwind of purple smoke shrouded Corcra's body. Sound went still, as if consumed by that thunder. The Purple Dragon, shading from deepest black on his dorsal spines to palest lilac on his belly, launched himself into the sky on purple wings.

The Dragon turned to align himself across the advancing host. Brilliant white-hot flame cooling to blue and orange at its front spewed from his gaping mouth, covering the writhing maelstrom of advancing black bodies.

The Demons shrieked in agony and writhed as they burned.

The portal shrank in size as the three decimated the attackers. Half of a Demon flopped onto the sand, cut in two by the portal as the bridge between worlds snapped out of existence.

The Dragon banked at the end of his flight and flew back, fire streaming, burning and charring Demon bodies into ash. He pulled up and hung over the caravan, huge billows of sand lifting into the air from the downdraft as he beat his wings. He swung his great head from side to side. Cold amber eyes glittered.

The fire from HellScream and SunWalker faded into nothingness.

Purple smoke wreathed the Dragon as he lowered himself, hind legs first, to the ground. Corcra emerged from the smoke, his clothing as pristine as ever.

Breanna watched him, mind gibbering. She'd been fighting Demons inside the Keep when Aeden took her Dragon form, incinerating the Demon enemies in the forecourt during the first battle of the war. She'd never seen anything like this.

She swallowed on a dry throat, a little bit of fear tightening her body. *Maybe a lot of fear* she admitted to herself. She dropped her gaze to the ground to hide that fear as Corcra swept his gaze over Marta, her, and down the line of wagons.

Breanna sheathed SunWalker. Questions swamped her mind. *Why had the Demons attacked? Did they know that Marta and I are here? That we've seen the rift in the Carpehg Desert that opens to their world? Why that portal? Didn't they know Corcra was here?* She shook her head in frustration.

Corcra faced the front of the caravan, raised his hand and sand flew away from the wagons to the south in a giant wave. Humans stood like pillars, shocked at Corcra's power. With slow deliberation and many glances at him, they returned to excavating their own vehicles from what sand remained. A murmur of conversations filled the air, most of them thankful, some filled with terror at what they'd seen.

Breanna retreated to the end of the vardo and moved to the other side where the animals sheltered under the tarp the drover and the girls had hung at the beginning of the storm. The sand had piled up a good five feet from the edge of the tarp. She cocked her head, remembering how snow piled up in the forecourt of Red Dragon's Keep when a blizzard swept the mountains, leaving a clear path as wide as the wall was tall along its edge.

The tarp rippled. Breanna gasped and stepped back in alarm. One of the animals under the tarp snorted. *Oh, thank the Three.* She hurried to the other side of the shelter and pulled the pins that secured the triangular flap at the side of the shelter from the ground. Flipping the edge up, she slipped between the vardo and the tarp into the warmth and smell of animals too long in one place. The two oxen and three horses turned their heads to look at her. The oxen pushed themselves to their feet, rump first then one front leg at a time. They rumbled out a greeting. Breanna reached out and rested her hand on the closest shoulder. The touch calmed her roiling mind.

The piles of hay in front of each animal were gone. Breanna ducked under the ropes tying each animal to the wagon and squatted down to reach under the vardo. Pushing her fingers under the corded binding of a bale of hay, she pulled it to her. Breanna broke it open, pushing her knee into the center and pulling the ends toward her body. Separating the flakes of compacted grass, she tossed them in front of each eagerly waiting animal.

As if a spigot had been opened, every ounce of energy drained out of Breanna. Too tired to think, she knelt on the ground and then curled up on top of the loose hay, letting the sound of grinding teeth of horse and oxen chewing lull her mind and body. She wrapped her mind with her shield and drifted into dreamless sleep.

# Chapter 18
# Death Spell

Marta went looking for Breanna when the wagons were almost cleared of sand. Drovers dug out wheels as the shapeshifter removed the sand in great windrows, hastily moving to the opposite side of the wagon as Corcra approached. The only humans willing to be near him were the caravan master and the trader. Neither spoke to him except by necessity.

Marta rounded the end of the wagon and rocked to a halt. The animal shelter that kept the horses and oxen alive during the sandstorm had been detached from the side of the vardo and folded away, the animals led off to be harnessed and saddled. Breanna slept on, oblivious to the noise.

Marta shook her head and stepping forward, bent down and shook her friend's shoulder. "Breanna, wake up. We're getting ready to move out."

Breanna squinted her eyes open. She stretched out her legs and pushed her arms over her head with a huge yawn, ending with a grunt. She yawned again and rolled up to sit on the hay under her.

She remembered.

Panic gripped her again. She couldn't speak. She couldn't reach out to her Sword or her Familiar. She tried drawing in long slow breaths, concentrating on the in and out. Her fear waned.

"Marta. Breanna. Come here."

Both looked toward the back of the wagon. Corcra's baritone voice ordered them to attend him. Marta looked back at her friend. She reached down and grasped Breanna's forearm, pulling her to her feet. They both stepped a few feet to the end of the wagon and stopped.

Corcra stood next to the small hill of destruction the women had pulled from the vardo. His booted foot moved some of the debris aside. He squatted down and slowly passed his hand over the wreckage, palm down. His fingers darted out to a small metal box partially buried by splinters of wood and glass. One corner bulging out, exposing a lining of maroon silk, its lid no longer tight.

He picked it up. "It's heavy," he murmured.

Breanna reached out and grabbed Marta's arm. Dread tightened her throat and stomach. Her breathing quickened. She could feel something evil connecting her to the box.

Corcra unfolded from his crouch, box in hand. He sketched a sigil in the air. The sounds of the caravan and the desert were gone in that moment as the three were shrouded in a mental shield that he formed around them. Breanna glanced to the left and right, looking for observers. There were none.

Corcra rested his fingers on the lid of the box. It began to rise. A putrid stench poured from the opening. With an oath, he dropped the box, taking several steps back. As it hit the ground, a black crystal wrapped in a rotting piece of heart rolled from the box. Breanna's mouth fell open.

Every joint in her body rebelled. Pain gripped her fingers and toes, wrists, elbows, and knees. Her heart stopped beating. The muscles around hips, spine, and shoulders spasmed, sending her to her knees. Her eyes rolled back in her head. Her body began to convulse, sending her into darkness.

§ § §

Breanna woke, lying on the floor of the wagon. Her sleeves and the legs of her trousers were rolled up. Marta sponged water on her forehead and arms. Every movement Breanna made sent jabs of pain through her body. Corcra stood at her feet. As she awakened, he spread his fingers and held his hand over her. She sighed with relief as his magic flowed and the pain immediately lessened.

"Thank you," she mouthed to him. He gave a nod and left the wagon.

"He destroyed the box, the crystal and that disgusting heart when you fell," Marta said. "I wish you could tell us what happened."

Breanna moved her hand as if holding a pen and writing. Marta cocked her head, then rose and went to a drawer in the cabinet that hadn't been destroyed at the head of the bunk beds. She pulled out several sheets of parchment, a pen, and a jar of ink. She set them on the table.

"Come on, let's get you up."

She knelt and helped Breanna to sit up. Standing, Marta grasped Breanna's forearm and pulled her to her feet.

Unsteady, Breanna stepped to the bench by the table and sat. She pulled the parchment to her and unscrewed the lid of the ink jar. She dipped the pen in the jar and began to write. Marta watched as Breanna started to communicate.

$$\$ \$ \$$$

The sun used the wagon's canvas roof as an anvil to hammer heat into the interior. The open windows, glass replaced with canvas, gave no relief. The only one who enjoyed lounging in the shadowed warmth at the open back door was Selgith. Her paws were tucked under her chest, her eyes shut, only the tip of her tail occasionally twitching.

Within a candlemark, Breanna had written down all that she could remember of the magic that attacked her. She sent a message to the caravan master, asking for a camel to ride. She had to get outside and out of the heat intensifying within the vardo. When it arrived, she mounted and guided the smelly beast to the side of the caravan to get out of the dust raised by wheel, hoof, and boot.

The jerking, rolling motion of the camel as it padded beside the caravan kept Breanna's stomach in a constant state of low-level nausea. Sweat ran down her face from under the cotton kufiyah covering her head. She could feel the beads of moisture roll down her back under the long-sleeved brown cotton shirt that covered her from neck to hips under a white cotton cape that captured any arrant breeze. Sturdy cotton twill trousers protected her legs from the camel's sides and saddle. The trader had gifted them with the clothing when they had left the meadow they had used as an oasis.

Worry pressed down on Breanna. She ached every-where. Shifting her body repeatedly, she searched for a place to sit without pain. Whatever had come out of that box had been meant for her. Neither Corcra nor Marta had been affected.

Breanna pulled back on the ropes connected to the camel's halter, slowing it down. She was too exhausted to continue. Corcra's horse pulled even with her. He reined it back to a walk.

"Do you need to return to the wagon?" he asked.

Breanna nodded. Corcra waved his arm at the driver and the wagon pulled to the side of the road, slowed, and stopped. Breanna tapped the camel's shoulder repeatedly with the thin camel stick, giving the command to kneel. Much groaning followed as it folded itself to the ground.

She dismounted and gasped as her feet hit the ground. She fell against the camel's side, panting with the pain.

Corcra swung down from his horse, dropped the reins, and lifted her into his arms. He carried her into the vardo and set her on the bench by the table. Breanna folded her arms around her belly and began to rock. She ducked her chin to her chest and gasped with pain. She felt Corcra's magic roll through her and sighed with relief as her stomach settled and muscles relaxed.

"We are within a day of Jafara," he told her. She nodded her thanks as he turned and left.

Breanna stumbled the short distance to the bottom bunk, using the furniture and wall for support, and slowly lowered herself to the mattress. She rolled to her back. *What should I do? What can I do?*

She imagined her meeting with the Sayathia of Fasach. Breanna pictured herself sitting silent and reserved, listening to Marta present her. Corcra stood at her back. *Maybe my best path is to listen and record everything, what's said, body language, the atmosphere, the players in the game. The first job is to find the amulet. Marta and I should 'dream' about it. Second is to find out about the Demons and the portal in the southwest of Fasach. Third, see if the Sayathia is ready for an alliance with father. That's going to be interesting.*

The swaying of the wagon and diminished pain lulled her into a quiet drift of her mind, despite the heat. Selgith padded to the bed and jumped up to lie at her feet. Breanna's eyes closed

# Chapter 19
# The King's Deception

Tom Arach and his wife Jennifer rode their horses toward the massive metal gates of Cathair Ri standing open to the traffic that was moving in and out of the capital. The beat of hooves and rumble of wheels on the paving stones echoed back and forth between the high walls lining the road. They had deliberately timed it to arrive very close to the end of the day and the closing of the gates. The granite walls and towers of the Castle of the Kings thrust skyward from the top of the hill on which it was built.

A grim smile twisted Tom's lips and his eyes narrowed. They had started out months ago at the king's command to advise him on a plan to beat back the Demons attacking Ard Ri. They'd been kidnapped half-way to the capital and imprisoned, then tortured and beaten at North Meall, the fortified manor held by turncoat Earl Tilden, and his son. Their escape had been harrowing, hunted by fey from the Darkened Forest and pursued relentlessly by Demons. Three Demons attacked their small band and, as the monsters leapt at them, the four Swords of Light that the Arachs and Gobhlans carried awoke and gave them the strength and dexterity to kill the Demons in sprays of caustic blood.

They'd raced for Aos Si, the home of Debra and Scott WindWalker, Jennifer and Anne's sister and her husband, encountering an army of fey from the Darkened Forest. They joined their sons Owen and Thomas, working with the elven Forest Lords, to battle the Dark Fey and went on to battle the Demon hordes attacking Aos Si. The Red Dragon, Aeden, had turned the tide from desperation to victory. The allies had won, at a very heavy cost.

Tom watched the four gate guards on either side of the massive gate with alert speculation, noting the pikes held at the ready by those furthest from the opening. He glanced at the top of the fully manned crenelated walls and frowned. Knocked arrows pointed at their cavalcade. *What is the king worried about this far from the borders?*

As they rode forward, a shudder passed down Tom's spine, raising the hair on his body. His grunt of surprise was echoed by the others. "What was that?" he muttered, his hand automatically reaching for the hilt of his sword. He clenched his teeth, remembering his Sword's retreat into itself for his protection.

"That might have been a magical barrier we just went through," Jennifer murmured.

"Makes sense," he said quietly from the side of his mouth. "All of you, keep your mental shields tight." Tom raised his hand, fist clenched, signaling the column to halt.

The guard to the left of the gate, a corporal by his insignia, lifted his hand as they reached it. "State your business," he barked.

The Arach and Gobhlan banners held by the two soldiers at the front of the column whipped and snapped in the steady breeze blowing through the causeway. Horses snorted and blew, stamping hooves on the stone road. Tom leaned forward and rested his crossed arms on the swell at the front of his saddle, his fingers loosely holding the reins. His eyes narrowed as he watched the gate guards. The banners should have been announcement enough of who they were.

"The Duke and Duchess of Red Dragon's Keep and the Duke and Duchess of Falcon's Spire to attend the king, by the king's order," the soldier holding the Arach banner on the left at the front of the column announced in a loud voice.

The pikes held by the rear guards wavered as the men showed their surprise at the news. Tom straightened in his saddle, his suspicions confirmed. These men thought he and the others were dead. He glanced at Jennifer and back at Jeremy and Anne. They acknowledged him with a barely noticeable dip of their heads. Jennifer's eyes held fury, her lips flat. He gave a tiny negative shake of his head. Her face went blank. He grinned.

The corporal stood nonplused. His raised hand slowly lowered to his side. His eyes darted from side to side, taking in the train of soldiers and wagons. Coming to a decision, he looked at his companion. "Go tell the watch captain that the Lords Arach and Gobhlan are here."

"My lords and ladies, if you would follow me?" He turned and motioned the pike bearers back against the walls on either side of the passage through the gates.

The column started forward and followed the corporal into a wide and long paved area to the left of the gates. It was lined with a row of buildings, doors standing open onto the parade ground. Tom looked at them curiously until he realized that these were barracks for the men on top of the walls and the gate guards. "Huh," he grunted. That probably meant that there were barracks like these at every gate and throughout the city. They made sense for quick response to any threat. Much had changed since he'd last been here.

Traders and merchants, wagons and mounted men streamed by now that the blockage of Tom's men cleared the road. An officer strode out of the door of the guard station at the far end of the open area. Silver lieutenant's tabs flashed on his collar. His uniform was immaculate, boots polished to a high sheen, the cover on his head precisely centered. Tom struggled to keep his face blank.

Either the man was a chair-sitter or brand new to his rank.

He came to a halt in front of the still-mounted column. He gave a half bow. "My lords and ladies, welcome to Caithar Ri. Arrangements for suitable quarters for you are in process." He turned with a frown to the privates who had joined him on his march across the parade ground. "Where are the welcome cups?"

"Sorry, sir. We weren't sure if these were imposters or not. We thought it best to wait for your direction," one of the men said.

The lieutenant glanced back at the party from Red Dragon's Keep and narrowed his eyes, as if that thought had never crossed his mind. He turned back to his men. "The welcome cup is extended to all high-born who arrive at Caithar Ri. The King's Mage will have the testing of them. Get the cups." He gestured toward the gatehouse. The privates hurried to do his bidding.

§ § §

Anne shook her damp hair, rubbing the towel she was using over her head and down the dark fall. She sat on a bench beside the large, tiled tub within the suite the Arachs and Gobhlans were shown to by the castle's seneschal. A short fussy man, he'd bowed repeatedly and wrung his hands in distress at the treatment they received on their arrival.

She stood and pulled on the clean shirt and trousers she'd carried from Aos Si. A knock on the door startled her. She reached for her Sword leaning against the wall. "Come in," she called.

Jeremy pushed the door open, halting as he saw her holding the Sword. A grin lit his face. "Jumpy, are we?"

"Aren't you, knowing what we know?"

Jeremy's grin faded. "You're right." He paused in thought. "We've been commanded to attend the king at dinner. I expect the King's Mage will be there. Meet me in the main room when you're done getting dressed."

Anne wrapped the sword belt around her waist but left the Sword leaning on its rack. Pushing her feet into her scuffed and worn boots, she wiggled her toes until her heels slid into place. She slid the small sheath with its dagger she'd begun to carry into the top of her right boot. She pulled the door closed behind her.

$$$

The four companions met in the great-room in front of huge doors standing open to a room large enough to hold a banquet. A servant stepped from the hallway to the left and gestured toward the right corridor leading from the hall.

"My Lords and Ladies, please follow me."

He guided them past a door on the right and two on the left. He turned into another doorway on the right. The room beyond held a dining table surrounded by eight chairs. Glowing orbs like those at Red Dragon's Keep rested in ornate sconces. The walls were covered with crimson velvet. A tall window behind the throne-like chair at the end of the table glowed with the last light of the setting sun. Tom followed him, trailed by the others. The servant pulled the door closed.

Two men stood behind chairs on either side of the table.

"Duke Arach, Duke Gobhlan, I'm glad to see you are safe and finally made it to Cathair Ri. Orley Mackey, Sand Ridge Keep. Not sure if you remember me from the conclave a couple of years ago." The tall thin man on the left approached, his right hand held out in greeting. He shook Tom's hand first and then Jeremy's.

"Come, all of you take a chair. The King will be late. The King's Mage is closeted with him about planning. Come, come. You remember Earl Peggin from Castle Asheford?" The other man gave a short bow.

Tom glanced at the others and gave a tiny nod. Tom and Jennifer moved up one side of the table, Jeremy and Anne up the other. When they were seated, another servant entered the room with a pitcher and proceeded to fill the glasses at each place with ruby red wine. "I'd like water," Anne murmured to the servant, "as I'm sure the others would too."

"What happened to you?" Lord Mackey asked. "We were sure you were dead after so long without contact."

"It's a long story," Tom's deep rumble filled the room. "I'd prefer to tell it only once. Let's wait until the King is here. What of you and Earl Peggin? What has been happening in the kingdom these past months?"

A frown lowered Mackay's brows as the corners of his mouth turned down. "A Demon War is truly underway," he said with a shake of his head. "The outlying villages and holdings are under attack almost every night. We've lost hundreds of people.

The door opened and a broad, tall guard stepped through. No emotion crossed his face as he scanned the room, searching for threats. Finding none, he stepped aside.

Rudraige Mór, the King of Ard Ri, walked into the room. Everyone bowed. His face lit with a smile as he waved his hand. "Sit. Sit. It's long past time that you arrived, Duke Arach, Duke Gobhlan. And your lovely ladies." The scarlet of his tunic over a cloth-of-gold shirt and black trousers shimmered as he walked to his chair.

Behind the king stood a man taller than all of them dressed in white silk robes that fell from his neck to the floor. Arcane symbols embroidered in gold covered the robe's hem and his sleeves' cuffs. Black hair swept back from his high forehead and fell to his shoulders. Rings of gold covered every finger. He followed the king into the room.

"This is Mannan, my mage." Rudraige waved the man forward. "Come. Sit next to me."

Eyes so dark that they seemed to drink the light glanced at each face as if burning them indelibly in his mind. The king sat. The others followed.

Tom felt pressure against his mental shield. Mannan caught his glance and held it. Tom tightened the protection further against the intrusion, his face as blank as he could make it. Jennifer jerked as if struck. Jeremy and Anne mirrored her movement. Tellingly, the others in the room did not.

Tom broke eye contact with Mannan, turning his head and touching Jennifer's shoulder. "Are you all right?" he murmured. She slanted him a look. "Fine," she muttered.

The mage made no sound as he glided to his chair at the king's side. As soon as he was seated, servants began to serve the meal.

"What happened to you?" the king asked as he used his knife to fold a piece of meat into his mouth. He lifted his goblet of wine and drank deeply.

"Sire, we were ambushed by bandits as we came out of the Dragon Spine Mountains on the way to Cathair Ri. They attacked at dawn as we were getting ready to break camp. The night before we discovered that our supplies were sabotaged, I sent men to the next town to buy more. The squad of guards I'd kept wasn't enough to keep the bandits back. They all died. Lady Jennifer took a sword cut to her thigh. Each of us was knocked unconscious as we fought. We were tied to our horses and hauled to North Meall and thrown into what passes for a dungeon."

Mackey and Peggin gasped.

"They tortured Tom and Jeremy," Jennifer added. "He'll never tell you, but I will. Those ...persons  paid for their mistakes." Her eyes glittered, her lips thinned, and nostrils flared as she almost bared her teeth. "We escaped." Her voice was a growl.

The king lowered his goblet and set it on the table as the story unfolded. Mannan had not eaten anything. His eyes fell almost closed as he listened.

"We made our way to Aos Si." Anne continued the tale. "Along the trail we were attacked by a pack of Demons and were able to fight them off. When we got to Aos Si, the Forest Lords had joined with Owen, Tom's second son, to fight a Demon horde that had almost overrun the compound. It was a hard fight, but the Forest Lords were the deciding factor. Then we came here." She shrugged and took a sip of water.

$ $ $

Jennifer watched the king and Mannan with her magic. She'd become quite good at reading people on their journey. The king's shield wasn't very well constructed. She let her perception sharpen as she followed the twists and turns as they presented themselves. Ha. She was in, under the shield.

Jennifer cut her meat and ate with mechanical precision, keeping her head down and looking at her plate. What she found under the shield almost made her gag. The king was controlled by thick bands of dull dark magic that anchored him to the man sitting beside him. Mannan. She carefully drew away, backing out the way she had gone in, leaving no trace behind.

The fork Jennifer held clattered to her plate. "Sire, I am suddenly ill." She felt the blood drain from her face. "I need to retire, if I may."

"Of course," the king acquiesced.

Tom's alarm reached out to her. "I'll go with her, Sire."

The king waved his hand. "You all must be exhausted. We'll speak of this later."

The companions stood and bowed. Tom put a hand under Jennifer's elbow and guided her from the room, the others following them.

# Chapter 20
# The Fasach Mage

The path beckoned to her as Breanna skimmed the edge of sleep. She pushed the gate open that signified the beginning of her DreamWalking. Her feet carried her smoothly beyond the first bend of the trail. No pain followed her into the dream as she moved.

Wrap my mind with threads of silk
Shroud my walk from notice.
Guide me to the sand King's dreams
Reveal his plans and patterns.

The familiar spell of veiling enveloped her dreaming mind, dampening its radiance to a tiny flicker to anyone else walking in their own dreams.

Breanna stopped and cocked her head in consternation. Instead of the aspen and lindens that normally bordered the path she followed, palm, Joshua, and fruit trees faded into the distance on either side. Shrubs grew under the taller trees, obstructing the view deeper into the grove.

Frowning and shaking her head, she continued down the path. *Maybe it's because we're in the desert now.* The trail split to the right and left. A golden light rose from the horizon to her right.

Breanna stopped at the junction of the two paths. She glanced to the left, sensing wisps of dreams. Nothing was close. She turned to the right and settled into an uneasy wait, searching the dreamscape as far out as she could extend her senses.

A sudden blaze at the very edge of her perception made Breanna twitch. Its power pulled at her, making her want to hurry toward it. Instead, she waited. *What is that?* With reluctant steps, she started walking toward the energy. It felt nothing like the grey Dragon she'd met before in the dreamscape.

She scanned around her, suddenly anxious that the monster might find her. Her heart sped up and began pounding with fear. *Stop. It is not here.* She breathed deep, slowing her panic.

She did not find that evil thing anywhere near. Instead, the golden glow pulled her toward it. As she drew closer, her steps slowed further. The trees were thinning, allowing her to peer between the trunks.

The light shimmered gold and red. An older man in the loose long cream-colored robes of a Bedouin, a shemagh draping his head and shoulders, stood as if waiting. Breanna stopped her advance, slipping completely behind the thick bole of one of the palms growing among the fruit trees.

"Child, you are well come. There is nothing to fear here. Your shields are strong. You are invited to sit with me and rest." He sank down onto a rug decorated with swirls of blue, red, and yellow rolled out at his feet, big enough for two to sit on.

Breanna began to shake. Fear tightened her belly. *Who is he? How can he know I am here?* After a few moments struggling with that fear, shoving it into a box in her mind, she made her way toward him with slow cautious steps and sat on the rug as close to the edge as possible.

"I am the Mage of the Marabout, like your Mages Enclave. I knew long ago that you would come. You were set on this path to arrive when Darkness walks in the day. Ah. I see the spell that has entrapped you."

Sudden hope surged in her heart. She leaned toward him. He shook his head.

"I cannot remove that which binds you. Nor the one that seeks to take your life. It is well that the binding was first as the second spell..." he paused and leaned toward her, inspecting her more closely, "It is well that the binding was first as the second spell, that spell is Demonborn."

Breanna recoiled.

*Demon-born? How did it get in the vardo? How could it know I was there? Why did it target me?*

She frowned. She pointed at herself, then raised her hand to shoulder height, palms up.

"What can you do?" The Mage put his elbow on his knee and cupped his chin with his hand. "I'm not sure." His eyes looked far away as he thought. He straightened and thumped his hands on his knees. "I will think on this and meet with you when you arrive in Jafara. Ask for me once you have greeted the Sayathia of Fasach."

The figure stood. Breanna scrambled to her feet as he bowed to her and faded into dream.

She felt the dreamlands begin to thin. She turned and began the walk to her gate. Her dream faded into true sleep.

# Chapter 21
# Sandcat Warning

The sandcat leaned against her companion's leg. An all-but- inaudible growl rumbled through her body. She lifted her nose to test the wind. It was here.

She tilted her head to look at the face of her bhanna, her chosen. She tried to reach Breanna's mind but failed again. Selgith could feel the danger lurking ahead. She had met the predator that lurked within when she was a small kit. Her mother had died under its twisted viciousness.

The rumble of the wheels and shuffle-thump of hoofs and feet faded into nothing as the caravan halted outside the gates of Jafara. The cloud of dust surrounding them slowly settled. The driver dropped the reins of the Vanner horses to the seat as he swung down the front of the vardo onto the ground, striding away toward the rear of the caravan. The women scrambled out the door they had been leaning through onto the seat, Breanna next to

Marta on the outside. Head turning from side to side, Breanna looked at the sandstone walls of the city rising above them and the camel trains and other travelers jostling to enter the hub of Fasach. A light haze of sand and dust filled the air, making Marta sneeze. The river Tanarut flowed northeast toward the largest lake in Ard An Tir east of Jafara, sending the smell of water and growing things through the air.

Selgith wiggled her way between the two women to sit on her haunches, flicking her tail with agitation. Her head came to her bhanna's chin. Breanna's fingers dug into the fur along her spine that was beginning to stand on end, raking through its softness, finding her skin. It was oddly calming to the cat.

She swiveled her ears, catching the thud of hoofbeats. She recognized the distinctive drag of one hoof of the shapeshifter's horse on the road, moving forward along the right side of the wagon. The caravan master made his way back along the left side of the line stretching away from the gate, stopping at each wagon to speak to the drivers. Beneath it all, she listened for the sliding *shhhhsh* susurrus of snakes burrowing under the sand.

Selgith eased back into the shadow of the wagon's overhang and into the vardo as the caravan master approached the two women. He gave a nod to them, lifting the corner of his lips in a smile not reaching his eyes. They remained cold and distant.

"We part ways here. Trader Soth Lahri invites you for last meal in her compound at the eighth hour. Ask anyone for directions."

"Please, thank..." Marta started to respond as he reined his horse away from the wagon, not waiting for her to speak. She closed her mouth and glanced at Breanna. "I'm tempted not to go at all," she muttered to her companion. Breanna narrowed her eyes, pursed her lips, and nodded twice in affirmation.

"I would not be so quick to spurn her invitation." Corcra pulled even with their seat on the other side. "Much can be learned during a meal." His amber eyes investigated Breanna's brown gaze. "Especially by one who cannot speak and appears...less." He quirked his left eyebrow up in question.

Breanna looked down at the footrest, her head bowed in thought. She looked up, nodding her head with slow acceptance.

Selgith cocked her head. She tried to send a thought to Breanna. She could not find that bright glow. Casting her thoughts wider, her mind recognized the cold blaze of her bhanna's Sword. She sent a picture of the threat held within the city to that intelligence.

The Sword's regard turned to her in an instant.

*What is this thing you show me?*

Selgith quailed from its intensity, crouching away from it, flattening her ears, lifting her lips in a silent snarl.

She quieted her instinctive fear with firm intent. The Sword damped down its power. *It is a horror from another world. It flies and chains others to its mind. It eats living and dead alike. I don't know its name. It seeks to build an army to rule the world. It killed my mother.* She sent a picture of the creature grabbing her mother by the neck and eviscerating her, then beginning to feed. *It lurks deep within the tunnels under the city, only daring to emerge in deepest night. Perhaps you can tell the other of the danger and pass it to my bhanna?*

SunWalker sent the information to HellScream, Marta, and Corcra.

Marta jerked and gasped. Corcra swore. Breanna looked up in alarm, reaching for her dagger, darting glances to left and right, searching for danger.

"Selgith showed SunWalker what waits in the city," Marta strangled out. "A monster."

$$$

Marta pulled the vanner horses to a stop in front of the livery stable doors. The sun had reached midday and heat was building. The smell of manure, hay, and wet straw hung heavy in the air. The women jumped down from the seat as a short bandy-legged man in much patched brown shirt and trousers slipped out between the doors. "What 'cher want?" he barked toward them, shuffling forward, and taking the horses by the reins next to the bits.

"Feed and water as well as a good brushing for all the horses. A place to keep the vardo while we're here. We've got eight more horses that can be turned into the corral," Marta answered crisply. "Do you have room?" Breanna began to unhitch the harnesses from the wagon, tossing the traces over the backs of the horses. She sneezed at the dust she raised.

"We'z room. Two silvers for each horse and ten f' the wagon. Yuz haul it next to those stalls." He held out his hand.

Marta dug into her pouch and fingered the coins into her palm. She pulled out the amount and handed it to the hostler. "We'll pay by the week," she told him. He put the money in his own pouch and walked the two horses into the stalls. Once they were tied to the mangers, he began to remove their harnesses.

Breanna shared a look with Marta and went to the shafts of the vardo, lifting the left side while Marta lifted the right. They backed the vardo into its place at the end of the stalls, then lifted further and rested the shafts against the face of the wagon.

Breanna hurried into the vardo to grab their travel sacks and the two Swords of Light, stepping lightly down the steps and keeping close to the side to hide the

Swords. The hostler stomped down the center aisle, calling for his stable hands to come and groom the horses.

*HellScream, would you ward the doors and windows of the vardo? Set them to warn us if anyone tries to enter.* She paused in thought as Breanna passed her the Sword, then continued, *also if anyone tries to move the vardo.*

*It is done,* the Sword of Light replied. *What of the sandcat?*

*Ask her what she wants to do. I think staying in the wagon might be a good idea, especially with the 'monster' here.*

*She wishes to remain in the wagon, but asks for water and food, and a way to leave the wagon if she so chooses,* the Sword responded. Marta gave a sharp nod and saw to provisions for Selgith.

*Tell her we'll be back after last meal to check on everything and make plans for our next steps,* Marta sent to her Sword.

Corcra entered the stable, leading his horse. Breanna and Marta turned to look at him. The animals in their stalls shifted uneasily, sensing danger. He stood quietly, waiting for them to settle.

"What is your plan?" Corcra's deep voice filled the quiet.

Breanna reached into her tunic and pulled out a piece of paper, shoving it into Marta's hands. Marta unfolded it and glanced at its contents.

"Breanna says that she must find the Fasach Mage after we meet with the Sayathia and establish ourselves as ambassadors. She had a dream that the mage might be able to help her." She refolded the paper and tapped it against her hand while she thought.

"We need to find a tavern to stay at and get ready for last meal with Trader Soth Lahri. Do you know a place?" she asked, hope in her voice.

Corcra led his horse into the empty stall next to the vardo. He stripped the saddle from its back and slipped the bridle over its head.

"I asked for information while you dealt with the hostler. There are three tavern inns that would suit us. The Wandering Camel is much recommended."

Marta grinned. Breanna snorted.

"Let's go to the Wandering Camel, by all means."

The women shouldered their travel sacks and followed the shape-shifter out of the stable.

Scanning up and down the street, Breanna pointed to the left. Marta raised her hand to shade her eyes. Breanna saw a crudely drawn black camel on a faded wooden sign mounted above one of the openings in the mudbrick walls of shops lining the hard-pan of the road. The sign swung back and forth in the air currents curling down the street. Dust hung in the air.

The road was crowded with traders, animals, and vendors urging passers-by to sample this or that. The companions made their way to the entrance, where the murmur of voices and thumps of plates and crockery spilled out. Corcra stepped into the room beyond, Marta and Breanna close on his heels.

The air was filled with the smell of stewing lamb and fresh bread. Breanna's mouth watered. It had been a long time since breakfast. Corcra made his way to the counter at the end of the room behind which the innkeeper stood taking orders for drinks and bowls of stew topped with hunks of flatbread.

"Do you have rooms available?" Corcra asked, the volume of noise in the room fell slightly as he spoke, the rose to even higher levels as customers made note of the strangers.

The inn keeper eyed the three carefully. "Aye, we've two rooms. Ten silver a room. Meals are five coppers for each of you."

Marta reached into her pouch and felt for the coins she needed. Pulling them out, she placed them on the bar. A brisk nod accompanied the motion of his hand, and he swept up the coins and made them disappear somewhere under the bar.

"There's cider and stew if you want to eat now."

Corcra nodded, turned, and made his way to a table against the wall closest to the door, sitting so that he could watch the room and the entrance. Breanna sat to his right, Marta to his left.

A woman of indeterminate age in sturdy trousers and shirt, probably the cook at this late hour after mid-meal, brought their stew and cider to the table, thumping down the bowls and almost spilling the cider. Her face held a sneer at their bedraggled appearance. Breanna looked at her with narrowed eyes. The woman left, back rigid with whatever had set her off.

Marta tilted her head in concentration, her face blank. Breanna knew she was talking with her Sword. With a satisfied nod, she pulled a bowl of stew in front of her, slid the cider over and using a piece of the bread, began to scoop the stew into her mouth. "She's angry because we've taken her bed for tonight," she mumbled around the stew filling her mouth. She has to sleep in the kitchen now."

Breanna reached for her own bowl of stew, cider, and flatbread, pulling them toward her. Corcra joined the women in emptying his bowl with quick efficiency.

A group of men entered the tavern, excitement threading through their voices. Breanna recognized several of them from the caravan.

"There was a wagon from up north traveling with us. Remember the tales of shapeshifters who were Dragons?" one of the men started the story.

"Well, guess what? The tales are true. One of them was a shapeshifter. He used his magic to move the sand from the storm that buried us two days out of Jafara."

The group tromped up to the bar and gave their orders to the barkeep for cider or beer.

"And then Demons attacked us, and he turned into a real Dragon and destroyed the Demons. He flamed them! The women with him used magic swords as whips that threw flames from the ends to kill any demons that got by him." The room had grown silent, listening.

One of the men leaned his back against the bar, scanning the room absently. His gaze passed over their table, then whipped back to them. His face went slack as his body stiffened. He elbowed the man next to him who turned and noticed his pallor. Turning to the room, his glance locked on Corcra.

"It's him. It's them!

Every head turned to look at their table. Marta dropped her chin to her chest, shaking her head.

"So much for keeping a low profile," she muttered.

Breanna closed her eyes. Corcra slowly rose from his seat and looked around the room. Wide eyes were riveted on him.

"My name is Corcra. This is Marta Haloran and Breanna Arach, envoys from Red Dragon's Keep, a duchy in the far north. What he has told you," he nodded at the storyteller, "is true."

The room erupted into chaos. Some of the customers hastily left the inn. Others called for calm. Still others started to tell their companions stories they had heard of Dragons.

"Lord Corcra, why are you here?" the storyteller shouted over the noise. Those in the room fell silent again.

Corcra looked at everyone, choosing his words carefully. "We are here to warn Fasach of a Demon War that is even now being fought across Ard An Tir."

Everyone sat in stunned stillness. "What does that mean?" one of the drovers at the bar choked out.

"The Demons we fought on the trail were but a small part of what is coming. We will meet with Sayathia Khan Maruk and his Mage as soon as possible."

The room broke out into multiple conversations, as customers turned to each other to talk about this news. The storyteller pushed through the crowd to stand before their table.

"Lord, we never thanked you and the ladies for saving us. If you need anything, we have your back."

Corcra looked affronted, "We don't..."

Marta's hand on his arm stopped him mid-sentence.

"Thank you, sir. We'll call if we need you," she told the man.

He nodded and made his way back to his friends with a final glance at Corcra.

Marta looked up at the shapeshifter.

"Any help with this mess is welcome," she said.

# Chapter 22
# Dragon Lands

Cameron flowed into the next Dragon kata. His body was covered in sweat, short, dark blond hair plastered to his head. The other young Dragon shapeshifters followed his lead, sinking into a deep lunge, arms outstretched, heel of hands thrust forward. Holding the kata for a count of thirty, he waited for his ki to flow through his body. When the flow stabilized, he moved into the next kata.

After an hour of training, he felt full of energy waiting to be released. He bowed deeply to their trainer. Working for almost a year with Neulach and the other shifters had taught him control of his body, mind, and most important, his magic.

Cameron scooped up the towel that he'd tossed on the benches lining the left wall of the training hall before the class. His companions followed suit, several making their way to cluster around him. The human mage was a popular figure with the Dragons.

His best friend Kennett punched him in the arm.

"Good workout. I didn't think you had it in you to go the whole series."

Cameron scowled and punched him back, then grinned. His amber eyes glittered with glee.

"Better than you did the last time, Kennett. Tripping over your own feet wasn't pretty."

"That was just to make you look good," his friend responded with an arrogant sniff, nose in the air.

He pulled the leather thong that tied his blue-black hair out of the way, releasing it and shook his head.

"Seriously, I'm glad to train with you."

An eerie wailing filled the training hall. Every Dragon went rigid, the inhale of shocked breath clearly audible.

"What *is* that," Cameron gasped.

"We are invaded!" Kennett hissed.

Cameron's eyes went huge.

"Who would be stupid enough to try for Dragon Lands? They've got to know that you can all fly and burn things to a crisp."

"Not to mention our own magic," Kennett muttered darkly, a snarl in his voice.

One of the older shapeshifters dressed in black leather vest and breeches, knee-high boots shining, strode through the door of the training hall and made his way to the center of the room. The trainees turned as one to face him.

"A portal has been opened on the southwest of the peninsula. Demons are pouring through and spreading out across the plain, almost to the mountains."

A crooked smile flitted across his face.

"This is what we've trained for all these years. Assemble with your battle groups and prepare to fight. You know what to do: now do it."

He turned and made his way out of the room.

A moment of shock, then a roar of anger and defiance echoed through the room. The shapeshifters gathered into clusters, most guided by friendship or age-mates. The groups moved off the training floor and hurried down the corridors and caverns under Dragon Mountain.

Cameron felt like he was frozen to the floor. He hadn't yet been assigned to a battle group. He had no age-mates. Kennett had already left with his. He didn't know what to do.

Clenching his fists, he shook himself out of the paralysis that held him in its grip. *I'll find Neulach. He'll know what I should do.* A frisson of fear worked its way down his spine.

"I hope I can do something to help," he whispered.

# Chapter 23
# Jafara

Breanna walked down the street from the tavern, following Marta and Corcra. She noted the sandcat slinking along the sides of the buildings, shadowing them, out of the corner of her eye, but did not turn her head. She rested her hand on the hilt of the Sword hanging at her hip. She'd stopped trying to contact HellScream not long after the spell of silence had wrapped her in its magic. Attempting to reach out stole her strength and gave her a headache.

People jammed the walkway and street, hurrying about their business. Breanna extended her stride to catch up with her companions and reached out, tugging on Marta's sleeve. The young woman glanced at her and turned to scan the street, keeping watch.

"I feel it too. Someone is following us, watching us. Some of the travelers from the tavern are behind us, but they aren't a threat."

The noise of a disturbance down the street grew as it drew closer. Corcra stopped and held out his arm to bar their way. The crack of whips sounded clearly over the turmoil. The crowd melted to the sides of the road, hugging the walls of the buildings. "News traveled fast," Marta muttered.

Before them, a cavalcade of twelve Jafaran guards advanced, mounted on the most beautiful horses Breanna had ever seen. Pure white with refined heads, large dark eyes, ears that almost met at the tips when pricked forward, dainty hooves that barely touched the ground and thin legs carried their riders with ease. The riders wore leather cuirasses and bracers over linen tunics. Linen trousers and tall leather boots protected their feet and legs. Brown burnooses bound around their heads with leather cords flowed down their backs.

The rider in front signaled the troop to stop in front of the travelers. "We seek the envoy from Red Dragon's Keep with an invitation to meet with Sayathia Khan Maruk, Sheik of Fasach. Are you those travelers?"

"We are the envoys you seek," Corcra's strong voice rumbled.

"We will show you to the Citadel Al Jafar."

"Lead on," Corcra responded.

$ $ $

Breanna tried to take in everything as they walked to the Citadel. Most of the men were dressed in long white or cream tunics, loose trousers. a head scarf bound across the forehead with a black cord, and sandals. There were very few women about. The ones she spotted were either completely covered with white or blue robes–only their eyes visible-or wore robes and head scarves. No one wore trousers and tunics as she and Marta did, or carried a sword. The smell of cooking lamb and bread drifted out of some of the shops they passed. She caught a glimpse of fabric and beads through an open door. Another shop held clay bowls and brass pots.

Again she caught the feeling of being watched by something inimical - the skin across her shoulders itched.

Within a quarter candlemark, the column reached the Citadel. Massive metal gates swung open as they approached. A building made of huge blocks of sandstone fronted the courtyard they moved into. A very short man in striped robes walked through the main doorway shaped like a minaret, pointed at the top and curving out and down on either side, and made his way to them with quick mincing steps.

He stopped in front of them and bowed, hands clasped at his waist. "Welcome guests. The Sheik of Fasach, Sayathia Khan Maruk, looks forward to greeting you shortly. I will show you to your rooms where you may refresh yourselves and prepare. Please follow me."

He turned away and started back through the doorway. The three visitors exchanged a glance. Marta
shrugged and they all followed quickly after the strange
little man.

He led them through the cool interior halls of the Citadel laid in blue, green, and white tiles set in intricate
patterns. Arched doorways through walls a forearm thick
opened into rooms filled with cushions and low tables.
The seneschal, for such Breanna judged him to be,
stopped in front of a doorway at the end of the hall.

"Your rooms, gentle guests." He gestured with a gran-
diose sweep of his arm and a deep bow. "There is a
hammam across the hall, should you wish to refresh
yourselves." He bowed again and turned to leave. "The
Sheik will see you in two candlemarks. Someone will return then to show you the way."

Breanna put her hand on his arm and looked at Marta.
"Soth Lahri" she mouthed. Marta nodded and spoke as
Breanna dropped her hand. "The caravan owner, Maaike
Soth Lahri, invited us to last meal. If you could send her
our regrets?"

The seneschal nodded once. "It shall be done."

Breanna turned and walked into the rose and gold
room. With a tired sigh, she shrugged her travel bag off
her shoulder and dumped it on the ground next to the
pile of cushions covered in gold lame sitting on the floor.
Marta followed her lead and put her bag next to

Breanna's, giving a grunt as she sat on one of the cushions.

Corcra paced to the arched window framed by thin
rose-colored curtains and looked out. Two tall carved al-
abaster vases filled with stems of feathery green river
grass softened the lines of the window.

Two windows set into the deep wall on either side of
the main one where Corcra stood made the room appear
open and airy. Between them, ornately carved tables
were laden with gold trays holding elegant pitches and
carafes.

Breanna made her way to the table on the right and
poured three goblets of juice that smelled like raspber-
ries. She gathered them up and handed one to Corcra on
her way back to Marta.

"I feel great magic within these walls," he told the
women. He stepped aside as Selgith sailed through the
opening. He took a sip of the juice. Selgith seemed to
float to the floor before she landed. Breanna's surprise
stilled her body.

Marta gasped, then began to laugh. Breanna joined in
silently. She sat down next to the cat and hugged her,
leaning her forehead against Selgith's neck.

The sandcat pushed her head against Breanna's shoulder. Wiggling loose, she made a circuit of the suite of
rooms that they'd been given, sticking her nose into every
nook and cranny. She stopped at the curtains that hung

on either side of the window she'd come through. She looked over at Breanna, catching her gaze, then looked back, riveting her attention on either the curtain or something behind it.

"It would be wise to watch our words in this room." Corcra stood by the window, putting the goblet back on the table and clasped his hands behind his back, "Perhaps within the entire Citadel. There is a magical device behind that curtain."

Breanna pulled paper and pen from under her tunic. "I'm not surprised," she wrote. "We have spy holes in the walls of Red Dragon's Keep."

"I for one am going to bathe and change into clean clothes." Marta pushed to her feet and rooted around in her bag. "Coming?" she asked her friend.

$$$

Breanna toweled her hair dry and shrugged into the formal gown she'd brought with her. She'd rolled it as carefully as she could when she'd packed it, but it was still twisted into a myriad of wrinkles. She shook her head at the image she faced in the long mirror mounted on the wall at one end of the bathing pool. She stamped her foot in frustration. *This will never do for the representative of the Duke of Red Dragon's Keep!*

Marta looked over from her own preparations and snorted. "Maybe Corcra can do something. I'll ask him," she told her.

The women walked across the hallway to their suite. "Corcra, is there anything you can do to remove the wrinkles?" Marta asked.

The shapeshifter looked offended for a moment, then shook his head in resignation. He wrapped Breanna in magic. The color of her dress deepened from sky blue to deep navy, panels of gold between the blue smoothed out. The slippers on her feet shed the dirt that was embedded in the fabric, leaving them a blue to match the dress. A golden veil covered her hair. Breanna staggered a little as his magic left her.

Corcra looked critically at Marta's dress. "May I?" Wide-eyed, Marta nodded, and he wrapped her in his magic. Black and white panels emerged from the grey that they had become, white slippers on her feet, a white veil covering her black hair.

"I believe these are now suitable," he told them.

Marta stood stunned, her mouth open. Breanna grabbed his arm and mouthed "Thank you."

"This should be interesting," Marta sighed.

Selgith skittered behind the draperies as someone called out through the curtains at the door "Are you ready?"

$$$

The Sheik of Fasach lounged on a pile of huge silk covered pillows on a dais that raised him three steps above the floor. He was dressed in brilliantly white trousers and a kurta stiff with gold thread embroidery that gleamed so much it hurt Breanna's eyes. His swarthy complexion contrasted sharply with the clothing.

The white shemagh draping his head was held in place by a thin strip of gold. The gaze of cold deadly eyes from a face weathered by the sun to a dark mahogany brown sent a shiver down her spine. Gold rings set with precious stones perched on every finger.

Those fingers chose a bunch of grapes from a tray held out to him by a male slave. He bit into one of them, all the while staring at the three.

"Sayathia Khan Maruk, I bring you the envoy from Red Dragon's Keep of Ard Ri, the Gentle Breanna Arach, daughter of Duke Tom Arach," the seneschal introduced her.

Breanna sank into a deep curtsey in front of the Sheik, then rose.

"Comes with her the Gentle Marta Haloran as her emissary." He hesitated, then spoke in a rush. "And the Dragon shifter, Corcra." He bowed to his sheik and hurriedly backed to the side of the room to remove himself from the line of fire.

Marta curtsied. Corcra gave a shallow bow, keeping his eyes on those of the Sheik. Anger kindled in the Khan's gaze as he stiffened at this introduction. Eyes narrowed, but nothing else showed on his face.

The tableau held for what seemed to Breanna to be forever, tension building.

"Welcome to my kingdom." The Sheik spoke in a surprisingly light tenor. "Why have you come to my lands?" He spoke directly to Breanna, ignoring the other two.

Breanna gestured with easy grace toward Marta and raised her chin.

"My Lord Sheik, the Lady Arach is unable to speak. We have come to warn you and your kingdom of the Demon War that has found its way here and to ask for an alliance with Fasach against the Demons. Do you have any information about the Demons or how to fight them?"

The Sheik's gaze lingered on Breanna a heartbeat too long for comfort, menacing and filled with contempt, then switched to Marta.

"You know more about fighting this evil than we do. You were attacked and fought them on your way here. Is there something else that you wish to know? Something, perhaps, that the...*Dragon*...can't tell you?" Mockery filled his voice.

Breanna's stomach tightened with apprehension. *Why is he asking? Does he know about the amulets? Does he think that we are naïve enough to blurt out everything we know? Why is he so scornful of Corcra?* She kept her face still and calm, noting everything that the Sheik did and spoke.

"Have any other attacks taken place in Fasach?" Marta asked.

The Sheik's lips thinned, and a deep frown furrowed his brows, as if he searched his mind.

"We have had none until this attack on your caravan. Perhaps the Dragon drew them." His firm statement was belied by the shift of his glance toward his steward. Breanna kept her face blank with difficulty. Corcra stiffened beside her.

She felt a pressure against her mind, something she'd not felt since the spell of silence had activated. She scanned the people standing at the back and sides of the sheik's throne. A tall older man in native dress with a grey turban covering his head was staring at her with an intensity she found disturbing. Breanna had seen him in her dream, the Mage of Jafara. He gave a miniscule shake of his head, a warning.

"Thank you, my lord. We were hoping that your people would know more. It is only by good luck that we were able to win the day against the Demons with the help of our friend, Lord Corcra," Marta told the Sheik. "Is there anyone else who might know more? Do you have a Mages Enclave as we do in Ard Ri?

The Sheik allowed a look of dismay to cross his face. "We do. Unfortunately, the mages are on retreat and cannot be disturbed," he responded with a very slight shrug. "Should one become available, we will make sure to convene a meeting. Instead, you will be granted a tour of the castle of Jafara." He nodded at the steward, who hurried forward.

Recognizing their dismissal, Breanna and Marta curtseyed. Corcra nodded his head, his left eyebrow raised in defiance. The Sheik's gaze sharpened as his eyes narrowed. Corcra's black cape lined with purple silk flared wide as he turned his back to the Sheik and marched from the room followed by the two women.

Once back in their suite, Corcra raise a shield against eavesdropping. "He lies," the shapeshifter exclaimed. "His very body betrays him." His jaw clenched as he struggled to hold back the words he wanted to say.

With an apprehensive glance, Marta turned to Breanna and found her already with pen in hand, busy at her writing. She passed the paper to Marta. Glancing at it, Marta paused, then slowly read it aloud.

"The man behind the dais with the grey turban is the mage I met in my dream. He is their High Mage. I must speak with him," Marta recited. "He holds the key to the spell that's trying to kill me."

Corcra was silent. The sandcat slunk out of the girls' bed chamber that opened to the left of the main room, sat down next to Breanna, and flipped her tail over her toes. She yawned, her tongue curling, exposing sharp fangs and incisors. Breanna and Marta looked at each other, knowing the same thought filled both their minds.

"HellScream, could you ask Selgith if she knows who the High Mage is? Can she find him?" Marta asked her Sword. She made sure she projected a clear image of the man behind the dais.

"She says yes," the Sword responded. "The mages are not far from here. She found them when she went exploring." Marta repeated what the Sword told her. A broad smile crossed Breanna's face. Corcra snorted.

"It appears that everyone has forgotten what Dragons can do." He swung his hand above his head, palm facing outward. The High Mage of Fasach stood before them.

# Chapter 24
# Breaking the Spell

Selgith sprang away with a squall of outrage. Marta recoiled as if struck. Breanna raised both hands in front of her face. The High Mage glanced at each of them, shocked. He swayed, his height reminding Breanna of a tree in a stiff wind.

"I have brought you to us as Bre...Lady Arach...requested," the shapeshifter said.

The High Mage staggered to the settee piled with pillows beside the window, arms outstretched to maintain his balance, then used both hands to lean on the arm of the seat. His face was pale, and beads of sweat dampened his skin. "Lord of All," he gasped. He thumped down on the cushions.

Corcra crossed his arms over his chest. Marta marched up to him, face so red it looked as if it would burst into flame and swung her arm back. "How dare you," she almost shouted. "Do you have a brain in your head? You don't treat a mage like this! Especially the High Mage of Jafara!"

Corcra's eyes flared bright yellow. A rumble started in his chest as he raised his hand and caught hers as she brought it forward to slap him. Breanna sprang between them, pushing Marta back and away. She swung around to Corcra, planted her hands on his chest and mouthed "Stop it. Stop it."

Corcra dropped his eyes to hers. The anger that tightened his mouth, furrowed his brow, and sizzled in the room, slowly dissipated.

"Yes. Control is necessary." He faced the High Mage and gave a shallow bow. "I regret bringing you here in this manner."

The High Mage studied them each in turn as his breathing steadied. Breanna felt as if she stood in front of Aeden or one of her tutors or, horrors, her father after failing to complete an assignment. She wanted to hang her head and dig her toe into the rug.

"My name is Bahador al Mahdi. You I have seen in the dreaming lands." He used his chin to point at Breanna. He moved his head to look at Corcra. "Lord Dragon, thank you for your precipitous magic. I did despair of seeing you three without alerting the entire royal palace. This is much better." He straightened from his slump on the settee.

"Have you found a spell?" Bahador looked at Breanna.

She slowly shook her head.

"What do you mean?" Marta's question was as sharp as a knife.

"When last your companion and I spoke, we talked of finding a way to nullify the death spell that shrouds her. I have thought long on this and may have a solution.

A death magic chant to counteract the death spell is what is needed. The other will dissipate when you have learned the lesson it is meant to teach. Cleverly done, I must say."

Breanna cocked her head to one side. *What is the lesson? How to not talk? To think before I speak? I think I've learned* that. *What's a death magic chant?*

"What's a death magic chant?" Marta queried, right on que.

Bahador reached into his tunic and withdrew a tightly rolled parchment scroll. "I have found the answer to your problem within our Shadow Scrolls. I have kept this with me since I found it to prevent...an accidental loss. It is grey magic, meant to reflect the death spell back upon the one who created it. There are certain things we must collect, and we will wait two days for the waning of the moon."

"What do you need? Perhaps we already have it," Corcra began.

"No. No, Lord Dragon. I shall bring everything. We will meet here at sunset two days hence. Could you return me where you brought me from? I was at the Mages Túir."

Corcra bowed. The women's eyebrows rose. Corcra flicked his fingers, and the High Mage was gone.

"Huh," Marta grunted.

§ § §

Breanna's mind was exhausted. She had repeated the High Mage's words again and again, searching for a clue to what he proposed. Finally, she ran the familiar pattern for setting up her mental shield before sleep. She could neither feel it nor tell if it was working. It had become habit, one that she faithfully followed each night.

> "To sleep, perhaps to dream,
> Capture eyes and make them see,
> The things that hide around me.
> Show the air and show the land,
> Reflect the image that I planned.
> Keep me safe, three by three,
> With harm to none, so mote it be."

The comforting knowledge that she was protected, though she still couldn't feel it, helped her drift into the margin between sleep and dream. She pictured her path into the dreamworld, setting her feet briskly on the crushed rock path, moving quickly toward the white picket gate.

*Can I find Marta in the dreamlands?* She cast her thoughts toward her friend. A faint flicker in the distance drew her. She flowed across the sand letting the path guide her. She saw Marta walking along the path.

Breanna knew she couldn't talk to Marta, only let her know that she was still able to DreamWalk. She wanted her to know that Marta would speak for her. Marta moved away, intent on her own dreaming.

Breanna continued to follow the path through drifts of sand, blocking her view of the surrounding land. Not a tree or growing thing graced her dreamscape. The land felt utterly alien, without life. She knew a quick death awaited her if she lost the path. She felt the danger pressing down on her.

The sandstone walls of Jafara slowly lifted their bulk above the dunes in her dream. With no interval, she stood before its gates. Again, with no interval, she stood at the doors guarding the Sheik's chambers. She watched intently as he gave orders to his seneschal to take the envoys from Ard Ri to the caverns beneath the city and leave them for the demons. The seneschal bowed low.

Fear rode her dreaming. *What kind of demon? Can we survive?*

She looked to the left of the path, disoriented by the rapid scene changes. *What now?*

Breanna started along the path; each stride felt like she traveled a mile. The beating of a heart punctuated each stride. Scanning the horizon before her, she saw a bank of fog rising before her. A flash of light within the fog dazzled her eyes. She threw up an arm to shield them. It felt like Corcra's aura, only twisted somehow.

She jerked awake, breath coming in a rush, heart pounding. She sat bolt upright, clutching the bed covering. *I was right. The Sheik is the enemy and I think the amulet lies out in the desert sands.*

She left her bed and shrugged into a silk robe. Tying it closed, she made her way to the table in the salon that sat before the window holding carafes of water and juice as well as dates, figs, and other fruits on a silver tray. She poured herself a tall glass of water and gulped it down. She poured a glass of citrus juice and sipped.

Gazing out the window at night, her mind skittered with thoughts of Demons and amulets.

*Is the Sheik in league with them? And where is the amulet?*

$ $ $

The sun rested low on the horizon, its soft light coloring the room in sunset colors. The fan of sunlight streaming from the horizon washed the sky with violet, red, orange and peach. Breanna stood at the farthest window, drawing in the peace. She withdrew into herself, calming after passing her written pages of description of the dream to Marta. She and Corcra stood together, reading them.

Though she had prepared for his coming, she couldn't suppress a start when the High Mage materialized in front of her outside the window. The drawstrings of a heavily laden canvas bag looped over his shoulder. Marta and Corcra joined her.

The mage muttered a spell that Breanna could not hear. The wall below the window faded into nothingness. Selgith padded to the opening, cautiously extending her nose through the emptiness. With a gay flick of her tail, she bounded through and beelined to the mage, winding around him, stropping herself against his legs. He smiled in delight at her antics.

"You have a sandcat. What a companion. I've not seen one in many years."

"Lady Breanna has the cat. They bonded on the trail as we turned from the Dragon Spine mountains. She it was who warned us of the sandstorm before it arrived. She has also warned us of something deadly within this palace," Marta clarified.

The mage's smile disappeared as if it had never been. He dropped his hand to Selgith's head. She stilled.

"So," the mage breathed out. The soft sibilant shivered its way down Breanna's spine.

"This is something I have heard of but never sensed. Extraordinary power has kept it invisible to us. A question is: Who has that power? Another: How did they use it without our knowing? This reeks of traitors in our midst."

With a snort, Bahador shook himself. "We will explore this later, after the banishing spell, the Death Magic Chant. Let us prepare."

The companions joined him through the window opening. Again, he murmured a spell and the opening under the window returned to normal. Marta's eyes were wide. Breanna shook her head.

The mage led them across the open space surrounding the castle and followed the curve of a wall that bordered it, gradually sinking to only a brick high. They were hidden from spying eyes when they reached a small orchard of fig, lemon, and other trees that Breanna didn't recognize. Marta reached up and pulled a ripe fig from one tree, taking a bite. "This is good!"

"Do not let the Sheik know that you stole one of his figs," Bahador warned them. Defiantly, Marta finished eating. Bahador smiled.

In the center of the orchard a small meadow of short dry grass opened before them "This space will do."

He stopped within the deepening darkness under the first row of trees surrounding the meadow. The colors of the sky blended from purple along the horizon into the blue and black of twilight. The sweet scent of ripe fruit filled the air.

He swung the canvas bag from his shoulder and set it on the ground. Bending over, Bahador pulled a highly polished mirror of silver rimmed with gold, four black candles, and a scroll from the bag. He handed each of them a black candle. A wand appeared in his hand.

"If you please, madam sandcat, please stay outside of this magic." Without protest, Selgith stretched out beneath one of the trees, her eyes beginning to gleam in the light of the rising crescent moon. The tip of her tail twitched rhythmically as she set herself to guard them.

"We will light our candles and set them at the points of the compass. At my command, you must think of the verse on the scroll. Lend her your power." He nodded at Corcra and Marta. Bahador handed the scroll to Breanna.

"Stand within the circle that I cast. Do not leave it."

With a flourish of the wand, he scribed a circle around them. A faint glow followed the tip of the wand as the circle enclosed them. As the beginning met the end, closing the circle, he called the four Quarters.

> "I call upon Earth, the power to make,
> I call upon Air, the power to take,
> I call upon Fire, the power to grow,
> I call upon Water, the power to flow.
> Brown and blue, green, and gold,
> Here the power I must hold.
> Quarter's mighty, strong, and sound,
> Four winds weave the circle round,
> Between the worlds the power be bound,

Until I release it at the last,
Guardians keep it strong and fast."

As he spoke each command, a tremor shivered the north, south, east, and west. Breanna could almost see vast figures taking their places at the cardinal points of the circle. A swirl of wind circled them.

"Light your candles and set them north, east, south, and west."

Flame flared as the candles were placed.

Bahador set the mirror, face up, in the center of the circle.

"Read the chant as I speak it," he commanded.

Breanna carefully unrolled the scroll and held it so she and Marta could see it in the dim light cast by the moon. Bahador's deep voice echoed around the circle and spread to the edges of the clearing.

"In the name of the Gods and all the Spirits,
In the name of the Green Man, and the light,
And the dark, and the gods of the Netherworld.
Remove this curse that stings
from my heart and my mind.
Whosoever has cast this curse against me,
Let them suffer what they have set in motion.
Let these candles be their candles,
This burning be their burning,
This curse be their curse.
Let the pain they have caused me and mine
fall upon themselves."

As they finished, the moon's light gathered by the mirror shot toward the sky in a brilliant beam. The Quarter's guardians raised swords that flashed with gathered starlight. Their light joined the moon's and flashed aloft. The candles flared high, consuming themselves in wanton abandon until nothing was left. With a suddenness that left the participants staggering, including Bahador, the lights winked out.

Breanna caught her balance and drew a deep breath. Bahador turned to her with a searching look. She looked within herself and felt a lightening of her spirit, as if a weight on her had been lifted away.

"The spell is broken! Well done, all of you. We will release the Quarters now and dissolve the circle."

"Thank the Gods and all the Spirits
The Green Man, the Light and Dark,
The Gods of the Netherworld, all who gave us aid,
We release you.
Now has come time for the circle to end,
Guardian of the East, with powerful Wind,
We release you back to your realm, with thanks."

The shadowy figure raised its sword and faded into nothing.

"Guardian of the South, with fire so bright,
We release you back to your realm, with thanks."

The figure to the south became flame and faded to nothing.

"Guardian of the West, with water of Life,
We release you back to your realm, with thanks."

A crystalline shower of blue diamonds broke apart and faded to nothing.

"Guardian of the North, maker of all,
We release you back to your realm, with thanks."

Gentle warmth filled the participants and gradually receded.

The heaviness that had filled the circle lifted. Bahador traced the circle counterclockwise, releasing all the power he had gathered.

Breanna slumped to the ground, weary beyond anything she'd ever experienced. Marta collapsed.

# Chapter 25
# Catacombs

A soft breeze rippled across the circle where they'd worked their magic, bringing the scent of damp ground from the canals that divided the land around Jafara into fields growing food for the city. Breanna stretched out flat on the grass. Her head ached with a fierce pounding matching the beating of her heart. She felt as if she'd been smacked with stone masons' hammers. Her arms and legs pressed to the ground as if stones were stacked on them.

"I can't move," Marta mumbled, stretched out next to her. Breanna grunted with pain as she reached out and patted her companion's arm. Marta turned her head and looked at her friend. "Me, too," Breanna mouthed.

She looked up at the darkening night sky as stars began to glimmer in its depths. Tracing the familiar patterns of the Crow, the Snake, and Warrior, homesickness stabbed through her heart. *I miss mother and father,*

*Owen, and Thomas. I miss the Keep and Aeden.* She felt tears gathering.

Turning her head, Breanna looked at Bahador. He sat on the ground to their left, back straight, chin touching his chest, hands resting on his knees. His eyes were closed. Corcra stood to the right, staring straight ahead at nothing, hands clasped behind his back. She watched as Selgith rose from the shadows of the fruit trees and padded to her side, stretching out beside her. Breanna shivered, realizing that she was cold. With a groan, she pushed herself over and rolled to sit up.

She crossed her arms on her knees and rested her head on them. A gusty sigh escaped. Selgith sat up next to her and pressed close against her side. Breanna felt a gentle warmth flow into her. She turned her head and eyed the cat. *Is that you?*

What felt like an affirmative brushed her mind. Selgith rubbed the top of her head against Breanna's cheek.

She sat up straight with a jerk.

"Can I speak?" she tried.

Disappointment crushed down on her. Pressing her lips together, she stopped. She looked up and caught Bahador's eyes studying her. Her gaze fell away to her lap.

"One has been mastered. The rest will follow. Patience, young one."

Effortlessly, the High Mage rose to his feet. Corcra turned to face him.

"That was enlightening," Corcra said with slow dignity. "Dragon magic is within us. We have no need of circles or guardians or rituals. I did not know such beings existed. That was very well done. I hope the person who set the death spell has well and truly received their reward."

Marta sat up with a groan. "By the Three Gods, I've been beaten and hung out to dry." She raised her arm toward Corcra. He grasped it and pulled her to her feet. He turned and held out his hand to Breanna. She looked at it and then up into his eyes. She saw compassion warring with impatience. Her lips thinned in response as she grasped his outstretched palm.

A shiver of apprehension slithered down her spine. She looked around the clearing, searching. *What is wrong? Something is wrong!*

Corcra scanned the meadow. "What do you feel? I don't sense anything."

Frustration ripped through her. *Why did we leave the Swords in the room?* She wanted to scream and stamp her feet. She clamped down on those feelings and reached into her tunic for her paper and pen. She wrote with quick urgent movements. *There is something wrong. It waits in the shadows for us to move away from this safe space!* She shoved the paper into Corcra's hands.

The shapeshifter scanned the page then raised his head and slowly probed the shadows under the trees with eyes and magic, looking for any movement. Sudden tension caused him to crumple the paper and stiffened his stance. "Something comes."

Two shadows launched themselves from the upper branches of the trees farthest from them. The smachtmaistirs unfurled giant black wings that occluded the light of the full moon. They rose high in the sky, then folded their wings to arrow toward the group, talons extending to take them. Not so safe a space after all.

Bahador stood ready to cast a spell, arms half-raised. Corcra called the purple smoke and shifted to his Dragon form between one breath and the next.

Breanna, Marta, and Selgith surged into a run toward the castle. A deafening roar rose behind them. The three skidded to a halt and whirled, Breanna preparing what magic she might still have to fight back.

The two flying demons split up, one arrowing toward the women, the other toward the mage and Dragon. The Dragon roared again, then inhaled. Without pause, he exhaled, incandescent blue, white, and gold flames riding the release of his breath. The smachtmaistir burned, shrieking as it fell apart in the sky and plummeted to the earth.

Bahador thrust his arms apart and opened a hole in the sky between the women and the flying horror. The hole, blacker than the night itself, began to rotate, pulling the beast into it. It beat its wings with frantic haste, trying to get away, until, with a final rotation, the hole snapped shut with a rumble of thunder.

The breeze fled. The night held no sound. Silence waited for many heartbeats. The sounds of insects began again with hesitant intermittent buzzes and clicks. Corcra called the smoke and walked out a man. He stepped to the mage and put a hand on his shoulder. "Well done. I would know how you did that."

"Come, let us return to the castle and the wished-for safety of your rooms." The mage patted Corcra on the back. "There is still the tour of the castle to endure tomorrow. Let us go. I will teach you what I can."

Corcra nodded and joined him as they walked to the women. Breanna and Marta stood, slowly standing down from their readiness to fight. Breathing returned to normal. Heartbeats slowed.

"I want to know about the portals, too. Maybe we can use them," Breanna told them. They fell in step with the men, Selgith gliding next to Breanna, her ears folded flat against her head, tail occasionally lashing.

Once they reached their rooms, Bahador and Corcra spent candlemarks talking of magic. Corcra shared what lore he knew and Bahador showed him how to create portals to other places on Ard An Tir and other worlds.

"Dragons came from another world. Our own myths tell of a cataclysm that drove us to find a new place when we knew our sun was going to explode. This was the closest world we could reach with portals to save as many as we could. I do not know why we have remembered the tales but forgotten the spells." Corcra took a sip of water after sharing this.

"Perhaps it was to keep your history alive and to protect the Dragons from scattering. There is a price to be paid for creating a portal. You must give part of yourself to the gate. When it is closed, that part of you is gone forever. Without a well of magic to draw from, weakness and eventual death follows." Bahador's voice was deep and solemn. He took a small sip of the fruit wine he had chosen from the table.

Their talk continued late into the night.

$$$

The next morning, slaves brought covered trays to the main room and slid them onto to the tables between the windows. Breanna had finally realized they weren't servants like the skullies at home. She had already been to the hammam and sat on a chair next to one of the tables, combing her damp hair. No one had yet joined her.

The two slaves lifted the covers off the trays. The smell of olives, poached eggs, lamb, and pita bread filled the room. A third woman entered the room carrying a tray with an ornate long necked kaffea pot, cups, and tiny spoons. She carefully slid the tray onto the low table in front of the settee. The smell of cinnamon, cardamom, and saffron drifted from dishes on the tray.

Breanna's stomach twisted with hunger. After their adventures last night, Bahador had made sure they ordered pita bread filled with honey and fruit to help replace the energy they had spent on the spell. Corcra had sent the mage to his rooms with no one in the castle the wiser.

She watched as the slave filled the small cups with kaffea. Breanna had heard of kaffea but never tasted it. The sweet-bitter smell was intriguing. She walked to the low table in front of the settee and watched the woman prepare a cup. Holding it out, she gestured at the spice dishes. Breanna tilted her head, then pointed to the dish containing cinnamon. A tiny amount was added to the cup.

She took the offered dish and held it to her nose. The rising steam carried a delicious buttery spiciness that made her stomach growl. She took a tiny sip, afraid of burning her mouth. Surprise flitted across her face as the flavors exploded across her tongue. She took a bigger sip. A wide smile lifted the corners of her mouth in delight. *This is good! Why don't we have this in Ard Ri? This would be a great trade item.*

Looking at the woman, she nodded her head in thanks. She motioned toward the door, dismissing the slave. The woman bowed to her and left.

Breanna turned her attention to the trays of food. She loaded a plate with black and green olives, what looked like fava beans and chickpeas mixed with chopped on-ions and two pita bread rounds. She sat on a cushion on the floor next to the table holding the kaffea and began to spoon the beans into her mouth with the pita bread.

Marta and Corcra entered the salon from their rooms. Marta rubbed her face, brushing away sleep. Corcra walked straight to the food trays and began his selection. Marta joined him and they made their way to Breanna's table. No voice was raised as they filled the clambering holes in their stomachs.

Finally full, Breanna reached back and pulled several cushions behind her, stacked them up and leaned back to relax. A loud burp forced its way out of her mouth. Her cheeks reddened.

*Excuse me*, she mouthed and mumbled.

Shocked, she sat up straight. She tried to reach out with her mind but received only a faint buzzing. She tried to grasp it and bring it close.

Marta and Corcra whipped their heads toward her.

*What was that? Is the spell waning? I'm afraid*, Breanna admitted to herself. Not speaking had become a habit, something to just live with. It made her feel invisible, protected somehow.

"Can you speak?" Marta leaned over and put her hand on her friend's arm. Breanna's insides trembling in fear and excitement. Her breathing quickened.

Breanna gave a quick shake of her head. "I don't know."

The sound that emerged was a cross between a croak and a grunt. But it was a sound. Tears gathered in her eyes and ran down her cheeks. She clapped her hands over her mouth.

"No time," Corcra reminded them both. "The seneschal will be here soon to lead us on the tour of the castle. We need to prepare."

Breanna rolled her eyes to look at the ceiling, stopping the tears that still fell. She brushed them from her eyes and cheeks, pulling in deep breaths to calm herself.

Corcra tilted his head and stared at her. She could almost hear his thoughts as he watched.

"Don't try to speak. This is something we can still use. Keep watch as you have been. People often slip when they think a person is weak or disabled," he told her.

*I won't have a problem with that. I still can't speak!* Breanna stood and made her way to the sword stand that held HellScream, SunWalker, and Corcra's sword. She stood in front of the Swords for what seemed like candle-marks. She reached out with tentative fingers and rested them on SunWalker. The buzzing in her head grew louder.

Selgith padded into the room and glided straight to Breanna, shoving her head under Breanna's other hand. Contact with SunWalker and Selgith roared into her brain. She staggered away from both, hands clutching her head. She bent forward at the waist, eyes closed in pain.

As quick as that, the roar decreased to buzzing again. She opened her eyes to slits as she slowly straightened her stance. She shook her head in disbelief. She grabbed the hilt of her Sword and lifted it from the rack. A very faint, very quiet voice filled her mind. *You are back.*

Breanna gasped, her heart immediately hammering. She turned to the others and raised the Sword. *I can hear them!*

Marta jumped to her feet and strode to her friend. She grabbed Breanna in a hug, squeezing tight.

"Finally. The High Mage was right. Let's hope the lesson has been learned." Corcra spoke from where he was still seated, finishing his breakfast.

Breanna set her Sword on the rack and followed Marta back to the cushions. She did not try to respond. She cocked her head to the right and looked at Corcra. *I hope so too.*

Startled, Corcra looked back at her, eyes glittering. "I heard that!"

Breanna grinned, then lost it as the beads hanging at the door rattled.

"My Lord and Gentles, are you ready for your tour?" the seneschal announced, stepping into the room, and bowing deeply.

"Soon," Corcra responded.

$ $ $

Breanna rested her hand on the comforting weight of SunWalker hanging at her side. She had seldom worn it when her link to it had been severed. Having it on her hip again made her feel much more secure. She'd decided to bring her pack to make sure they had water on their tour. Knowing what the Sheik planned had all taking steps to prepare.

She followed the seneschal with her companions through the confusion of hallways that made up the interior of the Fasach capitol. It didn't help that every hallway looked the same: same stone, same colors, same number of doorways. The only thing that might give her a clue to their location were the murals painted on the walls between the doors.

A tiny nudge to her mind had her turning her head just a little, catching a glimpse of Selgith as she ghosted along the wall. Breanna jumped and looked at him when Corcra touched her shoulder. *I made very sure that no one can see her.* Breanna heard his quiet voice in her mind.

*Thank you* she responded. His touch fell away.

She quieted her thoughts, imagining grounding her magic as she had before all of this had started. A faint weak echo of what she expected from SunWalker danced just beyond her reach. A sharp jab of pain behind her eyes almost made her gasp. She shut down her attempt to reach out. Now was not the time.

The seneschal halted at the head of a stairwell descending below the ground floor of the castle. A shiver of unease raced up Breanna's spine. Her grip tightened on SunWalker's pommel. She frowned and reached out to Marta, tempted to pull her away from the stairs.

"We have completed the tour of the upper levels of Jafara Castle as the Sayathia Khan ordered. The only thing left is the lower levels and catacombs that hold the wine cellar and supplies for the castle. He specifically wants you to see the wine cellars." The seneschal started down the stairs, his short legs taking each step individually.

Marta put her hand over Breanna's. She gave a tiny nod, almost imperceptible. *Good. She knows something's wrong.*

She started down the stairs, following their guide, Marta trailing her followed by Corcra. A faint growling reached her ears. She could well imagine Selgith's fear and rage without seeing the sandcat.

Mage lights mounted near the ceiling flared to life as they walked down the corridor that opened before them at the bottom of the stairs. Breanna shuddered as she remembered the labyrinth of cellars at Red Dragon's Keep and the horror they hid.

Pillars of stone rose into yawning aches along the passage extending into the darkness before them. Motes of dust filled the air, tickling Breanna's nose, thick enough to make her want to sneeze. The seneschal stopped in front of one of the archways.

"Here we have the wine cellars reserved for our honored guests." He gestured to the room filled with racks of wine bottles. "Please feel free to investigate and choose bottles for tonight's banquet the Sheik has ordered for you. I must return to my duties in preparation. I will send a servant to guide you back."

A jolt of alarm stiffened Breanna's spine. Marta and Corcra stepped closer to her as the seneschal scurried away from them, back toward the stairs.

*It is here* Selgith sent, a note of fear in that faint mental contact.

Breanna knew that no servant was coming to guide them. She slowly drew SunWalker from its sheath. Corcra and Marta followed suit. She motioned at the archway.

"Do we go back?" Marta asked. Both women looked at Corcra.

"No," he said. "Going back is unwise. The Sheik will try to imprison you. Let's go forward and face that which they sent us down here to find. We have a Dragon with us, after all." A small smile lifted the corners of his mouth.

The three and Selgith started off down the corridor, the cat slinking along the wall, ears laid flat, hackles raised all along her neck and spine. They approached each archway carefully, sending light into each one. They soon became worked stone instead of brick. Caution dogged their steps, Corcra making use of his magic to check the rooms for demons and other creatures. The mage lights marking their progress flickered and died.

Pitch darkness pressed down. Marta and Corcra immediately created their own balls of mage light, much dimmer than those on the wall. They set them floating in front of them.

*What did that? What monsters do we face?* Breanna's heart raced. She held out her left hand and tried to form a sphere of light. Her hand shook with tremors. A spark flared, then failed. No light She clenched her fingers into a fist and held it against her chest. Her right hand tightened on the hilt of SunWalker. She raised the blade across her body, the heft of it calming her nerves.

*Look out!* Selgith raced between them, sending them staggering toward the walls as the massive black head of a Demon at the end of a thick, scaled neck thrust out with lightning speed from the doorway on the right, missing all of them. Corcra threw a bolt of flame at the leviathan. It splashed harmlessly off the Demon's face.

Red eyes bisected by black pupils glared at them. Teeth longer than Breanna's arm from elbow to wrist dripped saliva to the floor. The monster lashed its head back and forth against the walls, seeking to crush them. The Demon's thrashing caught Corcra and threw him head-first into the tunnel wall. He slumped to the floor and didn't stand up.

The sandcat squalled, leaping on the monster's black head, biting into an eye, clawing deep furrows into its face with the razor-sharp claws on her hind feet. Breanna crouched below it, thrusting SunWalker up into its neck, slicing sideways across the tough scales, as it writhed.

Demon blood splattered as the beast shrieked, a deep grunting growl that rose in volume as it whipped its head back and forth, trying to dislodge the cat, pounding against the walls and ceiling, its long thick neck flailing.

Breanna crouched in terror against the left wall. She kept low and began crawling toward the end of the corridor, away from the battle. Thrown against the right wall in Selgith's charge, Marta rolled across the corridor and followed her friend. The head of the monster, nostrils lined with deep red flared wide, eye as large as her head, landed on the floor next to her, then whipped back up. The Demon's mouth opened wide as it howled with rage.

Corcra lay still on the floor against the right wall. Breanna saw his body and her heart plummeted. *Lady of Light, help me get him.* She scuttled across the corridor and grabbed his collar, pulling with all her might. His body barely moved. She shifted her grip to under his arm and pulled again. Marta's willing hands joined hers, yanking hard.

They pulled Corcra across the open expanse and pushed him against the left wall as far from the Demon as they could get, shielding him with their own bodies. Breanna peered back at the battle.

Selgith had clawed her way up to the demon's earhole. Her hind claws raked at the monster's throat where the jaws met the neck. Shreds of skin hung from the Demon's face, runnels of blood flying everywhere.

One of her claws caught the carotid artery and sliced it open in a long slash, as clean as any knife. Blood gushed out over the walls and floor and companions as the Demon bled out. The head and neck landed on the floor next to them, grazing Marta and Breanna as it fell. Breanna grunted with pain. Marta watched as the eye next to her went dim and rolled upward in death. She gagged. The smell of rotting flesh and acrid blood filled the air. Flames began to crawl up the Demon's face and neck.

Selgith leapt clear of the dead monster. She shook her body, sending smoking blood flying. She rolled her tongue again and again, spitting out the taste. Breanna reached out with a hesitant hand, then slowly pulled it back. SunWalker's magic swept over her, removing the Demon blood that had started to burn on her skin. She shoved the Sword into its scabbard.

A groan sounded under her. She pushed up from where she lay on top of Corcra, rolling to sit on the floor next to him. Marta pushed herself to her knees, wiped Demon blood from HellScream, then struggled to slip her Sword of Light into its sheath. Corcra pulled his arms under his body and lifted himself to his elbows. His head hanging almost to the floor, he groaned again.

"Selgith killed the Demon," Marta said in a quiet voice. "We're safe for now."

"We have to move. This much noise, they'll soon send someone down to find out what happened." Breanna's voice was a whisper, hoarse and raspy with disuse.

Marta looked at her as a broad grin crossed her tired face. "Let's get him up on his feet and moving that way." She pointed with her chin toward the end of the corridor where a single archway stood blocked by a door illuminated by the burning Demon blood.

The women hooked an arm under each of Corcra's and helped him to his feet. They slung his arms over their shoulders. He grunted with pain, leaning heavily on them as they started toward the door. His head hung down as he stumbled along.

Selgith came bounding down the corridor behind them. She slid to a stop in front of the door, sat down and looked up. The light was going out as the blood and monster in the corridor burned to ash. Breanna and Marta coughed, trying to clear their lungs.

Breanna reached out and put her palm on the door. A surge of magic pulsed from deep within her. The door separated into two halves, starting at the apex of the frame, and continuing to the floor. Breanna snatched her hand back, fear shaking her mind. Marta used her foot, pushing against the panel on her side. The doors slowly opened, showing a stone staircase rising before them. Clean air flowed down the stairs, giving a respite to all.

The three shuffled forward and started up the stairs, one step at a time. Selgith trotted up ahead, soon out of sight. After twenty stairs, Breanna gasped. "I can't go any more. We need to take a break." She stopped and leaned against the wall of the stairwell. She slipped Corcra's arm from around her shoulders and let it fall to his side. Her hand on his back helped him to remain stable. Marta followed suit.

Corcra lowered himself to sit on the stairs with their help. Breanna and Marta sat on either side, trying to catch their breath. Breanna pulled her pack off her shoulders and untied its fastenings. She pulled a small leather skin filled with water and fruit juice from its depths and uncorked it, taking a small slip. She passed it to Corcra, steadying it when his trembling hand was finally able to grasp it. "Small sips," she croaked.

Marta reached out and sipped her share. Soon the skin was empty as they passed it back and forth. Corcra seemed stronger.

"What happened?" Marta questioned him.

"The last thing I remember is that Demon's head coming out of the door. I think it might have clipped me with its jaw or thrown me against the wall head-first. My eyes don't want to track, there's ringing in my ears, and I have a bad headache. Nothing like this has ever happened before." He started to shake his head, winced in pain, and returned to holding his head in his hands, elbows resting on his knees.

Breanna looked at them. Demon blood drenched their clothing. Breanna's hair was stiff with it. She shook her head, glad that SunWalker had removed most of it from her skin, and surprised that her clothes hadn't burned.

"We can't stop now. To go back is to die. Can you make it?" Her whispered words shuddered with anxiety.

Corcra responded after a long silence. "Yes," was his simple reply.

"Breanna, listen!" Marta hissed, reaching out and taking Breanna's arm, shaking it with a trembling hand.

They fell silent, straining to hear. The rub of scales against stone carried up the stairwell. Selgith crouched on the stairs below them, tail lashing, ears laid flat, hackles raised. She sent an image of a huge Demon, massive wings folded tight to its body, fanged mouth below a wrinkled snout, under enormous glittering red eyes. Its feet were armed with scimitar-sharp claws meant to slice and tear.

They looked at each other, then surged to their feet, pulling Corcra to his and pounded up the remaining stairs. Panting from the exertion, they reached the top. A wooden doorway framing a stone wall blocked their way.

Breanna leaned against it in defeat. Marta ran her hands over the stones on her side of the stairwell. "Hurry," she urged.

Breanna put out her hand and pushed against stone after stone, searching for any movement. Right where a knob would be, the stone moved back with a slight grating sound. "Here," she murmured, wanting to shout.

She pushed again, harder this time. The stone slid farther back, partially into the wall. Her hand free hand slipped along the edge of the frame, leaving a gash on her palm. Leaning against the stone lock, she pushed with all her strength. She took both hands and placed them on the stone, shoving it all the way into the wall.

Corcra and Marta threw their weight against the door. The bottom grated against the floor, slowly shifting outward. The early evening sky spread before them, letting cooling air into the stairwell. The three and Selgith slipped out onto a stone platform. Breanna twisted around, trying to figure out where they were. "Quick, close the door," she croaked. She threw her weight against the stone. The others joined her as the door moved back to fill the opening into what would have been their tomb.

Breanna stepped back and tilted her head, looking up at the expanse of the outer wall of Jafara, rose-gold in the setting sun. She twisted around and looked out at the desert stretching uninterrupted to the horizon. Before them, at the bottom of a steep hill, stood the High Mage of Fasach holding the reins of their horses and halter ropes of two pack mules.

# Chapter 26
# Desert Sands

Breanna started down the hill, sidestepping with care not to twist her ankles. She leaned back, braced herself as Corcra started down, using her shoulders for his balance. His knees kept trying to fold, threatening to send him tumbling down the slope. Marta followed him, pulling back on his tunic as a check from moving too fast.

Reaching the bottom of the hill, Breanna tried to wipe the flakes of dried demon-blood from her face, shifted her shoulders to re-settle her tunic and pack, then bowed to the High Mage. Corcra thumped down with a clumsy jump to stand next to her. Marta slid the last two feet with lithe grace, taking her place next to him.

Bahador al Mahdi stood before them. His arms were crossed, hands hidden in the sleeves of his white robes bordered by arcane hieroglyphs in black and silver thread.

"I am pleased you made it through the gauntlet of the underground. *It* is dead?"

"Yes." Breanna's voice emerged as a shadow of itself, but it was becoming stronger.

"Selgith killed it," Marta contributed. "With help from us. But she killed it."

Awe tinged her voice.

"There's something else down there. We heard it when we were resting on the stairs. Selgith showed us an image of it."

HellScream sent the image to Bahador.

"I thought I felt a spike in magic when your creature died," replied the High Mage. "The other is now exposed. We will deal with it. Now, for your own safety, you must leave. Go southwest into the desert. Your ...Swords..." he gave a tiny nod toward them, "will help with direction. There is a legend that travelers tell of an abandoned palace brooding in the desert, appearing when most needed. Or not. Perhaps it may aid you in your journey."

"I saw something within a fog bank in a dream before we did the Death Chant. Do you think that palace might be what I saw?" she asked Bahador.

"Perhaps," he responded after giving it some thought.

Breanna crossed her arms, grasping her elbows, brows furrowed. *What does he want? He doesn't want to confront the Sheik. Is he sending us to our deaths?*

*Not so, Lady. Your journey continues. There is much for you to learn and experience. I wish you well.*

The mage spoke in her mind. Breanna flinched, then steadied, a broad grin spreading across her face.

*The spell is finally broken,* she exclaimed to him. He nodded and held out the reins of the horses to her. She took them from him, sorted them out, and handed them to her companions.

"Thank you for your help," she told the mage. "I would be pleased to call you ally. If you ever need anything, call on me, and I will fulfill it if I can."

"I would call you friend," Bahador replied. "Should I find myself in need of help, I will surely ask you."

Breanna mounted her horse, the same brown gelding she had ridden from Red Dragon's Keep, and firmly checked him when he thought to buck. As the others mounted their horses, she nodded to the mage.

"Would you store our vardo? Or better yet, send it back to Red Dragon's Keep? Maaike Soth Lahri, the trader who guided us here, could use it on her return."

"I will do it. Now go before the Sheik sends his sataba to hunt you down."

§ § §

No one followed them from Jafara. As the city disappeared behind them, Breanna gave a silent prayer of thanks for that mercy.

She shifted her weight to her left leg, trying to ease her back and seat pain. After spending four days riding across the desert, she reeled with exhaustion. It was a constant battle making sure the thin sand-colored burnoose the High Mage had provided covered her from head to toe. The nights were spent shivering through the desert cold at the oasis' spaced a long day's ride apart.

A gentle wind billowed the burnoose around her. Selgith rode on a makeshift pad she'd shaped from a spare blanket and attached behind the saddle's cantle. The cat could not keep pace with their horses.

Breanna gathered her reins and signaled a halt.

The sun had set long ago, giving welcome relief from its heat as the companions continued to ride to the west. There was no moon to give light, but starshine was enough to navigate by. The sky was gradually obscured by clouds the longer they rode.

"I've got to rest," Breanna stated, her voice a dry croak.

"We need to find a place to stop or return to the oasis from last night."

Lifting the water skin hanging from the saddle next to her leg, the mouthful she allowed herself was warm and tasted of leather. Pulling the drawstrings closed and winding them about the top, she looked at Marta.

Her friend slumped in her saddle, eyes glassy, face reddened from the sun even though she too wore a burnoose. Corcra sat straight and tall, swathed in pale lavender linen, his face empty of emotion, body adapting to the motion of his horse without thought. The horse stopped next to Breanna's.

"Corcra. Corcra. Come back," she muttered to him, reaching out to place her hand on his arm.

Corcra threw his arm up with a violent flinch, flinging her hand away. His horse danced sideways. Breana's mount swung his head up and sideways to avoid the sudden movement above him. Corcra's sword hissed from its scabbard as he drew it. Marta shouted in alarm.

Awareness returned to Corcra's eyes. He lowered the sword with slow precision, then re-sheathed it.

"I'm sorry. I was far away. Why have we stopped?"

Breanna shook her head. Weariness pressed down on her.

"We need to stop. I need to stop." She sent a thought to SunWalker. *Is there anywhere near that we can use for shelter?*

*Look to your left. The shadow palace that the High Mage foretold is there.*

# Chapter 27
# City of Silence

Breanna stopped breathing. She had not looked to the south, focusing with rigid attention on the west. Out of a misty fog that billowed in ripples and curtains on the desert sands rose the vague outlines of the walls of a city, a castle tower rising in its center.

The walls were gray stone, fading in and out of sight, as if trying to hide. No hint of air movement touched her face. A shiver raced down her spine.

"Is this real? Are you all seeing this?"

She looked at Marta. Her friend sat on her horse, mouth agape. With an audible gulp, Marta answered her.

"I think so."

"Corcra, what do you see?"

"There is a gray city moving in and out of our reality," was his slow response. "I cannot feel it with my magic."

"Do we dare try to enter?" asked Breanna. "At night?"

"Can you and Marta create shields for yourselves?" he asked.

"I... I think so. Marta?"

Marta nodded her head, mute with wonder and fear.

Breanna visualized a clear wall surrounding her body and her horse and sent a trickle of power through it. She checked to make sure that Marta had done the same. Breanna nudged her horse toward the gates of the city. No sound broke the stillness around them.

Breanna put her hand on her Sword of Light. A faint tingle let her know that the Sword was aware. The others followed.

They rode through the gate and halted on the other side. Shadow figures moved around them, oblivious to their existence, all color leached away.

"They are out of our past," exclaimed Corcra. "We had best not stay here. We might be trapped."

"Is there any place where we can rest?" Marta asked in a small voice.

"Perhaps outside near the wall, although I did not see an oasis," Corcra answered.

"Maybe there's one on the other side of this city," said Breanna. "Can we go straight through, or do we have to ride around?"

"We can make our way straight through. We should avoid the tower," he told them.

The women started forward, resting their hands on sword pommels. They rode for what felt like an eternity through the winding streets of the ghost city. The inhabitants were not ghosts, able to go through them. Instead, they avoided any contact, walking around the three travelers.

A very faint clicking followed them, gaining strength as they passed the walls of the castle, then faded away as they approached a gate at the end of the main street, this one blocked by a heavy wooden panel cross-braced with iron bands.

The horses slowed and stopped. Corcra rode forward, left hand raised. Breanna felt his magic rising. The gate began to vibrate, the iron bands beating against the wood, as it rolled slowly to the left of the opening.

Breanna urged her horse through it. Marta followed close behind, so close that Breanna's horse pinned its ears back and gave a little crow-hop, warning the other horse away.

Corcra rode through, releasing his magic as he moved. The heavy gate rushed back into place with a whoosh of displaced air, locking them out.

Marta saw the tall palm trees of the oasis first.

"There," she pointed ahead and to the right of their path. Breanna swung around and sighed with relief. They could stop and rest.

$ $ $

Breanna lifted her dripping face from the watering trough, eyes closed, felt along its edge, pulling the burnoose she had removed up to pat the cool water off. She used the damp fabric to pat the back of her neck and then her neck and chest. Selgith crouched at the edge of the small pool a few feet from the trough, slaking her thirst.

They'd watered the horses first, then made their way to a small patch of dry brittle grass under the palm trees surrounding the trough, a tiny pool of water, and a stack of dried fronds from the trees. The horses started grazing as they were untacked and hobbled.

Breanna's stomach grumbled loudly. She trudged back to their tiny campfire. Marta used her magic to start a small fire in a ring of stones and set their travel cauldron filled with water on it. The scent of lamb stew they had traded for at the last oasis soon drifted in the air. Breanna's mouth watered.

Marta spread the saddle blankets on the sand in front of each saddle.

"I feel like I could eat a horse," she said, sitting down next to her saddle with a tired grunt. Selgith slipped into camp, arrowing toward Breanna.

*I have eaten well,* she told her bhanna, sending a picture of a scrawny desert hare.

*If you need more, I'll share my stew with you,* Breanna sent back. She laid SunWalker next to her own blanket, ready should she need the Sword. Her hand shook as she dipped her bowl in the pot and sat, using the saddle as a backrest.

A light breeze from the west rustled the leaves on the palm trees and carried the metallic scent of hot sand.

"I wonder why no one else is here, not that I'm complaining," Marta asked. "The fewer people who know we're traveling, the better."

Breanna looked at Corcra standing at the edge of the grass, arms crossed, gazing across the sand as the sun set in a cloudless sky, curious if he had an answer. When none was forthcoming, she ventured a guess. "Maybe the city keeps them away or maybe they can't see it because of the city."

Turning away from the desert, he said "It is neither. There is no one close to this quarter. There is something far away in that direction." He pointed to the southwest, "and something back there" pointing at the city as he made his way to the fire, boots crunching across the sand and gravel.

He settled to the ground in front of his gear after dipping a bowl into the stew pot, taking the last portion.

Breanna finished her meal and set the little that remained in front of Selgith who licked the bowl clean.

"What do you mean, 'there's something back there?' What's in the city?"

Marta collected the dishes and the pot, taking the few steps to the pool. She scrubbed the dishes clean with sand, then dipped them into the water to rinse. The dry air removed the moisture within minutes.

Putting the bowls in the pot, Marta returned and stuffed everything in her saddlebag. She sat down and crossed her legs, resting her elbows on her knees. "What should we do tomorrow?"

*There is an amulet in the City of Silence.* SunWalker and HellScream spoke in all their minds.

"Oh Gods," Breanna mumbled, dropping her chin to her chest. "Well, that answers your question. We go back."

# Chapter 28
# Grasslands

Owen shook his head in frustration. He ran the stem of grass he had plucked from the stand of waving grain in front of him through his fingers. What he really wanted to do was charge into the meeting of the Fearmhar Commanders of the Nations and force them to understand the danger they were in.

The Demon War was happening as they wasted time, regardless of what the seven leaders of Fearmhar thought, regardless of their desire to deny it.

Owen had fought Demons on the Windward Range and at the Battle for Aos Si. His skin shuddered and goosebumps rose at the remembered viciousness and utter ruthlessness of the monsters from another world. He had closed a portal to that world at great personal cost.

Saleth ghosted up on his left and Owen jumped. "Could you please make some noise when you sneak up on me?" he snapped.

"Frustrated are you," the elf shot back, his statement bringing Owen's mind to a halt. Owen's lips pursed as a sudden thought caught him. "Maybe that's their goal," he murmured.

"I believe so," Saleth replied. "The warriors are intrigues with both of us and those we travel with. They are aware of the threat the Demons represent. There have been minor incursions from Fasach. They have been warned. They know."

A semi-permanent settlement surrounded the monolithic Meeting Stone that jutted into the sky at the center of the area. A low-level hum from the stone was always present in the back of his mind. Owen scanned the settlement and the prairie beyond. Something beyond his frustration was bothering him.

He opened his mind and reached for HeartStriker. *Can you sense anything coming or already here?*

"Do you feel anything off?" Owen asked Saleth.

Saleth shrugged. "Nothing beyond the taint in the magic of the land." His voice trailed off as his own attention was caught by that strangeness.

*There is something deep under the ground,* HeartStriker responded slowly. *I cannot tell what it is, but it is large and incredibly angry.*

Owen repeated HeartStriker's thoughts. Saleth stiffened, alarm narrowed his eyes and tightened his fists.

His body went still, his face went blank. Owen felt him using his magic to probe the ground.

With a swiftness that rocked Owen back on his heels, Saleth's awareness returned.

"There *is* something there and it is coming *here*," he exclaimed. Owen grabbed his arm and pulled him toward the half-timbered meeting hall.

He pushed his way past the guard at the door and shoved aside the warriors standing in a circle around the commanders. Exclamations of annoyance followed their path.

Owen stepped before the men, still firmly gripping Saleth's arm.

"Forgive our presumption, but you need to know this. Both HeartStriker and Saleth have found a threat to you and your people. We do not know what it is, it is deep underground, and it is coming here, now."

A babble of voices erupted from the gathering. "Prove what you say," and "You're lying!"

*He speaks the truth.* HeartStriker spoke in everyone's mind. Instant silence crushed down on the meeting.

"What do...what can we do?" quavered an old man in the circle.

"Have any of your shamans felt anything?"

The leader of the Commanders of Nations this cycle stood. He looked toward a man leaning against the wall who wore beaded buckskins that reminded Owen of the decorated robes mages wore. A black raven sat on his head. Owen assumed it was a headdress until the raven moved its head and looked at him.

Owen shuddered. He slammed his shields into place and reached for HeartStriker, drawing it from its scabbard with a *shing* of metal on metal. The Sword burst into flame.

Chaos ruled. Shouts of panic filled the room as people tried to move back and leave the space.

The leader crossed his arms, waiting for the turmoil to subside.

"Lord Owen, thank you for the warning. You need fear nothing in this room."

The deep, deep voice of the shaman rang out. "Calm yourselves. You are an embarrassment to Fearmhar."

He pushed away from the wall. Quiet and order was quickly restored.

"Indeed, we have felt something in the magic of Fearmhar. It is amorphous at best and not easily recognized. In ancient times past, there was a protector of the land, but we have not seen it for centuries. We do not even know what it is or what it looks like. Perhaps this is the power that you feel."

"Well, whatever it is, it should be here today. This is your land, but were I you, I would prepare to honor it or defend against it," Owen told the gathering.

"I am Kajika, leader of Fearmhar for this cycle of the Sun." He used his chin to point at the shaman. "He is Gaa-gii."

HeartStriker dampened his flame. Owen returned the Sword to its scabbard. He gave a short bow to the two men.

"Join us to talk of the threat and its future," Kajika invited them.

# Chapter 29
# Chaos

Breanna rolled up in her saddle blanket, then set shields around her mind. The desert cooled quickly after sunset, making it easier to fall asleep. Left without blankets, she'd be shivering by the middle of the night. She hoped that her sleep would be dreamless.

The path to the dreamlands opened before her. She hesitated, resisting the pull. Heavy grey fog obscured the gate, rolling over the trees and ground that usually stood beyond it. She took a step back.

The greyness billowed and crept past the gate onto the path. That had never happened before. With a suddenness that shocked her, the fog almost leapt at her. Her shriek of fear startled her awake and sent her bolting from her blankets.

Marta and Corcra scrambled up to join her. Breanna pointed toward the grey fog that was rolling from the city walls toward the oasis.

"Shield yourselves," Corcra snapped.

Breanna felt him raising his with swift efficiency. The women followed suit. Plunging their awareness into the earth to ground themselves, they raised mental protections around their minds and bodies as well as those of the mules and horses.

The fog slithered closer as if it was a predator preparing to attack. It churned and roiled along the sand in front of them.

"Stad go tobann." Corcra spoke the quiet command to stop.

The menacing fog halted as if it was touched by the fingers of winter.

"Bailigh leat!"

His command to leave rang with power. The grey fog melted away like ice in summer.

Corcra staggered forward and fell to his knees. His hands thrust into the sand, keeping him from falling flat. He groaned.

Breanna dropped her shields and scuttled to his side, touching his shoulder. She shared her power as quickly as she could. Marta joined her, gripping his other shoulder, and poured out her magic.

Corcra rocked back to his knees, hands resting palms up on his thighs. "Thank you," he gasped.

"That is enough."

The women released his shoulders.

"What happened?" Breanna panted, dropping to her knees.

"There is some great Demon within the tower," he mumbled, not yet recovered. "It tried to take me over."

Marta and Breanna were still, breathing suspended.

"What?" Breanna whispered.

"A Demon in the Tower." Corcra's voice gained strength with every second that passed. "We must pass it to find the amulet."

Marta sat down on her blanket with a weary sigh.

"Could we have just one day with no menace to kill us? Time to rest and recover our strength?"

Corcra regarded her, then darted his gaze to Breanna, noting their exhaustion.

"Perhaps we should take a day. Repair our gear, eat well. As she says, rest and recuperate."

"Agreed." Their voices spoke as one.

$ $ $

Breanna slid her whetstone along SunWalker's length, almost finished sharpening the Sword. The steady whisk the stone made along the steel blade was oddly calming. The rhythm of her movements contributed to her serenity.

I needed this time, she thought.

As did we all, responded her Sword.

With a final run of the stone along its length, Breanna dropped it into the pouch hanging from her belt, picked up the oiled cloth lying on the blanket beside her and wiped the Sword clean. Placing the Sword in front of her, Breanna folded the cloth and pushed it into the pouch next to the whetstone. She'd blocked the noise with a spell so as not to disturb the others.

She rolled to her feet and put her hands on her hips, releasing the spell. Scanning the horizon, she looked for threats, anything out of place. Nothing moved in the growing heat of early morning.

After the terror of the night, Breanna surprised herself by sleeping soundly. When she woke, she felt energized, ready to face anything.

She glanced around the campsite, taking in the sleeping mounds of her companions. Gathering the things needed for a meal, she started a small fire, brought water from the pool in their pot, and placed it over the fire. Using the oats meant for both horses and humans, she poured them into the water. There. Breakfast started.

Breanna wondered what the day would bring. The day of rest had helped. She wasn't looking forward to going back into the city. She clenched her teeth in determination, fisting her hands. She...they... needed to get the amulet. That had been the goal for the entire trip.

Selgith slipped into camp, her mind radiating satisfaction after a successful hunt. Breanna grinned. Better than the oats we're having.

Selgith made a gagging sound. *Do we go back today?*

*We must. You can stay here if you want to.*

*No, I will come to guard your back* the sandcat answered.

*"Thank you,"* Breanna murmured.

Marta gave a huge yawn and stretched in her blankets. At the noise she made, Corcra stirred as well.

The sun rose higher as they prepared for the day. Breanna saddled horses, Marta repacked the mules, and Corcra buried the fire and cleaned their camp.

"What should we expect?" Breanna's question stilled the other two.

"Perhaps Selgith could scout ahead for us," Marta suggested.

Corcra strode through the sand to join them.

"We should leave the horses and mules outside the walls. I think Selgith should stay and guard them. If we do not return, they will eventually break free and return to Jafara or one of the oases' where we stopped."

Breanna looked at the sandcat. *Would you stay with the horses? It is your choice.*

*I will. There is danger under the sand that I will deal with if needed.*

Breanna put her hand on the cat's shoulder, letting gratitude flow.

"There is this," Corcra continued. "I have been probing with my magic and found a back way into the tower. I do not think this Demon is as powerful as the one we fought beneath Jafara."

"It tried to take you over," Breanna exclaimed.

"Yet it could not," he responded. "With our Swords and our magic, I believe we can succeed. Should we need more, Selgith can send us what magic she can." He pulled his belt knife and squatted down, swiftly outlining the city, castle and tower in the sand, and the path they must take.

"This City of Silence is an enigma. Why does it shift in and out of our reality? What allows this to happen? Is it the amulet? Will it remain if we take the amulet? Can we escape again? I do not know exactly where the amulet is kept, but it feels like the second or third floor of the tower."

"I agree," Breanna said. "I've been worried about taking the animals back in. This gives us more freedom of movement, should we need it."

Marta nodded.

Breanna swung up on her horse. The others followed her lead. She turned her horse's head and nudged him into a trot. The City of Silence was only a half-candlemark away.

# Chapter 30
# Tower

Breanna set her shoulder against the wall that wasn't there. Thank the Three that Selgith agreed to wait with the horses. Oh, she could feel the wall, all right; she just couldn't see it.

"Corcra," she whispered.

"Corcra!" a little louder.

"Stop!" This last loud enough for her to hear herself.

The figure moving away from her stopped, then swung around to face her.

"What?" The sharpness of his response quelled her rising anger.

"Where are we? Why can't I see this wall?"

A deep frown creased his brow. "You cannot see the wall?" Incredulity laced his voice. He swiveled his head toward the wall, then back at her.

"Use your magic."

"How?" Her blunt question stopped him before he could turn away.

*Sink your perception beneath the blankness. Know that there is a wall here, rough grey stone. Very little light.*

He sent her the aspect of what he perceived himself. He widened his sending to include Marta.

Breanna opened her mind to the possibility, using his image as a guide. There was indeed a wall of grey stone to her right. A wispy fog filled the corridor, still trying to obscure her vision. Corcra cocked his head in consternation.

"Are your shields up?"

"Yes," she replied.

"Marta, what do you see?" he asked.

"There was nothing there until your sending," she said with quiet dignity.

"The Demon's playing. We should move quickly now."

"Too late, Worm. I have you now. And the little girls playing at hero."

A deep voice boomed in the hallway they were using to approach the stairs to the tower's second floor.

*Shing* and *shing* echoed as Swords-of-Light left their scabbards. Light splashed around them as Sword-flame ignited. Something huge, black, and wet dripped slime on the floor at the end of the corridor. Sickly, pallid yellow eyes bisected by red pupils gleamed. Saliva foamed along teeth as long as Breanna's hand. She shuddered with fear and disgust.

"Think well before you strike, fiend," Corcra's voice was stern. "We come for a trinket and wish no battle with you."

"It is mine!" The Demon's voice rose to shrillness as it claimed their prize.

"Then we will take it from you," shouted the Dragon, calling the whirlwind.

Dust was sucked into the maelstrom, almost pulling Breanna and Marta into it. They took hasty steps backward, away from Corcra's power. The wind dropped to a whisper, and the Dragon filled the hall.

"Ha, ha, ha, ha, ha!" Burst from the Demon. "Think you that you can best ME?"

Without warning, it leaped at the Dragon. One bound and it was on him. Corcra didn't even have time to draw a breath. His muzzle was engulfed by the ever-widening gape of the Demon's mouth.

With a scream of rage, Breanna charged up next to Corcra's giant haunch and plunged SunWalker into the monster's side as it grappled with her friend, a friend who'd saved her time and time again. She pulled the Sword free and plunged it into the beast repeatedly. For all its power, the Sword barely scratched the Demon's hide.

Marta attacked the beast's shoulder opposite Breanna. She slashed at the neck and shoulder joint, hoping to hit something vital.

Breanna could feel the Dragon's strength and magic ebbing as the Demon tightened its jaws and jerked on Dragon's head, suffocating him as it consumed his magic.

The Demon stomped its feet, trying to catch its tiny tormenters and smash them. It thrashed its body back and forth.

*We can't win. It's too strong.* Despair gripped Breanna's heart.

*I should grab Marta and go back the way we came.*

She reached out toward Marta.

*Fight!* Selgith's thought stopped her in her tracks. *Fight! You are not done.*

Power triggered by the sandcat's words shuddered along her nerves; determination tightened her jaw. She *would* save her friend or die trying.

Breanna pulled SunWalker from the Demon's side and using the wall, flung herself as high as she could, searching for its throat.

There. Using her momentum, she shoved SunWalker through the thing's neck and pushed herself up and over its head. It acted as a fulcrum, and SunWalker ripped out the front of the Demon's neck, almost severing head from body.

Marta ran past the Dragon, threw herself to the stone floor and slid along it, raising HellScream vertically, slicing through the Demon's underbelly.

Breanna continued her roll, landing next to Marta. They raised their Swords to guard position, ready to leap in again.

The Demon was dead, eviscerated, and beheaded. Its mouth slid off the Dragon's muzzle as the head fell to the ground with a thud. Its body collapsed. The Dragon raised his head and shrieked in triumph.

The women slowly straightened. The Dragon began to shudder, then sank to the ground. Blood puddled under his head. Swearing, the women charged forward, laying their Swords along his neck, hands slamming into his shoulders, knees hammering to the ground.

HellScream and SunWalker sent magic roaring into his body, replacing that which the Demon had taken. Marta and Breanna struggled to contain and guide the torrent that would kill him if not controlled. The lacerations on Corcra's head and neck closed and healed.

The Dragon's eyes had dulled and lost their glimmer. His body began to jerk.

As the magic filled him, the jerking shudders slowly subsided. His eyes began to shine. The river of magic slowed, became a stream, became a trickle. It finally wisped away to nothing.

The women held their breath. Breanna's heart clenched. "Please," she prayed. "Please."

The Dragon took a deep breath and released it, followed by another, and another. His body twitched.

*I am here.*

# Chapter 31
# Portal

Corcra stood before them, completely healed. He set the Demon's body afire with Dragon flame once he'd recovered. It had taken three candle-marks before he could call the whirlwind to shapeshift into a man.

Breanna and Marta sat against the wall, Marta leaning her head on crossed arms braced on her knees, Breanna leaning her head back against the wall, both utterly exhausted. Neither wanted to try to stand, even supported with magic energy from their Swords.

"I am forever in your debt," Corcra said. "Thank you. I would have died without your help. I am humbled by your bravery."

He stood across the corridor, feet shoulder-width apart, arms crossed over his chest. His eyes glittered in the dim light.

"You're welcome," sounded faintly from Marta's direction.

"Uh," a tired grunt came from Breanna.

"What do you need? How can I help?" he asked.

Breanna's head snapped forward at his question.

She tried to moisten her mouth and croaked, "Water."

The saddlebags they had left with the horses appeared on the floor in front of them.

Breanna raised tired eyes to him. "Thank you."

Marta reached forward and dragged her bag to her side. She rooted around until she found the water bag, pulled it out, unstoppered it and raised it to her mouth. Breanna copied her.

"Slowly," Corcra reminded them.

Breanna dived back into her bag a pulled out the flat-bread wrapped in a napkin. She opened it and grabbed a piece, holding up the bundle to Corcra. He shook his head and she set it down on the floor.

"I've got some dried meat in here," Marta said.

Breanna held out her hand.

They ate every scrap in the bags and felt much better.

"Guess we were hungry," Marta said.

Breanna only grunted in agreement.

"Do you think you can move now? We should not stay here," Corcra reminded them.

"Should we try for the amulet?"

Breanna's tentative question made them all pause.

"Are there any other Demons here?"

"No. I've checked and that was the only one. At least for now," Corcra answered. "This one probably held the tower because of its size. Another will come to take its place when they realize it's dead."

"Then yes, let's get it and get out of this cursed place," Breanna responded.

She rolled to her feet and finished stuffing the detritus of her meal back in the bag. Marta followed suit and they stood together, ready to go.

"Which way," asked Marta.

Corcra pointed to the right.

"The stairs are there."

The three quickly walked along the hall, leaving the place of their battle. They came to the stairwell and began the climb to the next floor. Bones and skulls littered the stairs and they stepped carefully to avoid them.

The stairwell opened to another corridor, this one filled with bones as well. A great battle had been fought here. Breanna wondered who had fought and why. Surely it wasn't because of the amulet.

She sent a tendril of magic out, testing to see if she could find it.

*Draw me* SunWalker demanded.

Holding the Sword upright by its grip in front of her, Breanna followed the faint directions that tugged her toward the end of the hall and the room on the left. As she entered it, a muted blaze of magic reached her. A wooden chest sat at the foot of the bed that almost filled the room, its coverings in shreds.

She made her way across the room to the trunk, leaning SunWalker against the bedframe. The others crowded into the room behind her. She lifted the lid of the trunk.

Magic emanated from something bundled in silk. She drew a deep breath, trying to still the frantic beating of her heart. Reaching out a shaking hand, she lifted the bundle from the trunk and began to unwrap it. As the last bit of fabric fell away, a blaze of power filled the room. Light and heat followed. Corcra and Marta stepped back, throwing up their arms to protect their faces. Breanna squinted her eyes in reaction, almost dropping the amulet.

It was a triangle of stone, sharp edged on the sides, smooth on the bottom edge and underside of the shape, about the length of her first finger, half that wide across at the broad end. It was thin. On its top, tiny pieces of amethyst were laid in an intricate pattern resembling dragon scales. From tip to bottom, a thin strip of gold covered the amethyst. Small chips of ruby, indigo gabbro, serpentine, fire agate and dragon stone were set into the gold. The edges of the amulet looked as if it had been broken from a larger piece.

"The third amulet," breathed Corcra. "The tales are true. I can feel it calling even now with only one."

Breanna snatched up the silk and wrapped it around the amulet. The magic, heat, and light decreased as the thickness grew. Only a murmur was evident when she was done. She looked up at Corcra and Marta, shaken to her core.

"This must not fall into Demon hands. How did that thing miss it?" she wondered.

"I don't think it did. It feels like background magic now," Corcra responded with slow deliberation. "It would not know that the bundle was special. Perhaps it was claiming all magic in the tower."

Breanna shrugged the strap of her bag off her shoulder and carefully slipped the bundle into a pocket. At least she had something to carry it in. She straightened and faced the other two.

"We've got to get this back to the Keep as quick as we can. I've been thinking. Corcra, do you think you could make a portal that would take us there like Bahador did to the Smachtmaistir?"

He frowned. "I'm not sure I have the power to do it. Bahador explained how, but..." he hesitated.

"What if all of us did it together, even our Swords, and Selgith?" Marta asked.

"We can but try," Corcra agreed.

The three strode purposefully through the tower and out into the city. It remained a City of Silence, people going about their own business, colors leached away, avoiding any contact. Corcra led them single file to the gate beyond which waited their horses and Selgith.

The women fed Corcra magic as he used his to open the wooden gate in the wall. It slid aside much easier than before. They slipped through quickly and the gate shut as Corcra released his magic.

Selgith rushed to Breanna and butted her to the ground. A rumbling purr filled her ears. "I guess you missed me," Breanna smiled.

*I was aware of the fight. You are very lucky. As is the Dragon.*

"Enough of that. We were all incredibly lucky. I think we're going to need some more." She hesitated, then rushed on. "We're going to try to 'portal' to Red Dragon's Keep."

Selgith sat down, head cocked to the side. *Is this possible?*

*Well, Bahador showed us how. We need to get the amulet home safely and quickly.*

*I will help*, the sandcat responded.

$ $ $

The companions rode back to the oasis. It was almost dusk, and their task best begun before then.

The oasis still stood empty. Breanna was surprised at that. She shrugged.

Corcra chose a place on the side of a dune facing toward its bottom before a second dune rose on the other side. A running start made sense. "Remember the forecourt?" she asked. "Bahador specifically said we should not go anywhere we hadn't seen, or we could get lost. I'm sorry. My nerves are making me babble," Breanna told them.

"Send me your magic now," Corcra said.

He gathered the threads of magic as each Sword sent them, then Selgith's, Breanna's, and Marta's. He started to glow, swollen with power. With a tiny rotating gesture of his hand, he opened a portal for the very first time. Beyond it he could see the forecourt in which he had landed so long ago. He gestured again and the portal continued to grow.

"Go," he commanded.

Breanna booted her horse into a gallop, down the dune and through the portal followed by Selgith and Marta. Corcra stepped through leading his horse into a chaos of alarm bells and soldiers running toward them. They should have sent a warning first.

# Chapter 32
# Kinship

Breanna threw up a shield around them all as soon as she recognized their danger. Horses danced with fear and surprise, shoes striking sparks from the paving stones. Her chagrin at her failure to send a warning would have caused her to lash out before this trip, but she had changed. *There wasn't time to send a warning.*

Thomas and Aeden raced through the doors of the Keep, swords drawn, slowing to a halt as they recognized Corcra, then Breanna and Marta.

"Sorry. I didn't think to send a warning through the portal first," Breanna shouted. Selgith pressed herself against Breanna's legs. Breanna's hand dropped to the cat's head.

*Nothing to fear. My brother and our resident Dragon, Aeden,* she told her. Selgith snorted, sat down by her feet, and curled her tail around her toes. Ears flicked back and forth as she used them to investigate this new place.

Breanna dropped the shield as their horses calmed and soldiers stopped charging toward them, bent on mayhem. Thomas and Aeden stopped on the stairs and waited as the companions approached.

"What are you doing here? How..." Thomas stammered.

"We learned to 'portal'," Breanna said, laughter filling her voice. "And we found the real third amulet."

Thomas strode down the remaining stairs in a rush. He grabbed Breanna in a tight hug.

"Thank the Three Gods you're safe." His eyes locked on to Marta over Breanna's shoulder. "Thank Them that you are all safe."

He released Breanna but kept his arm over her shoulders. "You all look like you've been in a battle and barely won," he told them bluntly.

"We have," she told him. "Killed a Demon, or two, or three. It's been an..." she searched for the right word, "interesting trip. There is much to tell."

Her head reeled as the time of day hit her. It had been almost dusk in Fasach. Here, it was just past midday. She looked at Marta and Corcra, watching as the same awareness filtered past their euphoria at creating a successful portal.

Thomas dropped his arm from her shoulders and set steadying hands on both arms. She shuddered with reaction.

*Stop.* Selgith and both Swords spoke in all their minds. Aeden joined the group. *There is nothing to be concerned about* SunWalker continued. *We are here and we are safe. Let that be enough for now. You fail in your duty by not introducing your companion, cara mór.*

Breanna hung onto the Sword's words. They steadied her mind and her heart. Stronger, she focused on the sandcat.

"Thomas, Aeden. This is Selgith. She is a sandcat from the far south of Ard Ri, near the border of Fasach. She saved me from a rattlesnake, and many times since. Oh, what a tale we have for you!"

Thomas stepped back from Breanna and gave a short bow to the cat.

"Welcome, Selgith. Thank you for watching over my sister. May you find joy at Red Dragon's Keep," he greeted her.

Selgith's scrutiny of her brother was intimidating, as Breanna well knew. Finally, the cat gave a regal nod.

*Well met, brother of my bhanna. May we dwell in peace.*

Breanna stared down at Selgith. She unfocused her eyes and looked at each person in the group without moving her head, watching reactions.

Astonishment was primary. Amazement from Corcra was the most hilarious. Breanna schooled her face to mild interest and looked up. Aeden was watching her, left eyebrow raised. She gave her teacher a bland smile.

Grooms were approaching to take charge of the horses and mules. Breanna handed the reins to the one nearest her. She pulled her pack off the saddle. A tired sigh escaped. Thomas heard.

"Let's not stand around the forecourt. Come. I'm sure there's something to eat while rooms are prepared for everyone. Thomas held out his arm and gestured up the stairs.

As she put one foot in front of the other, Breanna tried to sort out what she was feeling. She was home, but strangely it didn't feel like home. She noticed for the first time how time-worn the stairs were. How many had taken these up to the Keep causing a depression in the stone where she placed her own feet? The Red Dragon laid in stone up the side of the tower drew her eye. She'd never noticed before how the colors of the stone blocks created an illusion of movement, as if the Dragon was about to spring away from the tower and take flight. She shook her head with wonder.

At the top of the stairs, Aeden stopped Corcra. He stood before her, hands clasped behind his back, much as a recruit stood at-ease before his sergeant. Breanna took note of the tableau, then walked through the double doors and entered the greatroom. She turned to keep an eye on them.

*Is everything all right?* she sent to Corcra. His glance flicked to her, then away. *The interrogation is unpleasant, but I am fine. There are things I will leave for your telling.*

She nodded to him as she turned back to the room. The dais where the high table sat looked shorter to her, the table smaller than she remembered. So much had changed.

Breanna looked around the room for Marta. There she was, next to the stairway to the kitchen, talking with Thomas, brows lowered in a frown. She waited for a pause in their conversation. *Everything ok?*

*Someone thinks he's in charge of me. This is not going to end well,* Marta sent back.

*It appears there's a lot of that going around. We'll deal with it.* She sent a picture of the tavern room in Fasach as the customers realized just who was in their midst. At Marta's sudden smile, she congratulated herself for diffusing the situation.

"Where is Gregory? Why don't I have a welcoming cup in my hand?" Breanna asked of no one in particular. As she spoke, she glanced down the hall and saw the seneschal hurrying toward the greatroom. A smile spread across her face as she moved forward to greet him.

A skully came up the stairs from the kitchen, squeezing past Marta and Thomas, and made his way to the high table with a tray of cheese, bread, cups, and pitchers with something wet inside.

Breanna held her hands out and Gregory took them in his. His normally shoulder-length hair had turned totally white. Breanna struggled to mask her shock at the change in his appearance. Deep lines grooved from his nose to the outsides of his lips. Frown lines slashed between his eyebrows and furrows crossed his forehead. He still stood straight, but there was a slight curve to his upper spine. His hands had become wrinkled and deeply veined.

Sudden dread filled her. What had changed with her parents? With her brothers? She looked closely at Thomas, hoping to see the same young man who had sent her on her quest. He had changed as well. She wondered what the others saw when they looked at her.

She led Gregory to the high table. She checked each pitcher and found one with the deep red wine that he preferred and poured a cup. She poured one for herself and sat in one of the chairs, gesturing for him to take one as well. "We have a story to tell, and you should hear it," she told him.

*Everyone, there is food and drink at the high table. We should all come together to share it and tell our stories only once,* she sent.

Aeden and Corcra entered through the doors to the great hall from the forecourt. Thomas and Marta made their way up the dais stairs and joined her at the table. "Good suggestion, Breanna," Thomas told her.

The gentle confusion of serving themselves was soon settled and everyone found a place to sit.

Breanna pulled her pack onto the table and flipped open the buckles that held it closed. She reached into the side pocket and gingerly pulled out the silk wrapped bundle she had placed there this afternoon in the City of Silence. Utter quiet fell around the table. With careful hands, she unwrapped that which she held until the final fold fell away. Indrawn breath greeted the first glimpse of the Fasach Amulet, the Third piece of the Cumhacht ar Draigoini–The Power of Dragons Talisman.

Breanna could feel its power through her hands. It shivered through her awareness. Its impact was felt by everyone, even Gregory, who was not sensitive to magic at all.

*Huh. I wonder if it's magnified by the other two pieces we already have.*

Aeden reached out with a tentative move of her hand, then withdrew it, shaking her head.

"What?" questioned Breanna.

"No Dragon should touch this. Not until the amulets are re-united. Tell us what happened."

Breanna smiled and began the tale.

# Chapter 33
# Magic

Power shuddered through the Aether. Mannan's heart hesitated, began to pound. What had changed? Desperate to betray nothing to those around him, he raised his arm in a signal to hold, waiting for those at the King's table to quiet.

"We have been long at this discussion and made some progress. Let us pause for now and think on what more should be done," he told the attendees. "Let us meet again in a week."

Tom and Jenni, Anne and Jeremy shared a glance. It had been weeks since their arrival at Cathair Ri. Discussions among the king's council about how to prosecute the war against Demons had been fruitless.

They pushed back their chairs and stood, bowing to the King and the High Mage.

"Thank you. I for one, am weary and need time to think. Until the next meeting, then," Tom said.

The four left the room and followed the hallways to their chambers.

"Join us for some food and wine," Tom invited Jeremy and Anne into the salon of their suite. Refreshments already rested on trays placed on tables around the room.

*Did you feel that?*

*What was it?*

*What happened?*

"Whatever it was, it unnerved Mannon."

Satisfaction laced Jenni's words.

"We'll know soon enough, but this is big. Bigger than we can possibly imagine."

# Chapter 1
# Book of Shadows

A broad nose shoved Cameron between his shoulder blades.

Absently, Cameron reached behind him and smacked the scaled muzzle of the Dragon that had pushed him. He was engrossed in reading the Book of Shadows he held. Sitting in the late afternoon sun on the low wall between the training grounds and paths that led to the lower caves of the mountain, he was wholly involved in reading the spells contained in the book.

Its pages were brittle with age, the ink faded. The spell lock on the book had not been renewed and was easy to manipulate. The bookplate on the first page bore the name Maghnus.

He'd found it in the Dragon's Library on the top shelf among other old books. As his fingers passed over its spine, they'd tingled. He'd reached forward and pulled it from its place between a book about cooking and another about horse training.

The library took up two levels in the Arach Dubh's caisléan. Called Arach Baile, the caisléan stood in splendid isolation on the flattened peak of Dragon Mountain in the far north of Ard An Tir. Raised by Dragon magic in ancient times when Dragons had first come to the world of men, it stood sentinel against evil and a beacon of hope to the people of the world, though not many remembered the dwelling place of the shapeshifters.

Two days ago, the invasion alarm shrilled through the caverns under the mountains, calling all Dragons to wing in defense of their land. The thunder of their leaving had shaken the ground for many minutes. Not a Dragon remained in the entire citadel.

Cameron found the library as he wandered the corridors of Neulach's home for hours, searching for the man he thought of as his teacher and mentor, wanting to help but not knowing how. He hadn't found the king.

Kennett's snout shoved him again. Cameron slipped his finger between pages to mark his spot and turned to his best friend with ill temper.

"What do you want?" A grumpy snarl snapped out.

Cameron did a double-take, realizing that Kennett had returned.

"You're here! Finally! What happened?" He jumped to his feet.

*Let me change shape, and I'll tell you all about it,* Kennett spoke in his mind.

A whirlwind formed around Kennett's Dragon body, growing from a tiny zephyr to a roaring cyclone in moments. Cameron raised his arm and buried his face in its crook to protect his eyes. As the whirlwind fell to nothing, Cameron's friend stood where the Dragon had been.

Cameron punched him in the shoulder. "Well?"

Kennett punched him back, then draped his arm over the young mage's shoulder.

"Eleven mages opened three portals from the Demon world into the south of our land. Neulach thinks the mages are from all over Ard An Tir. The Demons were flooding out and making their way north. The mages shot leven-bolts from cross-bows at us and ripped five dragon wings apart. We stayed in formation and laid down fire. They burned nicely. Stupid demons."

Cameron heard the shaking in Kennett's voice. He reached up and patted his friend's shoulder. "Anyone we know get hurt?"

"No. The trainees were too far away."

"Good. You've been gone for two days, and I'll bet you're hungry. Let's go eat."

§ § §

"I found something interesting while you were gone. There was nothing else to do, so I searched the library and found an old Book of Shadows." He put a proprietary hand on the book on the table beside him. "It's got some fascinating spells that are hard to understand. I'll take it to Neulach when he gets back. How long do you think until he gets here?"

Kennett finished the last piece of venison steak on his plate and drank from his cup. He'd put away two plates of food and a gallon of water.

"I think he may already be here. Word came down from those in charge: he closed the portals and captured one of the mages who took off on horses when we started killing Demons."

Cameron pushed back from the table and stood up.

"Come with me?" he asked his friend.

"Sure," Kennett told him. "Why not go corner the King of the Dragons after he's been fighting mages and Demons for two days. Just what I wanted to do."

He pushed back from the table and came around to Cameron's side. "You have no idea how special you are–to all of us."

Cameron's face flushed to his hairline. "Stop. Just stop." He hooked his arm through Kennett's. "Come on, let's go."

They walked through the halls of Dragon Home to the king's chambers and knocked on the door.

"Come."

Cameron pushed the door open and pulled Kennett into the room after him.

"My lord, I hope I'm not interrupting. Have you eaten?"

"I have. You're not interrupting. I'm sorry we left you alone." The king leaned back in his chair, setting the pen he held down on the papers on his desk.

"That's ok," Cameron said. "I was wondering if there's a possibility..." his voice trailed off. "Am I going to be assigned to a duo? Is that even possible? I want to help."

Resting his elbows on the desk, Neulach laced his fingers together and leaned his chin on them. He looked at the two young men standing in front of him.

"It is possible. Cameron, you would have to learn to ride a Dragon. Kennett, would you allow that? Having a mage on your back as you fly, throwing spells around?"

Neulach watched with interest as his idea took hold of their imaginations.

"Oh, my," Cameron murmured faintly.

Kennett swiveled his head to look at Cameron. He cocked it, a question in his eyes.

"Just how good are you with those spells," he asked, doubt lacing his words.

"I can drill a hole in a steel shield every time," Cameron replied with some heat. "I don't know if I can do it while I'm riding a Dragon," honesty compelled him to answer.

Cameron shivered with sudden apprehension.

"I was bored and went to the library while you were gone," Cameron added. "I found a Book of Shadows." He held the book out across the desk.

Neulach took the book. A heavy frown drew his eyebrows together. He flipped the cover open and read the bookplate.

"Maghnus," he murmured. "I've not seen that name for ages."

He slowly raised his head, staring at nothing for several moments.

"Where *is* that Dragon? I've not seen him for ages," he repeated.

Neulach pushed to his feet.

Cameron took a step back in alarm. He stumbled into Kennett behind him. The sound of rushing bootheels striking the hallway floor outside the king's offices jerked him toward the door. It burst open and thudded against the wall as a fully armored Dragon guard burst through.

The guard's eyes swept the room, looking for threats.

"Thank you for coming so quickly, Darius. Please have the mage prisoner brought to the tower for questioning. Questions must be asked...and answered."

# Acknowledgements

When a book is finished, it's the culmination of a dream and very hard work. The words capture parts of everything an author has experienced. I swear that "Universe" literally sends the story to my brain and out my fingers. I write as if I'm watching a movie.

Thank you, "Universe".

With that said, I'd like to thank everyone who has inspired me. Family tolerates me reading passages to them and offers excellent suggestions.

The Rocky Mountain Fiction Writers critique group has helped me all along my writing journey, from Red Dragon's Keep, through WindRunner, and now, with DreamWalker. Thanks to John Campbell, Anita Bunten, Fran Scannell, Mindy Kinneman, Joseph Caldera, Suzanne Clark, Karen Call, Benson Sullivan, and Nick Davis. Thank you for your excellent critiques and suggestions.

Susan Hicks and Donna Lawrence helped catch lots of problems and issues. Thank you both so much.

I keep forgetting the elephant in the room. COVID19. I literally could not write while the lockdown was in progress. I tried. Oh, how I tried. Nothing. All of that wasted time! I got a lot of cleaning done, though.

Thank you to every one of my readers. Without you, I wouldn't have anyone to tell my stories to.

So, it's time to set DreamWalker free and see what happens. I hope you like it!

# About Natli VanDerWerken

Natli VanDerWerken loves Dragons. She has more than 30 that she collected, many while serving in the Navy as a meteorologist and ASW specialist in Okinawa. She was the first woman petty officer stationed in the meteorology office there.

Natli has written two Amazon #1 Best Sellers as well as international multiple award-winning novels.

The Dragon's Children was inspired by a fairytale Natli told her grandchildren one Christmas Eve. The main character in each story is based on one of them.

Natli is a native Coloradan living in Aurora. She holds an MS in computer information systems, develops websites, shows Shetland Sheepdogs, and creates quilts in her non-existent spare time.

Find her at: natlivanderwerken.com

facebook.com/natlivanderwerken.author

Twitter-@CODragonLady

Instagram-codragonlady

# Other Novels by Natli VanDerWerken

The Dragon's Children: Red Dragon's Keep
(Book 1 - 2017)

The Dragon's Children: WindRunner
(Book 2 - 2019)

The Dragon's Children: DreamWalker
(Book 3 - 2024)

The Dragon's Children: Falcon's Spire
(Book 4 - forthcoming)

The Dragon's Children: Talisman
(Book 5 - forthcoming)

# Characters

Agni – ancient magical creatures resembling a cross between a horse and goat. They carry the Forest Lords during the Great Hunt
Alberick – High King of the Forest Lords
Aos Si – manor house of the WindWalkers, related to the Arach's by marriage

Bahador al Mahdi – High Mage of Fasach

Duke Sir Tom Arach
Duchess Lady Jennifer Arach
Thomas Arach
Owen Arach
Breanna Arach
Lord John Arach – grandfather of Tom Arach
Lady Eirin Arach – grandmother of Tom Arach

Duke Sir Jeremy Gobhlan
Duchess Lady Anne Gobhlan

Cameron Gobhlan

Evan Gobhlan

Duke Sir Scott WindWalker

Duchess Lady Debra WindWalker

Captain Braden - appointed captain of the guard after Captain Mathin leaves

Captain Mathin - captain of the guard. Killed in the
Darkened Forest by the Myrmidae

Cathair Ri - The King's City - Capital of Ard An Tir

Ciardha Demon - Demons of the Dark

Claiomh Solas - Swords of Light

    BattleSworn - Lord Tom Arach's sword

    FireGuard – Lady Jenni's sword

    BloodForged - Lord Jeremy's sword

    StormBringer -Lady Anne's sword

    HellReaver - chooses Thomas

    HeartStriker- chooses Owen

    SunWalker - chooses Breanna

    GhostWalker - chooses Cameron

    ShadowSworn - chooses Evan

    HellScream - chooses Marta

    OathKeeper - Aeden's sword

Corcra – the Purple Dragon

Falcon's Spire - home of the Gobhlan's. Duchy southwest of Red Dragon's Keep,

Garan Tilden - squire, son of Earl Tildon of North Meall
Gregory Anur– Red Dragon's Keep seneschal
Faolan Haloran - Steader, former Master Sergeant of the King's Army
Jaiman Haloran – oldest son of Faolan
Kevin Haloran – youngest son of Faolan
Marta Haloran – daughter of Faolan
Raina Haloran - Faolan's wife
Rand Haloran - grandfather of Marta. Killed by Demons during the retreat to Red Dragon's Keep

Idris – scout from Red Dragon's Keep
Jago – Gregory's clerk
Jalyn – head cook. Traitor.
Jory Quinn – sergeant in the Keep's army

Kennett – Cameron's best friend – Shapeshifter. Means Born of Fire and Flame.

Lady Aeden - Dragon/Mage/Sword Mistress

Maaike Soth Lahri – Fasach trader/spy sent to watch and sabotage the Arachs

Centak Soth Lahri – trader, deceased father of Maaike

Maccon - squire – friend

Mannan - High Draiolc - High Mage suborned by the Ciardha Demon

Moirra - the Keep wise-woman/healer


Neulach – King of the Dragons, Aeden's Father

North Meall - northern mounds – badlands – held by Earl Tilden and his son, Garan


Khaled Qadir – caravan master for Maaike Soth Lahri


Red Dragon's Keep - home of the Arachs

Rudraige Mór – King of Ard Ri


Saleth – scout for the Tua Dé

Samhanach – dire wolf companion to Saleth

Sayathia Khan Maruk – King of Fasach – Sayathia means Sheik

Seleigh Soren - Demon created by the High Draiolc to attack and kill those that are its designated prey.

The one imprisoned in the Keep woke the Swords of
Light
Selgith – (Sell git) Breanna's sandcat
Sharley – (Shar – lay) the Sorceress's apprentice
Simon - chamberlain
Stefan - squire – friend
Siubhan – (Shu - vawn) the King's Sorceress


Tiarna Geal - Lords of Light
Tua Dé – Lords of the Trees. Elves


WindRunners – magical creatures using the power
of the wind for speed
    Ajillech – Debra's WindRunner
    Anial – Tom's WindRunner
    Cridhe – Scott's WindRunner
    Gaoth – Anne's WindRunner
    Lubach – Jenni's WindRunner
    Navar – Owen's WindRunner
    Siomh – Jeremy's WindRunner


Windward Range – Lands of the WindWalkers

# Dictionary

Aeden - Fire

Arach - Dragon

Arach Ri – Dragon King

Arach Dubh – (arak duh) Black Dragon- King of the Dragons, Neulach

Ard An Tir - The Shining Lands

Ard Ri - King's Land

An bhaile – (ahn wail) townsmen

Aos Si – (ā ōs see) ancient lands of the WindWalkers, the Windward Range

Faoi bhanna – bond between a human and animal

Bhanna – bonded one

Bailigh leat! – Leave Now!

Bolscaire bhaile – (bols care wail) town crier

Cailleach – (cal yish) – witch

Cara mór – (kara moor) – best friend

Ciardha - (Kay r da) - the Dark - source of all Demons

Claiomh Solas - (Klay m So las) - Swords of Light

    BattleSworn - Lord Tom Arach's sword

    FireGuard – Lady Jenni's sword

    BloodForged - Lord Jeremy's sword

    StormBringer -Lady Anne's sword

    HellReaver - chooses Thomas

    HeartStriker- chooses Owen

    SunWalker - chooses Breanna

    GhostWalker - chooses Cameron

    ShadowSworn - chooses Evan

    HellScream - chooses Marta

    OathKeeper - Aeden's sword

Coimeadai – (ko mi dye) – Guardian

Corcra – purple. Name of the Purple Dragon

Cosain Morroin - (ko sane Mo ro in) - Shield Lands

Crionna baen - (kron a bay en) – wise-woman

Cumhacht ar Draigoini – (come act ar drago in i) - Power of Dragons

Candlemark – a measurement of time marked on a special candle that burns at a specific rate. Equal to one hour.

Demon – (dee man) – Demon

Demon Marfoir – (dee man mar fo ear) – Demon Killer

Dorcha Dubh – (dorka dew) - Deepest Black

Draiochta - (dray ok ta) - magic

Draiolc - (Dray olc) - dark wizard

Foraois - Forest

Fuil - blood

Fuilba - (Fool ba) - dark bay color

Fanai – (fan eye) – Nomads

Fearmhar Tribes –

    Cheron

    Kran

    Marcach

    Stail

    Obhrai

    Coghadh

    Dair


Gaothsiuloir (Gwaysilor) – WindRunner

Gharda Machaire (Garda Makeda) Guardian Mountains


Hammam – bathing room in Fasach

Hold - small farm held by a holder

Holder - either indentured serf or small landholder be-
holden to a Steading


Ki - spiritual essence


Lands of Ard An Tir

    Ard Ri - King's Land

    Fearmhar (fear m har) - grasslands of the Horse Lords

    Talamh (Ta lem) - farmland Freeholders

Fasach (Fa sash) - desert kingdom south of Ard Ri

Lucid Dreaming – the ability to consciously observe and/or control one's dreams

Maraboute – Mages of Fasach, holy men

Midach - (Mi dak) – doctor

Mymarida - (My maŕ i du) (plural - ae (aye) Fairyfly wasp - huge flying Fey that paralyzes its victim, wraps the body in an egg case and holds it to eat or lay its eggs in

Neulach – The Black Dragon, King of the Dragons, father of Aeden-the Red Dragon

Peann – writing implement

Ri - (Ree) - King

Rivers
 Banuisk
 Caladen
 Samphir

Sabhdan – (Say dan) – sultan, ruler

Salle - (Sal) - weapons training hall

Sataba – unit of one hundred troops of the Sheik of Fasach army

Seleigh Soren - (Su lay so ren) - carnivorous Demon compelled by magic to devour flesh and soul

Skully - servant

Slieve Geal – (Sleeve Ga el) - Shining Mountain

Smachtmaistir – (Smawk t May stir) master Demon controller

Steading - large land holding granted by the Lord to a freeholder

Suibhan - (Su - van) – mage assigned to the High King by the Mages Enclave

Sword of Light - sword created by the first mages, imbued with their own personality, blades tempered by Dragon fire. Produced by Dragons to burn enemies

Téigh Trí Thine - The Last Burning – elven ceremony for the dead

Tiarna Geal - (Tee ar na Ga el) - Lords of Light

Tua Dé – Lords of the Forest

Vanner – small, solidly-built horse of cob conformation like a small Shire. It is often, but not always, piebald, or skewbald

Vardo – colorful wagon owned by a trader and used as a traveling home